World War III starts with a bang...

THE BESTSELLING NOVELS OF

TOM CLANCY

THE TEETH OF THE TIGER

*A new generation — Jack Ryan, Jr. — takes over in Tom Clancy's
extraordinary, and extraordinarily prescient, novel.*

"INCREDIBLY ADDICTIVE."   —*Daily Mail* (London)

RED RABBIT

*Tom Clancy returns to Jack Ryan's early days —
in an engrossing novel of global political drama . . .*

"A WILD, SATISFYING RIDE."   —*New York Daily News*

THE BEAR AND THE DRAGON

A clash of world powers. President Jack Ryan's trial by fire.

"HEART-STOPPING ACTION . . . CLANCY STILL
REIGNS."   —*The Washington Post*

RAINBOW SIX

*John Clark is used to doing the CIA's dirty work.
Now he's taking on the world . . .*

"ACTION-PACKED."   —*The New York Times Book Review*

EXECUTIVE ORDERS

*A devastating terrorist act leaves Jack Ryan
as President of the United States . . .*

"UNDOUBTEDLY CLANCY'S BEST YET."
        —*The Atlanta Journal-Constitution*

continued . . .

DEBT OF HONOR
It begins with the murder of an American woman
in the backstreets of Tokyo. It ends in war . . .

"A SHOCKER."   —*Entertainment Weekly*

THE HUNT FOR RED OCTOBER
The smash bestseller that launched Clancy's career—
the incredible search for a Soviet defector
and the nuclear submarine he commands . . .

"BREATHLESSLY EXCITING."   —*The Washington Post*

RED STORM RISING
The ultimate scenario for World War III—
the final battle for global control . . .

"THE ULTIMATE WAR GAME . . . BRILLIANT."
—*Newsweek*

PATRIOT GAMES
CIA analyst Jack Ryan stops an assassination—
and incurs the wrath of Irish terrorists . . .

"A HIGH PITCH OF EXCITEMENT."
—*The Wall Street Journal*

THE CARDINAL OF THE KREMLIN

The superpowers race for the ultimate Star Wars
missile defense system . . .

"*CARDINAL* EXCITES, ILLUMINATES . . . A REAL
PAGE-TURNER." —*Los Angeles Daily News*

CLEAR AND PRESENT DANGER

The killing of three U.S. officials in Colombia ignites the
American government's explosive, and top secret, response . . .

"A CRACKLING GOOD YARN." —*The Washington Post*

THE SUM OF ALL FEARS

The disappearance of an Israeli nuclear weapon threatens the
balance of power in the Middle East—and around the world . . .

"CLANCY AT HIS BEST . . . NOT TO BE MISSED."
—*The Dallas Morning News*

WITHOUT REMORSE

His code name is Mr. Clark. And his work for the CIA
is brilliant, cold-blooded, and efficient . . . but who is he really?

"HIGHLY ENTERTAINING." —*The Wall Street Journal*

Created by Tom Clancy and Steve Pieczenik

TOM CLANCY'S OP-CENTER
TOM CLANCY'S OP-CENTER: MIRROR IMAGE
TOM CLANCY'S OP-CENTER: GAMES OF STATE
TOM CLANCY'S OP-CENTER: ACTS OF WAR
TOM CLANCY'S OP-CENTER: BALANCE OF POWER
TOM CLANCY'S OP-CENTER: STATE OF SIEGE
TOM CLANCY'S OP-CENTER: DIVIDE AND CONQUER
TOM CLANCY'S OP-CENTER: LINE OF CONTROL
TOM CLANCY'S OP-CENTER: MISSION OF HONOR
TOM CLANCY'S OP-CENTER: SEA OF FIRE
TOM CLANCY'S OP-CENTER: CALL TO TREASON
TOM CLANCY'S OP-CENTER: WAR OF EAGLES

TOM CLANCY'S NET FORCE
TOM CLANCY'S NET FORCE: HIDDEN AGENDAS
TOM CLANCY'S NET FORCE: NIGHT MOVES
TOM CLANCY'S NET FORCE: BREAKING POINT
TOM CLANCY'S NET FORCE: POINT OF IMPACT
TOM CLANCY'S NET FORCE: CYBERNATION
TOM CLANCY'S NET FORCE: STATE OF WAR
TOM CLANCY'S NET FORCE: CHANGING OF THE GUARD
TOM CLANCY'S NET FORCE: SPRINGBOARD
TOM CLANCY'S NET FORCE: THE ARCHIMEDES EFFECT

Created by Tom Clancy and Martin Greenberg

TOM CLANCY'S POWER PLAYS: POLITIKA
TOM CLANCY'S POWER PLAYS: RUTHLESS.COM
TOM CLANCY'S POWER PLAYS: SHADOW WATCH
TOM CLANCY'S POWER PLAYS: BIO-STRIKE
TOM CLANCY'S POWER PLAYS: COLD WAR
TOM CLANCY'S POWER PLAYS: CUTTING EDGE
TOM CLANCY'S POWER PLAYS: ZERO HOUR
TOM CLANCY'S POWER PLAYS: WILD CARD

Tom Clancy's ENDWAR™

WRITTEN BY

DAVID MICHAELS

BERKLEY BOOKS, NEW YORK

THE BERKLEY PUBLISHING GROUP
Published by the Penguin Group
Penguin Group (USA) Inc.
375 Hudson Street, New York, New York 10014, USA
Penguin Group (Canada), 90 Eglinton Avenue East, Suite 700, Toronto, Ontario M4P 2Y3, Canada
(a division of Pearson Penguin Canada Inc.)
Penguin Books Ltd., 80 Strand, London WC2R 0RL, England
Penguin Group Ireland, 25 St. Stephen's Green, Dublin 2, Ireland (a division of Penguin Books Ltd.)
Penguin Group (Australia), 250 Camberwell Road, Camberwell, Victoria 3124, Australia
(a division of Pearson Australia Group Pty. Ltd.)
Penguin Books India Pvt. Ltd., 11 Community Centre, Panchsheel Park, New Delhi—110 017, India
Penguin Group (NZ), 67 Apollo Drive, Rosedale, North Shore 0632, New Zealand
(a division of Pearson New Zealand Ltd.)
Penguin Books (South Africa) (Pty.) Ltd., 24 Sturdee Avenue, Rosebank, Johannesburg 2196,
South Africa

Penguin Books Ltd., Registered Offices: 80 Strand, London WC2R 0RL, England

This is a work of fiction. Names, characters, places, and incidents either are the product of the author's
imagination or are used fictitiously, and any resemblance to actual persons, living or dead, business
establishments, events, or locales is entirely coincidental. The publisher does not have any control over
and does not assume any responsibility for author or third-party websites or their content.

TOM CLANCY'S ENDWAR™

A Berkley Book / published by arrangement with Rubicon, Inc.

PRINTING HISTORY
Berkley edition / February 2008

Copyright © 2008 by Rubicon, Inc.
EndWar, Ubisoft, and the Ubisoft logo are trademarks of Ubisoft in the U.S. and other countries. Tom
Clancy's EndWar copyright © 2008 by Ubisoft Entertainment S.A.
Cover design by Steven Ferlauto.
Interior text design by Kristin del Rosario.

All rights reserved.
No part of this book may be reproduced, scanned, or distributed in any printed or electronic form
without permission. Please do not participate in or encourage piracy of copyrighted materials in
violation of the author's rights. Purchase only authorized editions.
For information, address: The Berkley Publishing Group,
a division of Penguin Group (USA) Inc.,
375 Hudson Street, New York, New York 10014.

ISBN: 978-0-425-22214-0

BERKLEY®
Berkley Books are published by The Berkley Publishing Group,
a division of Penguin Group (USA) Inc.,
375 Hudson Street, New York, New York 10014.
BERKLEY® is a registered trademark of Penguin Group (USA) Inc.
The "B" design is a trademark belonging to Penguin Group (USA) Inc.

PRINTED IN THE UNITED STATES OF AMERICA

10 9 8 7 6 5 4 3 2 1

If you purchased this book without a cover, you should be aware that this book is stolen property. It was
reported as "unsold and destroyed" to the publisher, and neither the author nor the publisher has
received any payment for this "stripped book."

ACKNOWLEDGMENTS

The author would like to thank the following individuals whose assistance and support made this book possible:

Mr. Tom Colgan
Mr. Chris George
Ms. Sandra Harding
Chief Warrant Officer James Ide, USN (Ret.)
Major Mark Aitken, U.S. Army
Master Sergeant Randy McElwee, U.S. Army (Ret.)
Major William R. Reeves, U.S. Army
Major Craig Walker, USAF

FROM UBISOFT:
Joshua Meyer
Richard Dansky
Alexis Nolent
Olivier Henriot
Cedrick Delmas
The Ubisoft legal department

John Gonzalez

Audrey Leprince

Nathalie Paccard

Michael De Plater

FROM BLACKHAWK PRODUCTS GROUP:

Mr. Mike Noel, U.S. Navy SEAL (Ret.)

Mr. Tom O'Sullivan, U.S. Army (Ret.)

Mr. Michael Janich, U.S. Army (Ret.)

Mr. Steve Matulewicz, Command Master Chief (SEAL) (Ret.)

Mr. Brent Beshara, Canadian Special Forces (Ret.)

Mr. Michael Rigg, Paladin Press

Mr. Darrel Ralph, custom knife maker (www.darrelralph.com)

Dr. Rudy McDaniel, University of Central Florida

Mrs. Carole McDaniel (carole.mcdanieldesign.com)

Nancy, Lauren, and Kendall Telep

And there went out another horse that was red: and power was given to him that sat thereon to take peace from the earth, and that they should kill one another: and there was given unto him a great sword.

—REVELATION 6:4

I know not with what weapons World War III will be fought, but World War IV will be fought with sticks and stones.

—ALBERT EINSTEIN

CAST OF CHARACTERS

JOINT STRIKE FORCE (JSF) LEADERSHIP—U.S.

David Becerra, President ("American Eagle")

Roberta Santiago, National Security Advisor

Mark Hellenberg, White House Chief of Staff

General Laura Kennedy, Chairman of the Joint Chiefs of Staff (JCS)

General Rudolph McDaniel, Vice Chairman of the JCS

Major Alice Dennison, USMC, JSF Tactical Operations Specialist ("Hammer")

Charles Shakura (lead interrogator for JSF)

JOINT STRIKE FORCE, ODA SPECIAL FORCES

Team Sergeant Nathan Vatz ("Vortex"; "Bali")

Captain Tom Gerard, Detachment Commander

Chief Warrant Officer 3 Douglas Barnes, Assistant Detachment Commander

Sergeant Zack Murrow, Weapons Sergeant ("Volcano")

Captain Mike Godfrey, Detachment Commander (ODA 888, "Berserker Six")

Captain Manny Rodriguez, Detachment Commander (ODA 897, "Zodiac Six")

Chief Warrant Officer 3 Samson, Assistant Detachment Commander (ODA 888, "Black Bear")

Sergeant Jac Sasaki, Senior Medic (ODA 888, "Band-Aid")

Staff Sergeant Paul Dresden, Assistant Medic (ODA 888, "Beethoven")

JOINT STRIKE FORCE, MARINE EXPEDITIONARY FORCES

Colonel Stack, Company Commander

Staff Sergeant Raymond McAllen, Force Recon Team Leader ("Outlaw One")

Sergeant Terry Jones, Assistant Team Leader ("Outlaw Two")

Corporal Palladino, team scout/sniper ("Outlaw Three")

Corporal Szymanski, team scout ("Outlaw Four")

Lance Corporal Friskis, radio operator ("Outlaw Five")

Navy Corpsman Gutierrez, medic ("Outlaw Six")

Sergeant Scott Rule, New Assistant Team Leader ("Outlaw Two")

F-35 DETACHMENT, NORTHWEST TERRITORIES

Major Stephanie Halverson, USAF ("Siren")

Captain Jake Boyd, USAF ("Ghost Hawk")

Captain Lisa Johansson, USAF ("Sapphire")

STRYKER BRIGADE COMBAT TEAM

Captain Chuck Welch, Company Commander

Staff Sergeant Marc Rakken ("Sparta Six")

Sergeant Timothy Appleman, Vehicle Commander

Private First Class Penny Hassa, Vehicle Driver

USS *FLORIDA* SSN-805

Commander Jonathan Andreas

"Jack" (Operations Officer)

Senior Chief Radioman Sheldon

Chief Electronic Technician Burgess

"Dan" (Communications Officer)

JSF NAVY HIGH COMMAND, HONOLULU

Admiral Donald Stanton, Commander, Pacific Fleet (COMPACFLT)

Admiral Charles Harrison, Commander, Submarines, Pacific

"Smitty" USS *Florida*'s Submarine Squadron Commander

RUSSIAN FEDERATION

Vsevolod Vsevolodovich Kapalkin, President

General Sergei Izotov, Director of the *Glavnoje Razvedyvatel 'noje Upravlenije* (GRU)

Colonel Pavel Doletskaya (GRU)

Major Alexei Noskov, Tactical Operations Officer ("Werewolf")

Colonel Viktoria Antsyforov (GRU)

Commander Ivan Golova, commander of the *Ulyanovsk*

Captain Pravota, Ka-29 chopper pilot

Captain Second Rank Mikhail Anatolyevich Kolosov, commander of the *Romanov*

Alexi Vasiliev, aka William Bullard, Russian mole

EUROPEAN FEDERATION

President Nathalie Perreau

General Amadou Bankolé, EF Enforcers Corps

Capitaine Ilaria Cimino, EFEC Executive Officer

CANADA

Robert Emerson, Prime Minister

"Khaki," chopper pilot and ex–Canadian Special Forces

TERRORIST

Green Vox (symbolic head of the Green Brigade Transnational)

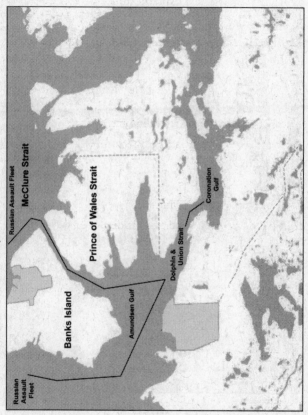

Map concept by James Ide
Graphic design by Carole McDaniel

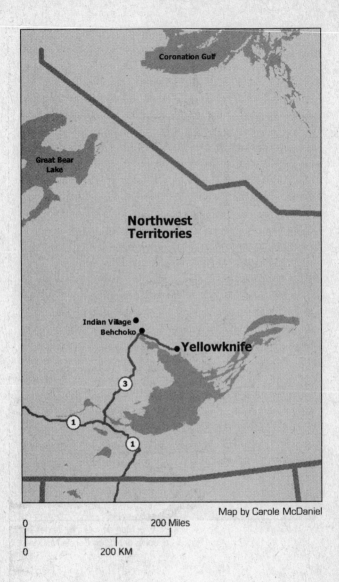

Map by Carole McDaniel

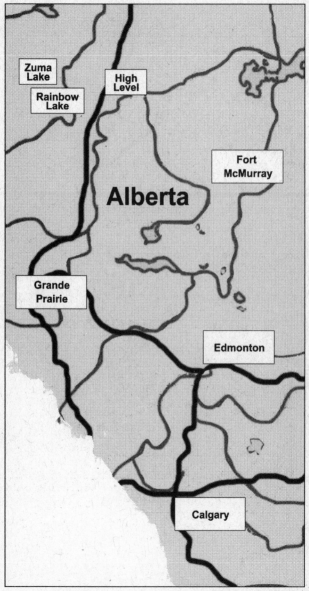

Map by Carole McDaniel

ONE

"He's coming around! Everybody get—"

Team Sergeant Nathan Vatz never finished his sentence. The Russian T-100 main battle tank on the opposite end of the intersection finished it for him.

Vatz slammed onto his gut, sliding across the rain-slick pavement as the office building fifty meters ahead exploded with a thunderous boom.

Shards of concrete, glass, and mangled metal arced into the cold night and fell in a hailstorm on the blackened remains of the HMMWVs and a pair of eight-wheeled Stryker infantry combat vehicles, behind which Vatz's special forces team had taken cover. A black rose of smoke backlit by fire bloomed across the intersection, driven by a wind thick with the stench of cordite.

With a sudden lurch, the fifty-ton tank rumbled

closer, its 152 mm smoothbore main gun swiveling menacingly, tracks grinding over the bodies of the rifle squad—the tank's first victims—who'd been hit as they'd dismounted from one of the Strykers.

Vatz wiped sweat from his eyes, cleared his throat, and spoke into the tiny voice-activated boom mike at his lips: "Victor Six, this is Vortex, over?"

His voice had cracked. *Calm down.* They just had to get the hell out of here. That was it.

But now their exfiltration had gone to hell. No bird to swoop in, land on the rooftop helipad, and whisk them to safety. No nothing.

And that tank wasn't operating alone. The rest of that platoon had to be nearby, with dismounted forces from the BMP-3 infantry fighting vehicles parked outside the gate.

"Victor Six, this is Vortex, over?"

Where was the rest of his twelve-man team? They'd been right behind him, and the captain had been holding up in that doorway, which was now empty.

Vatz bolted to his feet, darted back behind the still-burning hulk of a Mercedes SUV, and suddenly raised his pistol, about to fire—

When he realized the men down the alley were friendlies, his team, easy to mistake because of their Russian Spetsnaz uniforms.

Weapons Sergeant Zack Murrow had already shouldered the Javelin antitank missile they had recovered from one of the dead infantrymen and was moving toward the street, about to lie prone and get a bead on that tank.

Vatz rushed toward Zack; never breaking cover, he said in perfect Russian, "Don't miss."

The sergeant answered in English. "Right. But forget the Russian, Nathan. Our cover's been seriously blown."

Vatz and his colleagues were Joint Strike Force soldiers wearing enemy uniforms. They would be considered spies. They would not be taken prisoner. There would be no diplomatic negotiation for their release.

Hurrying farther along the wall, Vatz found the detachment commander, Captain Tom Gerard, and the assistant detachment commander, Chief Warrant Officer 3 Douglas Barnes, speaking softly, Gerard working an index finger over his pocket PC. Next to them were the team's two commo guys, and farther back were the two engineers and assistant weapons sergeant, Russian Varjag heavy pistols drawn as they covered the end of the alley. One of the two medics was positioned at the near side.

Somewhere in the distance voices lifted. The Spetsnaz dismounted forces were drawing closer. And the drizzle was beginning to get heavier, promising a downpour.

"Hey, Vatz," grunted the captain. "Heard you calling, but I was on the Shadowfire with higher."

"Bad news?"

Barnes, a round-faced man with more than twenty years of service, smiled broadly. "We have to fall back another half klick. Our friends across the street have pushed too far forward, and our bird can't get in here. She's already found a secure spot behind a parking garage near the old municipal airport."

"Couldn't be easy, huh?"

"Vatz, we're a Joint Strike Force team in the middle of Moscow. Operational Detachment Alpha. Special Forces. The world is at war. Damn. If you wanted easy, you should've joined the—"

"My cousin's in the Air Force."

"I was going to say the circus."

"We got one right here. What the hell happened? They were waiting for us."

Gerard and Barnes just shrugged.

Vatz swore under his breath. "Let's move."

As team sergeant, Vatz was responsible for the fighting men during combat situations, which freed up Barnes and Gerard to maintain close contact with their company commander and coordinate team movements within the larger battle plan.

At the moment, Vatz was all about giving one order: *Run!*

He called the others out of the alley, just as Zack announced that his missile was locked, his eye pressed tightly against the command launch unit's night-vision sight. A heartbeat later, he fired.

The missile ripped away with a terrific *whoosh* while a massive chute of fire extended from the launcher's tail.

Like a star in the night, the missile streaked up into the dark mantle of clouds. Even as Zack ditched the launcher and scrambled to his feet, the projectile abruptly changed course, coming straight down in top-attack mode. It struck the tank's turret with a powerful explosion that shattered nearby windows and, in turn, tore into the ammo compartment, creating several more explosions, white-hot shrapnel fountaining from the wreckage.

As more tongues of fire rose from the dead tank, Vatz signaled the others on down the avenue, then stole a glance at his wrist-mounted GPS. The captain had already programmed in their destination. All they had to do was leap over the debris and bodies, connect the dots, and they'd be home.

If you wanted easy.

The two medics, Patterson and Eck, were in charge of keeping the "package" in good shape, said package being one Pavel Doletskaya, a special forces colonel working for the *Glavnoje Razvedyvatel'noje Upravlenije* (GRU), or the Main Intelligence Directorate.

According to intel intercepted by the European Federation Enforcers Corps (EFEC), Doletskaya worked for the big man himself, General Sergei Izotov, the director of the GRU. The two were planning a covert operation with mention of the Amundsen Gulf region up in

Canada. The EFEC had tipped off the Joint Strike Force, and the team had gone into isolation until the opportunity arose to abduct the good colonel. Weeks of planning had resulted in a clean snatch as Doletskaya was leaving "The Aquarium" (the nickname for GRU headquarters) and heading home for the night.

Moreover, the team had done a fine job of wrapping their package. They had bound his wrists, taped his mouth, and placed a ballistic assault helmet with full visor over his head. They needed to protect that head. What he had in it could prove extremely valuable. They had also fitted him with a Dragon Skin armored vest composed of silver dollar–shaped pieces of silicon carbide ceramic. The pieces overlapped like fish scales to help dissipate a bullet's kinetic energy. Doletskaya was far better protected than any member of the team and, of course, worth a lot more to the JSF than they were.

Rifle fire suddenly erupted behind them, rounds burrowing into the wall just a meter behind Vatz.

He wanted to scream for the others to move faster, but that incoming was more than enough motivation.

They charged forward, Barnes and Gerard in the lead, the medics and Doletskaya and the rest right behind them. Vatz pulled up the rear.

Vatz raced to the next corner, dodged behind a wall, then rolled back and opened fire as Zack arrived at his side, adding more suppressing fire.

Six Spetsnaz troops were hustling across the road

about a block away, muzzles flashing as they cut loose another salvo.

Vatz and Zack fired a few more rounds that sent them into crouching positions; then Vatz urged Zack back and the sergeant nodded and took off.

The wind picked up and the rain finally came, hard and heavy, in time with Vatz's pulse.

Meanwhile, the team ducked right down another alley, heading for the next street, and a glance at his GPS told Vatz that the captain was taking a shortcut, probably getting word from Detachment Bravo. That Special Forces team was back at the tactical command post, monitoring their Blue Force Tracking screens and informing the captain that more soldiers were beginning to surround them.

Vatz got on the radio. "Victor Six, this is Vortex."

"Go ahead, Vortex."

"We have a squad in pursuit. Maybe more coming, over."

"Roger, there are at least a few guys coming from the west, along with a vehicle from the north."

"I figured. We'll break off and intercept the dismounts. Buy you a little time, over."

"Do it."

"On our way. Vortex, out."

Zack, who'd been listening over the channel, slowed as Vatz caught up with him. They continued straight up the street, toward a two-story warehouse or factory.

As they reached the corner, they jumped down a meter into a loading bay area, where collected rainwater nearly reached their knees.

Zack swore, slipped, fell face forward, and Vatz seized his arm and dragged him up. They trudged forward, out of the puddle, toward where flashlights—three to be exact—shone across the street from an alley that divided another two factory buildings in half.

Vatz tipped his head in that direction, and they sprinted off, able to reach the wall near the alley before the Spetsnaz troops emerged.

There they paused, and in the seconds it took to catch his breath, Vatz tapped his GPS, zooming in on his location to see if they should circle around the alley and come in from the back side or simply try a frontal approach.

A man's voice, low and heavily burred, echoed off the walls. The Russians were right there.

Zack's expression grew emphatic with the need for orders.

Vatz motioned Zack to crouch down, then whispered into his mike: "I got the first one."

"Okay."

The soldier reached the end of the alley, and Vatz already had his BlackHawk Caracara knife in hand, a black talon of steel that would cut silently and effortlessly through flesh.

The soldier came forward, waving his light—

Vatz sprang on him, drawing his blade across the soldier's neck in one fluid motion while cupping his hand over the man's mouth.

Even as the blood gushed from the Russian's severed carotid artery, Vatz gave the soldier a second punch—the kill shot to the spinal cord. He grew limp and crumpled.

One of the troops called out to his buddy.

Zack's eyes could not grow any wider.

Vatz nodded, and Zack whirled forward, into the alley, just as the second soldier drew near—

Yet even as Zack fired point-blank into the man's head, the third and final soldier fired before Vatz could.

It all happened so fast that Vatz wasn't sure what had happened until . . .

The two Spetsnaz soldiers collapsed to the puddles.

Followed by Zack.

"Aw, no . . ."

A hollow pang struck Vatz as he rushed to his friend, dropped to his knees, eyes already burning.

Zach had taken a round to the head. He was already gone.

Vatz froze. In shock. No time now. Just nothing. Emptiness. And suddenly, he thought of the day he and Zack had been sitting in the barracks and had heard the news about the nukes going off in Saudi Arabia and Iran, destroying both countries. People always asked: where were you on the day the nukes went off?

I was with my buddy Zack.

Vatz reached out, wanting to touch the man's cheek, when the captain's voice boomed in his ear: "Vortex, this is Victor Six. We're nearing the pickup zone, taking heavy fire, over!"

Vatz just breathed.

"Vortex, this is Victor Six, over!"

"Uh, Victor Six, this is Vortex."

"Taking heavy fire!"

"Roger that, Victor Six. We got those other guys but lost Volcano, over."

The captain's tone shifted. He swore then said, "Just rally on us now!"

Watching Zack die right there in the street got under Vatz's skin, that impenetrable Special Forces skin. And suddenly, he wasn't thirty-two years old anymore but just about eight, propelled by utter fear as he raced down the alley. He came out, glanced around, and began to hear the heavy whomping of the chopper. But it was accompanied by another sound, a whirling alarmlike noise that droned on.

He was at full sprint alongside the parking garage now, the chopper just on the other side, the alarm growing louder; and as he rounded the corner, he saw what was happening: a Russian BMP-3 was rolling up and blasting the team with its Long-Range Acoustical device. The sound was so loud that you couldn't help but cover your ears while the enemy gunned you down.

They hadn't opened fire with their big guns because they wanted their colonel back alive. But that didn't stop five or six dismounts from putting more selective rifle fire on the team, just as they reached the chopper's open bay doors.

The chopper's two door gunners did what they could, firing wildly, but they couldn't concentrate with that sound blaring in their ears. No helmets or plugs would help.

Vatz wasn't sure if he'd taken a round or not as he came in from the other side of the bird and launched himself into the air, crashing into the bay, someone shrieking in agony as the helicopter tipped its nose forward and suddenly took off, the gunfire still pinging off the fuselage.

The BMP-3 crew cut loose with their 7.62 mm machine guns, deciding that they'd take the risk and bring down the bird. But the team's pilot descended quickly to the other side of the garage, out of the line of fire, then suddenly banked right and headed back east, keeping low, weaving between buildings, heading for the front lines, for Joint Strike Force–held ground, for safety.

As he looked around the bay, entirely out of breath and bleary-eyed, Vatz realized that only Gerard, Barnes, one medic, and one engineer were onboard, along with Doletskaya.

"Where's everyone else? *Where are they?*"

The captain shook his head.

Barnes and the medic were no longer moving, and the engineer was clutching his leg, shot in the femoral artery and bleeding all over the bay floor.

Just then Gerard pulled open his bloody jacket and lifted his shirt, revealing a pair of dark holes in his chest. He wouldn't make it, and neither would the engineer.

"We need help!" Vatz cried to one of the door gunners.

The guy ignored him, tending to his own shoulder wound.

Gritting his teeth, Vatz pushed himself over to the Russian, wrenched up the man's visor, and grabbed him by the neck. "Are you worth it, you bastard?"

The Russian stared up with vacant eyes.

Vatz glanced back at the remains of his team, then glared at the colonel once more and screamed, *"Are you worth it?"*

TWO

"Obviously you don't remember my father," said General Sergei Izotov as he rose from his office chair. "He was a division commander and hero of the Motherland in World War II. To imply that there is a lack of intelligence in my family is going much too far."

Izotov felt certain that there was only one man in all of Russia who would take such a tone with President Vsevolod Vsevolodovich Kapalkin. He was not that man, but the chance that he might not survive such a conversation was not the point.

He would not allow Kapalkin to insult him or his family, no matter the cost. And he could not believe the insult had come from a man whose own father was a low-level functionary in the KGB, a man whose own fortune was amassed through smuggling personal computers, blue jeans, and other luxury items while attending university. How dare Kapalkin take such a tone with him!

Perhaps he would *not* survive the conversation!

Izotov glared at the president, who stared back at him from the computer screen. Kapalkin's pronounced jaw, penetrating eyes, and impeccably combed hair stripped a decade off his fifty-four years, as did his daily exercise regime of swimming, which kept his waist narrow, his shoulders broad.

The president began to shake his head. "I'll say it again. I'm shocked that your Spetsnaz and security units allowed such a breach. And now they have Doletskaya."

"We were addressing the breach, but they had help from the inside."

"Which is even more disturbing. And now you tell me the colonel's chip has been deactivated by the Americans? We can't kill him? If Doletskaya talks—"

"I think he will hold out for as long as possible. But it won't matter either way. There's nothing those cowboys can do to stop us. The wheels are already in motion. And I will plug this leak."

"General, I want to believe you're right. But then again, I believed your security was the best in the world."

Izotov snorted. "I'm right. Believe it."

President Kapalkin considered that. A smile nicked the corners of his lips as he glanced away at another screen. "The Americans are beginning to pull out of

Moscow. It seems Major Noskov is having more success than you are at the moment."

Izotov discerned a dismissal in the president's tone. "At the moment the major is doing quite well for himself and his unit, but we, too, will succeed. *Spasibo*, Vsevolod Vsevolodovich. Thank you."

The president nodded, and Izotov broke the link. Then he whirled around and smote a fist on the table, highly unlike him.

He wanted to call someone, vent his anger, but he had no real friends, just a shifting coterie of allies. Even his spartanly furnished office seemed to taunt him, to remind him that despite all the blood, sweat, and tears, there were still men like Kapalkin who would dismiss his sacrifices as cavalierly as they would a waiter.

What had he become?

The rumors had spread among his subordinates that he only slept one or two hours per day, that he was perhaps part machine, constructed by the government itself. Sometimes he felt that way.

And oh, he had served that government well, in the first and second Chechen wars, twice a hero back then. He had commanded the 6th Spetsnaz Brigade from 1998 to 2006, and was head of the *Vozdushno-Desantnye Voyska* (VDV), the Russian Airborne Troops, from 2007 to 2012. In 2012, he had assumed his post at the GRU and for the past eight years had expanded the directorate's power and purpose.

But had he focused too much on the work?

His subordinates even questioned his wife's death, wondered if he was somehow involved.

He would speak of it to no one, purge all thoughts of it from his mind.

He returned to his seat, leaned forward toward the computer screen, and reminded himself of the dream he shared with his subordinates, the dream he shared with the president:

There could be only one superpower. And he would do everything he could to ensure that.

Why? To restore the Motherland to greatness. To achieve a level of personal power nearly unimaginable.

And to be like his hero, Stalin, who never wore a personal sidearm yet boldly thrust out his chest against the Nazis. Stalin would know how to bring the European Federation and the American Joint Strike Force to their knees.

At sixty-one, there weren't many things left in this world that truly moved General Sergei Izotov.

War was one of them.

And while agonizing at times, it was still terribly fun.

THREE

Major Alice Dennison, USMC, wanted to speak to the prisoner herself, so she had caught a flight to Helsinki, where he was being temporarily housed at Vantaa Prison before being sent to Guantánamo Bay.

Two well-armed rifle squads of European Federation Enforcers Corps troops had been dispatched to reinforce security at the prison, and two sergeants stood at the gate, unflinching in the morning rain.

But as Dennison exited her armored SUV, their expressions shifted, eyes playing over her face and drifting down to her legs, despite the trench coat.

She was used to the ogling but never tolerated it. Her glare sent their gazes straight ahead, and she offered them a crisp and official-sounding, "Good morning."

"Morning, ma'am," they said in unison with thick accents.

Dennison was escorted into the building by a trio of heavily armed Joint Strike Force military police, along with a pair of her own personal security guards dressed in civilian clothes.

After passing through four separate checkpoints, they reached the small, ten-by-ten interrogation room.

The JSF had already sent in a team of six of their best interrogators, and they had already spent more than ten hours questioning Colonel Pavel Doletskaya.

Joint Strike Force doctrine gave the interrogators twenty-one approaches to "convince" prisoners of war to divulge critical intelligence. The approaches were designed to exploit the prisoner's personal history, morality, sense of duty, love of country, relationships with comrades, and even his sense of futility. Carefully applied in the correct combinations, the approaches were said to work on nearly everyone.

But during the flight over, Dennison had learned that Doletskaya had given up nothing. He made no attempt to invent information or misdirect the interrogators. He simply refused to cooperate and demanded that the consequences of such refusal be carried out immediately.

"Hello, Major," came a voice from behind her.

The lead interrogator, Charles Shakura, proffered his large hand and introduced himself. He was an impressive-looking black man despite his tattered business attire and the dull haze in his eyes.

"Nothing new since we last spoke?"

He shook his head and sighed in disgust. "I haven't been given authority to use enhanced measures."

"We'll go there, but only if it's absolutely necessary. I want to speak to him now." She headed toward the door, while Shakura motioned to one of the guards to unlock it.

Dennison stepped into the room, closed the door behind her.

The colonel sat at the head of a small, steel table bolted to the floor and kept his head lowered.

He had a graying crew cut, and from what she could tell from beneath his straight jacket, a barrel chest and thick arms. His face was flushed, the white stubble of a beard tracing his mouth. He was, in most respects, a beautiful man, a predator with his wings clipped.

"Colonel, look at me."

Slowly, his head rose, and his semi-vacant eyes began to focus, grow brighter. He spoke with a Russian accent, but his English was excellent: "Major Dennison, the most famous executive officer of the Joint Strike Force. And one of the youngest. You are more beautiful than all of the photos and videos I've studied. They do you no justice. How old are you? Twenty-nine?"

"What's going on up in the Amundsen Gulf?"

"You are thirty-four. I know how old you are. And

such a beautiful young woman given such a terrible job."

Dennison spoke through her teeth. "What's going on up there?"

"Nothing."

"What is Operation 2659? Who is Snegurochka?"

"Major, if you came to ask me those painfully obvious questions, you've wasted your time. Don't you want to know more about your adversary? Doesn't it fascinate you that I am here, in the flesh? I've studied you for a very long time. I know everything. Your father was an Air Force pilot. You went to Virginia Military Institute, graduated the class of 2005."

"Two thousand four," she corrected.

He smiled. "Of course. And then you went to the United States Naval Academy, got your B.S. in systems engineering, graduated summa cum laude. Very impressive. You've been in U.S. Naval intelligence and logistics and went on to serve in the U.S. Naval Special Warfare Command. I even know you were handpicked by General Scott Mitchell to join the JSF. Your favorite ice cream flavor is rocky road. And you watch that romantic comedy with . . . I don't remember the actor's name. You watch that over and over. Too many times."

Her face twisted into a deep frown. "I didn't know I had a Russian stalker."

"Stalker? Of course not. Details are my god. Know your enemy, keep him close, study him, learn his weaknesses, exploit them, then bring him down—if you want to call that *stalking*. I call it hunting."

"You're planning another attack. And you're going to tell us all about it."

"Please, Major. We know where this will go and how it will end. Fly home. Forget all about me."

She narrowed her gaze. "I'm going to get authorization to use enhanced methods to interrogate you. Do you know what that means?"

"This is where you promise to torture me, but it never comes because there are too many bleeding hearts in your government. If we had captured you, I would have already strip-searched you—and taken my time with that. And then we would stick a long needle in your arm. Do you know what SP-18 is?"

"I thought it was seventeen."

"This is the new serum, more potent; but like the old, it's tasteless, odorless, and has no side effects. Best of all, you would never remember our heart-to-heart talk. We use it on our own agents all the time, to ensure their loyalty. We would have what we want from you in one hour. I have been here a long time, twelve, fourteen hours? I do not know. They took my watch. And you have nothing after all that time, nothing except a team of dead soldiers, spies who deserved to die."

Dennison's chest grew tight, her breath shallow. She stood and came around the table, leaned over, and got into the colonel's face. "Those men gave their lives to bring you back here. Oh, you're going to talk. But first, I suspect, you're going to bleed. A lot."

"Like I said, you are a beautiful woman with a terrible job." He laughed again, under his breath.

Her fist connected with his nose, driving his head back, and she thought, *My God, I just punched him*, but there was no taking it back.

The door swung open and the guards rushed in, followed by Shakura. "Major, please, we have strict orders not—"

"I issued those orders," she said, rubbing her knuckles.

Doletskaya faced her, blood streaming over his mouth. "Thank you."

"For what?"

"For allowing me to bleed for my Motherland."

She cursed at him.

He smiled, blood filling the cracks of his teeth. "Major Dennison, you are apparently the only *man* here."

She regarded Shakura. "Clean him up. He's off to Cuba."

"I'm sorry, Major," said the colonel.

She frowned.

"I'm sorry we don't have more time to talk." The guards took the colonel by the arms and forced him to his feet. "I wanted to express my condolences about your mother," he added quickly.

"My mother?"

"The cancer. And yes, I wanted to tell you that you

should talk to your sister, that she is still your sister despite your political differences. And I wanted to tell you that it's okay to cry, late at night, like you do sometimes when you eat all the ice cream. The rocky road. It's okay."

She balled her hands into fists, glowered at him, flicked her glance to Shakura. "Get this . . . *freak* . . . out of here."

Doletskaya winked. "*Dosvidaniya*, Major."

Chills ripped across her shoulders as they shoved him out of the room, blood dripping from his chin.

She trembled violently now, began to lose her breath.

"Major?" called Shakura. "Are you all right?"

She closed her eyes.

Bared her teeth.

And inside, she screamed.

FOUR

"Oh, damn, Mick, we got only ten minutes till the Russians arrive."

Staff Sergeant Raymond McAllen, leader of a six-man USMC Force Reconnaissance team, didn't need his assistant, Sergeant Terry Jones, to remind him of that. He'd set his stopwatch within a minute after the eighteen-man platoon fast-roped down into the valley as their Black Hawk had thundered off to seek cover until they called her back.

"We got less time than that, Jonesy. But the crash site should be just over that ridge."

"Yeah, but it don't look good. No contact from them. We don't even know if this guy is still alive."

"Our job's to find out. Come on!"

The sun was beginning to set over the Sierra Maestra mountains in southern Cuba, and the shadows grew longer across slopes covered in mud from the midday rains. McAllen and his men had already shouldered their way through some dense jungle in sweltering, humid air, but they were almost at the site.

And no, this wasn't a run-of-the-mill TRAP (Tactical Recovery of Aircraft and Personnel) mission. Apparently, one of the passengers onboard the Learjet was a Russian colonel who'd been on his way to Guantánamo when the Russians had shot down his escort fighters. They'd also managed to strike a glancing blow to the jet, forcing it down into the mountains.

Fortunately, McAllen and his entire Force Recon company had been engaged in a weeklong, live-fire training exercise at Gitmo and been able to respond within minutes of the call.

Unfortunately, they'd been out in the field doing some physical training when the call had come, and they'd been forced to board the chopper with whatever they had, leaving behind their best high-tech toys— advanced body armor, weapons, and communications systems that were all part of the military's Future Force Warrior program.

They'd get by with just the conventional gear. McAllen believed that if you depended too much upon technology in the field, you'd become sloppy and soft, a kid at a convenience store who can't make change, a Marine who can't aim because the computer does it for him.

He waved on the others, Jonesy first; then his two recon scouts, Corporals Palladino and Szymanski; his radio operator, Lance Corporal Friskis; and finally the team's medic, Navy Corpsman Gutierrez, who carried the team's biggest gun, the Squad Automatic Weapon, because putting more steel on target was the best form of preventative medicine.

Palladino and Szymanski moved out ahead, walking point, ready to throw hand signals or call in via the intra-team radio at their first sign of contact.

Meanwhile, the other two six-man teams were about three kilometers west, moving to head off part of a company-size Russian ground force that had already inserted, minutes after the crash. A second Russian team was just north of the site, and higher was scrambling to put another Force Recon platoon on the ground there, but McAllen still bet that his team would reach the jet before the Russians did.

Their friends in Moscow were taking no chances and assuming nothing. They'd actually planned in advance to drop troops on the ground and ensure that this colonel was dead.

That certainly had McAllen's attention.

He pulled up the rear, sweeping the jungle with his carbine, head low, repeatedly stealing glances behind.

They stole their way even higher up the slope, boots digging deeper into the mud, as the mountain grew darker and the hoots and cries of birds seemed to drift off into an eerie silence, save for their footfalls. The stench of the crash grew stronger, a combination of mildew, smoke, and spilled fuel.

"Outlaw Three, this is Outlaw One, over," called McAllen over the radio.

"Go ahead, One," answered Palladino; he was also the team's sniper, six feet of muscle and hard heart.

"Got eyes on the site, over?"

"Just now, but we'll need to approach over that hill to the east. We can't get down this way. Too steep. Come on up and have a look, over."

"Coming up."

After reaching the ridge and jogging over to where Palladino and Szymanski were hunkered down, McAllen caught his breath and saw what the sniper was talking about.

The approach was far too steep. Even so, this perch afforded a perfect view of the valley below.

The Learjet had burrowed into the side of the mountain, yet most of the fuselage was intact. Its wings were gone, though, its side door open, smoke still pouring from its engines and the long, meter-deep furrow stretching out behind. They couldn't get to it, but circling around as Palladino had suggested would kill even more time.

"What do you want do, Sergeant?" asked Szymanski, his chiseled face and thick neck dappled with sweat.

"Shift around."

"Uh-oh," interrupted Palladino, staring through a pair of night-vision goggles into the gloom ahead. "Enemy contact, tree line north. At least six guys, maybe more. They're moving in."

McAllen tensed. So the Russians had beaten them to the site, but they hadn't reached the jet itself yet. He got on the radio: "Outlaw Team, this is One. I want Outlaws Three and Six up here on the ridge. I want sniper and SAW fire on that tree line. The rest of you come with me!"

Gutierrez hustled forward with his big machine gun, setting up a few meters away from Palladino, who dropped to lie prone with his M40A3 sniper rifle balanced on its bipod.

McAllen led Jonesy, Szymanski, and Friskis along the ridge, weaving through the palms and other trees until they reached the aforementioned hill east of their position. It, too, was particularly steep but draped in enough dense foliage to conceal their advance—and the possibility of a tumble down the hillside.

"Outlaw One, this is Outlaw Six," called Gutierrez. "They're breaking from the tree line, over."

"Let Outlaw Three take the first shot, and that's your signal to open up, over."

"Roger that."

McAllen imagined Palladino up there on the hill, staring through his scope, making hasty calculations—

When suddenly his rifle resounded, a great thunderclap echoing off the mountains.

A gasp later, Gutierrez began delivering his lecture, the Professor of Doom bathing himself in brass casings, the SAW *rat-tat-tat*ing loud and clear.

McAllen's group had a handful of seconds to make their break from the slope and weave a serpentine path toward the downed plane.

He ordered Szymanski and Friskis out first and they charged away, vanishing off into the trees, while he and Jonesy took a more westerly path, closer to the Russians in the tree line. McAllen figured that even if the enemy got closer, at least two of his men would make it to the plane, while he and Jonesy could intercept.

Up on the hill, Gutierrez and Palladino continued laying down fire, the Russians only answering with sporadic shots.

McAllen and Jonesy reached the Learjet, two seconds behind the other guys. "Stay out here," McAllen ordered Szymanski. "Mask up. Pop smoke. Friskis, stay with him. Call the PL, tell him we've reached the site."

"You got it, Sergeant."

McAllen and Jonesy slipped on their masks and McAllen followed Jonesy into the hazy confines of the jet, his rifle at the ready.

The cabin walls and ceiling were heavily scorched. He glanced right.

And wished he hadn't.

At least ten people were strewn about, their blackened limbs twisted at improbable angles. A few of them were dressed in the burned remains of civilian clothes while the others wore military uniforms, Navy mostly.

"Check the cockpit," he told Jonesy, then rushed forward to the nearest body, whose government ID had melted into his chest. There wasn't much left of his face, either, but it was clear he wasn't their Russian colonel. He was a black man, about middle age.

McAllen was about to move on to the next guy—

When the man's eyes snapped open, shocking the hell out of him. "Jesus!"

The survivor's voice came thin and cracked. "Help me."

McAllen leaned over the man. "Whoa, God, buddy, yeah, yeah, I will. And you help me. We're looking for a guy, a Russian colonel."

"Sergeant!" hollered Friskis from the doorway. "I think we got another squad. They're moving up!"

"Okay, get ready to fall back. We have a survivor here. Jonesy, check the others!"

McAllen's assistant emerged from the cockpit. "Roger that. Pilots are dead," he reported, his voice muffled by his mask.

The black man grabbed McAllen's arm. "Please, my daughters need me."

"Don't worry, buddy, I'll get you out of here. What's your name?"

"Charles Shakura."

"All right, Mr. Shakura, stay calm." McAllen carefully unfastened the man's seat belt. "But listen to me, man. The colonel. We need to know about that Russian colonel. He's supposed to be onboard."

Shakura grimaced.

Abruptly, gunfire began drumming on the outside of the fuselage—

And Jonesy came rushing forward from the back of the jet. "Looks like some civilians and officers, but no one's cuffed, Sergeant."

"Charlie, where's the Russian?"

Shakura swallowed.

McAllen seized him by the collar. "Where is he?"

Shakura slowly blinked. "He got here by sub. We're just the . . . just the decoy. He was never on this flight."

McAllen's shoulders slumped. He released Shakura and glanced over his shoulder at Jonesy.

"Well, I thought I was a Marine, not an actor," snapped Jonesy. "And I just love being expendable."

McAllen took a deep breath, composed himself. "All right. Doesn't matter what's going on here. Decoy, no decoy. We got a survivor. Help him out, get him strapped into a litter."

Jonesy sighed in disgust. "You got it."

Drawing in another deep breath, McAllen shifted outside, where Friskis and Szymanski had taken up firing position on their bellies alongside the fuselage, whose port side faced the tree line, now obscured in thick walls of gray smoke.

McAllen got on the radio with his platoon leader, shared the grim news that they were just part of a decoy mission but that they did have one survivor to rescue. The PL promised close air support within five minutes.

A pair of grenades exploded somewhere behind them. That would be the Russians trying to take out Gutierrez and his big gun. "Outlaw Six, this is One. Take Three and rally east to our second hill, over. We're bringing up a survivor."

"Roger that, One. On my way, out."

McAllen and Jonesy moved Shakura out of the Learjet. As Jonesy unfurled the portable litter he had removed from his pack, Friskis and Szymanski kept the Russians busy, triplets of fire drumming repeatedly.

Somewhere in the distance, the whomping of helicopters began to grow louder.

Once Shakura was strapped in, McAllen called back the scout and radio operator from their firing positions and gave them the unenviable task of hauling the injured man back up the hillside. He and Jonesy would remain behind to cover.

"Go now!" he cried, and while the two men took off

with their survivor, he and Jonesy set up on either side of the fuselage.

Not three seconds later, something remarkable and utterly breath-robbing occurred:

The damned Russians decided to storm the jet!

A wave of six troopers in masks appeared in the smoke not twenty meters away, running directly at McAllen, their rifles blazing, rounds punching into and ricocheting off the plane, popping in the mud, whizzing overhead.

Out of the corner of his eye, McAllen spotted at least as many troopers charging toward Jonesy.

"Oh my God, Ray! Here they come!" cried his assistant.

A terrible ache woke deep in McAllen's gut as he realized he couldn't get them all. Damn, there was too much life left in him. He hadn't even found the right woman . . .

And he'd worked so damned hard to get where he was, a Force Recon warrior—swift, silent, and deadly—the eyes and ears of his commander.

How many training missions? How many real operations, including that big one in the mountains of Bulgaria, fighting those terrorist bastards, the Green Brigade?

And now the big war had just started, maybe the war to end all wars, and he'd barely had a chance to make his contribution to the fight.

His life wasn't flashing before his eyes. That was a myth. But that ache, that solid, thick ache whispered like the Reaper in his ear, *This is it. Time's up. The bill's come due*.

He figured the best he could do was lay down some fire across their unarmored legs, try to drop all six of them as quickly as he could, and as they fell, he might be able to pan again with another salvo.

He set his teeth and squeezed the trigger of his carbine, striking the legs of the Russian to his far right, bringing that man down, though he could still recover and fire.

Yet before McAllen knew what was happening, Palladino's sniper rifle boomed once, blasting the head off one Russian, boomed again, tore off the shoulder of another. McAllen continued sweeping across the last three guys, dropping all of them.

Not a second after he did that, Gutierrez cut into them from above with his SAW.

McAllen exploited the moment to burst up from his position and charge toward the Russians attacking Jonesy's position. He already had a grenade loaded in his carbine's attached launcher, so he let it fly. Just as the grenade hit the mud and exploded, McAllen hit the deck himself, bringing up the rifle and raking their line with fire.

Suddenly, out of the smoke, came a lone Russian, blood pouring from his neck, his helmet gone. He screamed something at McAllen and swung his rifle around.

The roar of their Black Hawk was deafening now, the rotor wash suddenly hitting them, knocking the Russian back. As the enemy soldier lost his balance, one of the helicopter's door gunners opened up on him, and he jerked involuntarily before hitting the ground.

Since the valley was far too dense for the chopper's pilot to land, the bird continued to wheel overhead, door gunners cutting apart the tree line, giving the remaining Russians something to think about.

McAllen got to his feet and jogged past the dead troops to where Jonesy was lying on his gut.

Unmoving.

McAllen ripped off his mask and dropped to his knees, shaking his assistant. Then he ripped off Jonesy's mask and rolled the man over, seeing that he'd been shot in the face and neck.

McAllen rose, and all the anger and frustration suddenly funneled into his arms and legs. He hoisted Jonesy over his back in a fireman's carry and staggered away from the downed plane toward the hill. Friskis ran to meet him. "They got Jonesy," was all McAllen could say.

He told himself over and over that it didn't matter that the mission was a decoy and that they'd been pawns in a little game of deception. It didn't matter. It was a Marine Corps operation and Jonesy had done his job, as they all had.

But his mind raced with the what-ifs and with the names of the people he could hold responsible. If higher knew that the mission was a decoy, then why did they risk the lives of highly trained Marine Corps operators? Couldn't they have played wait and see or just attacked from the air? They probably wanted the decoy to look perfect, right down to the bogus rescue mission on the ground.

McAllen was left with only one hope: that Jonesy had died for something meaningful. Something important.

FIVE

Team Sergeant Nathan Vatz had Colonel Pavel Dolet-skaya strapped to an inclined board, his head lowered to about forty-five degrees. He'd wrapped cellophane over the colonel's face, allowing just a small gap for him to breathe.

Vatz picked up the hose and released some pressure, allowing a steady stream of water to flow over the colonel's head. Most prisoners lasted a handful of seconds, until the gag reflex kicked in, along with the fear of drowning; but the colonel didn't move, didn't flinch.

And this went on for more than two minutes until Vatz got so frustrated with the man that he threw away the hose, ripped off the cellophane, and screamed, "What's in your head that's so important? What do you know?"

The colonel's eyes widened. "What's in my head? The real question is what's in your head. And the answer is *me*."

"If I can't kill you, they will. You need to die."

"Nathan, please. I know exactly who you are. I know that you joined the Army because you were bullied all through school, that you somehow wanted to get revenge on them, to prove to them that you were more than just a punching bag. You thought you could be a man."

"Not true."

"Why did you kill your father?"

"What are you talking about?"

"You killed him when you joined the Army. Murdered him. Because he knew, deep down, the war was coming. And he loved his son. But you killed him."

"No!" Vatz beat a fist into his palm.

"And now you are alone. The diabetes took him. The alcohol took your mother. And I took all your friends, your brothers in arms. You're the only one left. Why were you spared? Do you think it's fate?"

"I don't know. It doesn't matter. I'm just having another nightmare about how much I want to kill you."

"Would that make you feel better?"

With a gasp and shudder, Vatz sat up in his bunk. He looked at his hands, which were still balled into fists.

Then he glanced up, out the window of his barracks. It was a beautiful morning, a cloudless sky sweeping over Fort Lewis, Washington.

He was back home with the 1st Special Forces Group (Airborne), and recently assigned to a new Operational Detachment Alpha team, ODA-888. The company commander wanted to keep him out of the field until he "healed," but he'd insisted that he was okay. There were those officers further up the chain of command who believed that his pain could be converted into a powerful weapon, especially during times like these, when the JSF's forces were spread so thinly around the globe.

"Hey, Nate, you want to get some chow?"

Staff Sergeant Marc Rakken stood in the doorway, lifting his chin at Vatz.

Rakken was about to turn thirty, already had a little gray in his sideburns, but his baby blue eyes and unwrinkled face made him look like a kid. He was assigned to the Stryker Brigade Combat Team and was a rifle squad leader in charge of eight other guys. They'd storm down the Stryker's rear ramp, divide into two teams, and raise serious hell on the enemy.

Ordinarily, a Special Forces operator like Vatz wouldn't socialize much with an infantryman because of differing schedules, billets, and because, well, some regular Army guys referred to Spec Ops as the "prima donnas" of the military, wild men and wasters of precious resources.

But Vatz's friendship with Rakken cut through all that. They'd met during basic training, since most Special

Forces guys started off in the regular Army. They'd talked about fishing and knife collecting and learned that they'd both been born and raised in Georgia, in small towns no more than a hundred miles from each other. Small world. They'd kept in touch over the years and eventually had both been assigned to Fort Lewis.

And while Vatz had come home to a few friendly faces, mostly acquaintances, Rakken was the only guy he'd call a friend, the only guy he'd talked to in the past few days.

"Marc, I don't feel so good. Maybe later."

"Bro, you don't look so good. Couldn't sleep again?"

Vatz shook his head.

"Come outside, get some air. At least get some coffee."

After rubbing the corners of his eyes, Vatz nodded, dragged himself from the bed, and pulled on his trousers.

They took the long path toward the mess hall, the snowcapped mountains on the horizon. Vatz squinted in the sun. "Any word on your next deployment?"

"None yet. The Euro ops have a lot to do with where we might get sent next. Who knows?"

Vatz nodded.

Up ahead stood the long, rectangular mess hall with a brick facade, a new facility constructed in just the past year. Vatz took another three steps—when the windows of the mess hall blew out with an ear-shattering boom.

He and Rakken hit the deck as the glass tumbled to the pavement and smoke began billowing from the jagged holes.

Rakken was already on his feet, sprinting toward the mess hall, with Vatz screaming for him to wait up, there could be more bombs.

They charged forward, over carpets of glass and pieces of blinds and other debris.

The pair of glass entrance doors had been blown off, and they couldn't see through the clouds of brown-and-gray smoke.

"Marc, it's not safe yet!"

"I don't care! Jesus, they hit us here?" Rakken gasped.

The question was who. The Russians? Any one of the hundreds of terrorist groups out there? Or was it just some grunt who'd gone insane and strapped himself with explosives before sitting down to breakfast?

After waiting another moment for the smoke to clear a little, Vatz followed Rakken into the mess; an oppressive wall of heat still emanated from the area. He held his breath, spotted a lance corporal on the ground, clutching his bleeding arm. He helped the guy to his feet, got him through the front, and led him to the grass. Then Vatz, coughing hard, his eyes burning, headed back into the mess.

The smoke and dust cleared a bit more, and it appeared that the blast had come from the center of the large dining area; there was a gaping crater in the concrete, tables upturned and shattered by the concussion.

And there were pieces of soldiers everywhere.

Vatz gagged. The rest of it became a blur of images accompanied by the sickly sweet odor of burned flesh. Someone shrieked, and the cry wouldn't stop echoing.

In the hours that followed, he and Rakken learned the truth: the Green Brigade terrorist group was responsible for the bombing.

Formed in 2012, they were a militant environmentalist/antiglobalist group with cells throughout the world but primarily in Europe and South America. From 2012 until 2018, they were credited with more than a thousand acts of violence, including acts of intimidation against factory and refinery workers and the kidnapping and murder of business executives, military personnel, and computer scientists.

One of their operatives had infiltrated the base and walked into the mess hall. He'd removed his uniform to reveal the explosives strapped to his chest. He'd made some announcement, but no one Vatz had spoken to remembered what he'd said before detonating his bomb.

At the same time, the terrorists had struck a motor pool at Fort Bragg and a dozen other facilities all over the globe, including a few more Euro military bases, a refinery in Venezuela, and even a Japanese whaler.

The group had gone silent after their leader, who dubbed himself "Green Vox," had been killed when his plane was destroyed by Spetsnaz forces late last year.

Oh, the man *portraying* Green Vox was dead. But the impassioned true believer who was next in line had simply assumed his place and his identity.

Green Vox was the ultimate terrorist.

You could never kill him.

There was always another one.

Vatz and Rakken had watched the bastard on one of the base's big screens, standing there in some undisclosed and heavily wooded location, wearing his green balaclava, shaking his gloved fist, and crying out in English but with a thick, German accent: "I am Green Vox. I am alive! I have returned! We are the Green Brigade Transnational. Today marks our return. We will not stop until the warmongers and tyrants raping our dear Gaia and threatening to scorch her from above are wiped out. We call for all free-minded citizens to join us in curing our green mother globe of this disease that will eventually kill us all."

Soldiers in the room began to throw paper cups and balled-up napkins at the screen, cursing and shouting at the terrorist.

Vatz drifted back to a chair in one corner, collapsed into the seat.

Rakken sat next to him. "I'm still in shock."

"You? I lose my entire team in Moscow and come home to this. Just who the hell did I piss off up there?"

"Piss off? You escaped death twice. Go play the lottery. We could both use the money."

"Marc, I should've died in Moscow."

"The survivor guilt is natural, man. You didn't die there. And you didn't die here. So that makes me believe you still have a lot of work to do."

"So it's fate?"

"I don't know."

Vatz sighed loudly in frustration. "I need to work this out, go for a run, do some boxing, something . . ."

"I hear you. And I don't know if I believe in fate, but I believe in faith. I got faith in you, faith in me. We'll get past this, move on. That's it, man."

Vatz nodded, took a deep breath, closed his eyes.

And there, in the darkness of his mind, stood Colonel Pavel Doletskaya, wearing a crooked grin. Beside him, materializing from the shadows, came the hooded Green Vox, who folded his arms across his chest.

SIX

They had given him the drugs.

They had spent hours questioning him.

They had grabbed him, shaken him, pummeled him, threatened to kill his wife.

And still, Colonel Pavel Doletskaya would tell them nothing.

Even he could not believe how long he'd held out. Surely, the drugs should have loosened his tongue.

Or maybe they had.

Maybe he'd already told them everything and had simply forgotten his betrayal of the Motherland.

The thought sent chills fanning across his shoulders.

He sat in the corner of his cell, elbows pressing against the painful confines of the straitjacket. He stared up at an energy-efficient fluorescent lightbulb glowing dimly from its socket.

That's what it was all about. Energy.

No changing that. And here he was. The end of his journey, perhaps. Major Dennison's people had shoved him into one of the JSF's submarines, a rather impressive little boat, and had secretly ferried him to Cuba. He'd managed to overhear something about the decoy flight being shot down but nothing more. He'd lost track of time; oddly, that bothered him more than anything. He'd spent his entire professional life chained to the clock, and now he was free of those shackles, only to have them replaced by a prison cell.

He nearly grinned over that irony as he glanced reflexively at his wrist, covered by the straitjacket. Some men had given up the watch, in favor of their phones, but not him.

General Sergei Izotov wore a watch as well, a watch that told him that Doletskaya was still a threat. The chip in Doletskaya's head had been their only way to silence him. Once the Americans had deactivated it, they had detached him from the system. Even if it took years, the Americans would try to extract intelligence from Doletskaya, one tooth at a time. Yes, Izotov knew that the Americans would keep Doletskaya alive, perhaps even use him as a negotiating tool, but Izotov and Kapalkin would not bargain.

This was his life now. He should resign himself to it.

But how does a warrior do that?

He didn't know. For now he turned his back on the present and looked to the past, the glorious past, if only to make himself feel better.

It was he and Izotov who'd come up with the brilliant plan to secretly fund the Green Brigade Transnational and train them to attack the *Freedom IV* lifter at the John F. Kennedy Space Center in Cape Canaveral. The plan was to prevent the Americans from completing the *Freedom Star* Space Station from which three companies of Marines could deploy anywhere on earth within ninety minutes. It was a simple matter of hiring terrorists to become your mercenaries. The difference was, the Green Brigade actually believed in what they were doing. Ideals were more important to them than money. As the Americans said, it was a win-win situation.

While the attack turned out to be a failure, it led to an unexpected and ultimately beneficial series of events. The JSF tracked Green Vox and his cronies to a training camp in the mountains of Bulgaria, but before they reached him, Izotov was able to plant information on the terrorists linking them to members of the European parliament.

The idea was to get the Americans to turn on the European Federation. Start a war between them. And then Izotov and Doletskaya would move in for the kill and seize all of Europe. Green Vox escaped that attack, but the JSF found the information planted by the GRU.

But then the situation turned once more. Green Vox holed himself up in the swamps of Belarus.

And that's when Doletskaya made his first mistake.

The Enforcers Corps had, in fact, captured Green Vox, but Doletskaya ordered his platoon leader to demand the turnover of Green Vox so that the Russians could deliver him to the United States because the Euros could not be trusted to do that. The Euros refused and, remarkably, wiped out Doletskaya's men.

And so Izotov and the president were forced to put another spin on the incident: European forces fired on Russian troops as they were attempting to capture Green Vox. As a consequence, Kapalkin stopped the flow of Russian oil and natural gas to Europe. Security forces at an Albanian refinery were overwhelmed by Russian forces, and some of the European shipments were restored.

Of course, blowback from the incident was severe. Russia was on the brink of war with the EF. And if the Euros managed to turn over Green Vox to the United States, he would crack under interrogation and reveal that he'd been funded by the GRU.

Both the EF and the United States would wage war against the Motherland.

That was hardly the plan.

Green Vox needed to die. And so Doletskaya had

assembled one of his best teams, who infiltrated Fort Campbell and reprogrammed the base's air defenses so that the plane carrying Green Vox was blown out of the sky before it could land.

Many bottles of vodka had been emptied in the hours following that crash.

Even better, the Americans were unable to identify Green Vox's assassins. Of course, Kapalkin was sure to point the finger at the European Federation. And Nathalie Perreau, that infuriatingly brilliant French woman who'd become the first president of the EF in 2016, was quick to return the accusation.

It was in the Motherland's best interests to drive a huge wedge between the United States and Europe, so Izotov and Doletskaya had come up with a final plan, which took them back to the beginning of it all:

Destroy the *Freedom IV* lifter, whose launch had been delayed because of the first Green Brigade attack.

Again, relying upon his cunning and two decades of tactical military experience, Doletskaya ordered a well-disguised team of Spetsnaz forces to seize control of a European air base in Finland. They killed everyone, erased all security data, and uploaded a virus into the European Federation's missile shield.

Hours later, when the *Freedom IV* lifted off, the virus caused Europe's laser satellites to misidentify the space-craft as a missile. The ship was incinerated, killing dozens of Americans onboard. To create even more confusion,

Doletskaya arranged for no less than ten terrorist groups to claim responsibility for the Finland base attack and destruction of the lifter.

More bottles of vodka were emptied.

And now there was great mistrust between the European Federation and the Americans.

No, it was not a total victory for the Motherland, but given how badly things could have gone, Doletskaya had been quite satisfied with the outcome.

Now another chapter in the war was about to be written, and it had begun with an elegant dinner and the company of a woman more beautiful and more intelligent than any Doletskaya had encountered.

"Hello, Colonel," she said, wearing a dark red dress, pearls, and a smile that left Doletskaya breathless. He helped her into her chair, returned to his; and as he sat, she hoisted her perfectly tweezed brows and tossed her jet-black hair out of her eyes. "Are you all right?"

"Yes, Colonel. I'm fine. It's just I've never seen you out of uniform."

Her eyes widened slightly. "Likewise."

He smiled. "You have a keen wit."

Viktoria Antsyforov was a colleague of Doletskaya's at the GRU, a woman who had recently proven her mettle by helping him coordinate several attacks on selected EF targets. She had worked her way up through the ranks, an impressive accomplishment and evidence of the more progressive policies instituted by the GRU.

The first time they had met, she had been quick to point out that Russian women had made major contributions to the defense of the Motherland.

The 1st Russian Women's Battalion of Death had formed during World War I, and while they'd never officially been part of the Motherland's other armies, their victories had been well documented. She had gone on to give him a history lesson that had proven quite fascinating.

Rumor had it that Antsyforov was an excellent marksman and that she had excelled in all of her martial arts training. Doletskaya hadn't taken much more time to do research into her background—that was, until she had invited him to dinner to discuss a few ideas.

And so he had learned that at thirty-six she had never been married, had a brother in the navy, and dedicated some of her free time to environmental causes. She also donated a lot of money to charities, particularly those that helped victims of radiation poisoning and those focusing on cancer research.

"You're still looking at me like something is wrong," she said.

"Nothing. I'm sorry." He'd lied. He was having painfully wrong thoughts about her.

The waiter arrived. They ordered vodka, appetizers, and lit up cigarettes.

He glanced around. She certainly knew how to pick a restaurant. The place was called Kupol, owned by the family of world-famous chef Anatoly Komm. The dining area offered a spectacular view of the Moscow river.

"I've never been here."

"Amazing, isn't it?"

"Even better when you're not picking up the check."

She laughed. "It's okay. I thought if I bought you a nice dinner, you might want to jump into bed with me."

"Oh, I see," he said, grinning himself.

"But your wife would not approve."

He shook his head. "Colonel, I'm in a good mood. And I'm going to let your little joke go unnoticed. I want to thank you for bringing me here. I suspect we will have a magnificent meal."

Her expression grew more serious. "Yes, we will."

They made small talk, drank some more, and ate like a king and queen. Not once did she mention any of her "ideas," and toward the end of the meal, Doletskaya, tipsy as he was, blurted out, "So was this a plan to seize my body . . . or my mind?"

"Maybe a little of both." She lowered her voice, leaned forward, and in a few carefully chosen sentences, unfolded a plan that left Doletskaya beaming.

She had taken the obvious, exploited it, turned it around, and made it all seem new again. Step by step she covered the details, as he did, trying to shoot holes in her assertions, but she countered his every attempt.

"I'm sure the Americans have considered this," he told her.

"Which is why I've worked their expectations into our plan. Pavel, a battle plan is like a narrative, a story that must be carefully constructed, familiar yet surprising."

"A story?"

"Yes. All stories are about *desire*."

When the word came out of her mouth, Doletskaya gasped. "Go on . . ."

"Our desire is to overcome the obstacles."

"And reach the goal," he concluded.

She nodded slowly. "But not before the climax."

"What is Operation 2659? Who is Snegurochka?"

Suddenly, Major Alice Dennison was now sitting at the table with them, demanding that Antsyforov tell her what she wanted to know.

"Please, Major," said Antsyforov. "We haven't even had dessert yet. I understand the ice cream here is incredible. You like ice cream, don't you?"

Dennison, an XO in the JSF and a woman almost always under complete control, would not do what she did. At least Doletskaya thought so. But this was his imagination, and he could imagine her doing anything he wanted.

So she lifted up the table, throwing everything onto the floor with a horrible crash and drawing the stares of everyone in the restaurant.

As a team of waiters came rushing over, she screamed at Doletskaya, "What is Operation 2659? Who is Snegurochka?"

He and Antsyforov exchanged a knowing grin.

And when Doletskaya opened his eyes, he was sitting in a chair and staring into the beefy, bearded face of one of his interrogators, who asked again, "What is Operation 2659? Who is Snegurochka?"

SEVEN

President of the United States David Becerra, fifty-six and the first Hispanic chief executive, was seated aboard Air Force One flying on a southwesterly heading at 38,500 feet above the Atlantic Ocean.

Recent news had left him with pain behind his eyes and a pit in his stomach; it seemed unlikely those discomforts would dissipate any time soon.

He was on a conference video call with Europe. The screens before him displayed European Federation President Nathalie Perreau, Enforcers Corps General Amadou de Bankolé, and Enforcers Corps Executive Officer Capitaine Ilaria Cimino.

Becerra had already greeted them and took a deep breath before speaking, determined to make the conversation go exactly where he wanted.

"As I'm sure you're aware, Madame President, three days ago the Russians sent up three cosmonauts to the International Space Station on what our intelligence sources concluded was a resupply and repair mission."

Perreau, just a few years younger than Becerra and an equally captivating speaker, glanced up from another screen set into her desk. "Yes, Mr. President. We monitored that launch, of course. And I'm still amazed that old station hasn't crashed into the ocean." Her English, though spoken with a French accent, was flawless.

"You're amazed, Madame President? The engineers who worked on the ISS are some of the best in the world. That station will far exceed its lifespan, and it became the springboard for everything we put into the new Freedom Star."

"If you've called to discuss *that*—" she began, immediately growing defensive. The Euros had been staunch opponents of Freedom Star, Perreau calling it "the beginning of a new insanity."

"No, ma'am. I'm not calling for that."

"Then, Mr. President, maybe you've called to explain why your ground forces pulled out of Moscow so quickly?"

The challenge came from General Amadou de Bankolé, commander of all special forces in Europe. He had even been involved in the design of the Enforcers Corps and possessed one of the most intimidating visages Becerra had ever seen: deep brown skin, a jaw that appeared to have been carved into shape with a bowie knife, and the cold, almost lifeless eyes of a shark.

Becerra carefully picked his words. "No, General, I'm not at liberty to discuss the specifics of those operations."

"I guess retreating is a bit embarrassing."

Tucking his fist into the seat, Becerra responded slowly, "I'll say this: any maneuver by the Joint Strike Force is carefully planned. Sometimes we trade space for time. And as the son of a Marine master sergeant and a Marine reservist myself, I understand that. As a military officer of your status, a man who has studied our tactics, techniques, and procedures, the situation and accompanying explanations should be obvious."

There, he'd insulted the bastard.

And before Bankolé could reply, another voice broke in. "Mr. President, could you answer a question for me?" Capitaine Ilaria Cimino raised her brows. She was in her mid-thirties, an attractive woman who'd already had a distinguished career with Italian special forces units. In some ways, she reminded Becerra of Major Alice Dennison.

"President Becerra, I asked Capitaine Cimino to join us because she and her team were responsible for intercepting the original transmission and decrypting what they could."

Becerra nodded. "Excellent work, Capitaine. I'm glad I have this opportunity to thank you."

She grinned. "I appreciate that. But now I must ask for all us—have you learned what Operation 2659 is? Who is Snegurochka?"

"We are still working on Doletskaya, but the interrogation has proven difficult."

"Torture him," snapped Bankolé. "And get what we need."

"It's not that simple, General."

He raised his voice. "Torture him."

"I didn't call this meeting to discuss Doletskaya or our justification for pulling out of Moscow. We have a serious problem, and I need your help."

General Bankolé sighed and began to shake his head, but President Perreau quickly said, "Mr. President, sorry for the interruptions. You have our complete attention."

Becerra sighed through a nod. "As I said, three cosmonauts headed up to the ISS on a repair and resupply mission. There are two other researchers up there right now: a Japanese scientist and an engineer from Brazil. About twenty hours ago we lost all contact with them and with the Russians, and shortly thereafter the station repositioned itself."

"Just a technical failure?" asked Perreau, her tone indicating that she already expected the worst.

"We had hoped. But following the communication break, we lost two key satellites, the early warning bird around the Arctic Circle and a comm satellite with ELF capability to communicate with submarines under the ice cap."

"Mr. President, what do you mean lost?" asked Cimino. "Lost communication?"

"No, Capitaine. I mean destroyed. We've picked up the debris fields. We're not sure if they—"

"Mr. President, if you believe the European Federation's laser satellites were somehow—"

"No, ma'am. Not at all. And I don't suggest that Spetsnaz forces have introduced a virus into your system. We've been down that dark road before."

"You're trying to make a connection between those cosmonauts on the ISS and your lost satellites," concluded Bankolé.

"Exactly. The data's being reviewed right now. But there's already speculation that the Russians used the ISS as a platform to take out our satellites. Our missile shield would stop anything they launch with a ground-based trajectory, but they could have smuggled up parts to construct a weapons system and fired it from the station. Could be laser- or projectile-based. We're uncertain at this time."

"What do you need from us?" asked President Perreau.

"If the Russians have seized control of the ISS, and if they have a space-based weapon onboard that station, one they could use to take out some of your lasers or our kinetic energy weapons, then we need to strike first."

"Oh, my God." Perreau gasped. "You want us to destroy the station?"

"No, if it comes to that, we'll do what's necessary. But right now I've got a blind spot up in the Arctic, and other stations have reported that the Russians have flown in some reconnaissance and communication aircraft. I need your lasers to take them out."

General Bankolé frowned deeply. "If I may interrupt. Mr. President, if the Russians have done as you say—smuggled up parts to construct a weapon on the ISS, then why would they use it on two of your more insignificant satellites? Why didn't they pick the obvious targets: your Rods from God and our lasers?"

"Thirty minutes ago I was sitting here, staring out the window, asking the same question. I don't know all the details, the science involved. Maybe they couldn't reposition the ISS to do so. Or maybe they took out the smaller satellites as a test. But believe me, we're working on it. We'll get the truth."

"Well, if you're right about the test, we should take out the station immediately," cried Bankolé.

Becerra recoiled. "The political fallout from that . . . I need proof of what happened up there. My hands are tied until I get it."

Bankolé's voice grew more stern. "Madame President, I suggest we direct one of our lasers on the ISS— as a precautionary measure."

"Mr. President, you will understand if we do that?"

"Absolutely. I'll send word. But you should be prepared to make a statement to the Brazilians and the Japanese if they discover what's happening."

"Of course."

"And you'll take out those spy planes?"

"With pleasure."

"If there's any change, I'll contact you immediately. General Bankolé? Capitaine Cimino? Our Joint Strike Force commanders will coordinate with you, as always."

"Mr. President," called Bankolé, "I hope that you are compensating for your satellite problem and still keeping a sharp eye on the Arctic."

"Rest assured, General. We are."

Becerra said his good-byes and ended the call.

Of course he'd failed to tell Bankolé that they'd now lost contact with one of their subs and were frantically reactivating the old Michigan ELF transmitter to reestablish ELF comms under the Arctic ice. The old system, shut down in 2010, took twenty minutes per character to transmit its three-letter alert.

"Mr. President?" called Mark Hellenberg, Becerra's chief of staff, from his laptop across the aisle. "Bad news from Paris. We lost General Smith. He was forced to call in a kinetic strike on his position. But the good news is that enemy forces were also destroyed and we're still holding the line there."

Becerra nodded, averted his gaze. "Smith was a good man."

"One of the best."

"Mark, I have a feeling the Russians are planning something even bigger."

Hellenberg's tone grew ominous. "So do the Joint Chiefs."

EIGHT

"Left standard rudder. Steady three-two-zero," ordered Commander Jonathan Andreas.

The USS *Florida*, SSN-805, a Virginia-class nuclear submarine, banked smartly to the left and steadied on her new northwesterly course, the third and final leg to refine the Ekelund range calculation to the target.

Ekelund calculations utilized listen-only sonar bearings to solve an equation: the distance to a target was nearly equal to the speed across the line-of-sight of the target divided by the bearing rate (change of bearing per minute, in degrees).

Andreas didn't just understand those calculations. As the commander of a nuclear submarine, they were part of his DNA. He liked to compete with the AN/BSY-1, the computer-based combat system designed to detect, classify, track, and launch weapons at enemy targets. It was man versus machine, and he truly appreciated the beauty inherent in mathematical formulas, an appreciation that had taken him far in his military career.

He was a Naval Academy grad with a B.S. in Marine Engineering, plus two years of postgrad school in Monterey, California, with a dual master's in Nuclear Engineering and International Relations. He was forty-three, from the Midwest, and married with requisite two kids, a boy and girl ages eleven and twelve respectively. He was on the fast track for captain and needed a deep-draft command such as an amphib, maybe even a nuclear carrier, to get his ticket punched. He was destined for a submarine division or squadron commander billet, even admiral if his political party snagged the White House and he could complete his Ph.D. after the Naval War College. His current rank of Commander guaranteed him thirty years in the Navy even if he was twice passed over for promotion, the automatic death knell for any naval officer.

Yes, it'd been a good life and a textbook career, most of it served during peacetime.

But this war, he had quickly learned, changed everything and those changes could begin with the smallest contact on a sonar display.

In fact, twenty minutes earlier the sub's BQQ-10 sonar processor had begun stacking dots on its waterfall display amid the background noise of Arctic shrimp.

Once the fire-control dot-stacker display had finished its stacking, the right target course and speed had been determined, and consequently they had a weapons firing solution on what they determined to be a multiship contact.

Andreas took a deep breath, forced himself to relax.

He had deliberately chosen the new course for his final leg, knowing it would bring him back to a nearby *polyna*, an area of open water surrounded by sea ice, where he could come up and sneak a peek at the contact, mixing the groan and screech of breaking ice with a cacophony of engine and screw noises.

Andreas was prepared to execute "emergency deep" if necessary, his crew automatically taking the sub down to 150 feet in a crash dive to avoid a collision or escape an aircraft attack.

For now, though, he ordered one of *Florida*'s two photonic masts extended. Each contained several high-resolution cameras with light-intensification and infrared sensors, an infrared laser rangefinder, and an integrated electronic support measures (ESM) array. Signals from the masts' sensors were transmitted through fiber-optic data lines through signal processors to the control center.

All the Virginia-class systems—weapon control, sensors, countermeasures, and navigation systems—were integrated into one computer and displayed on the Q-70 color common display console.

All right. They were fifteen miles due north of Banks Island, one of the Canadian arctic islands, and Andreas and his control center attack team now watched two columns of military assault ships glide through the frigid waters, each column preceded by a broad-hulled icebreaker.

Andreas's crew quickly identified the lead ship behind the smaller icebreaker as the *Varyag*, a former Russian aircraft carrier now converted into a command and control ship and flying the personal flag of a Red Banner Northern Fleet admiral headquartered in Severomorsk.

Astern of the *Varyag* was the *Ulyanovsk*, recently completed and modified as a helicopter assault ship. And behind her was the familiar amphibious assault ship *Ivan Rogov*.

The second column consisted of another icebreaker, an oiler, and an ammunition ship.

"XO, pull the manual and tell me what's flying on *Varyag*'s port yardarm and assure me that the Intel officer is recording every pixel on the Q-70 display."

After a moment, the XO reported his findings. "Captain, that's the personal pennant for a GRU general and a Spetsnaz field commander, and we're getting it all."

Just then, the two columns of ships began to split, the *Varyag* group continuing south along the west coast of Banks Island and the auxiliary column beginning to turn left into the McClure Strait and the east coast of the island.

"That's interesting," observed the XO.

"And smart," added Andreas. "He separates his volatile, slower assets and sends them through the Mc-Clure and down into calmer waters of the Prince of Wales Strait, where they'll probably rejoin in the Amundsen Gulf."

"Isn't that a little risky?" asked the Ops officer.

"Not really, Jack, he's got assault choppers to provide air cover. They could get across Banks Island in ten to fifteen minutes."

The Ops officer nodded.

Andreas cleared his throat. "Okay, gentlemen, let's get a slot buoy ready. I want a detailed SITREP. Advise Commander, Pacific Fleet we are in trail of the *Varyag* and add some pictures, space permitting. Plug in a one-hour transmit delay. We'll leave the buoy here in the *polyna*. I'm curious as hell to know what a GRU general and Spetsnaz field commander are doing out at sea with a Northern Fleet admiral.

"Officer of the Deck, take her down to five-four-three feet and fall in behind the column, rig for modified ultra-quiet." Andreas regarded his XO. "I believe an OPORDER is forthcoming. So have the Ops officer and Weapons officer in the wardroom in one hour with a plan to wipe out this Russian task force."

"Aye-aye, sir."

In his mind's eye, Andreas saw the sub's four UGM-84G Harpoon antiship missiles and the Mark 48 (MK-48) ADCAP torpedoes reduce those ships to burning buckets listing hopelessly until they sank to the cold depths.

NINE

The doorbell sent Major Alice Dennison bolting up from her sofa. She noticed the motion-sensor lights on the front porch had already clicked on.

Who the hell is that?

She grabbed her robe from one of the bar stools, slipped it on over her long nightgown, fastened the tie, then finger combed her hair.

It was 9:26 in the evening. No call had come from the gate, so it had to be one of her neighbors, right?

A quick glance around her 1930s bungalow made her grimace. The rugs had been pulled, the paintings removed, all the light fixtures unscrewed from the walls and ceiling.

And that was just the beginning. She'd ransacked

every room, every piece of furniture, looking for Doletskaya's bugs. She'd even removed the showerheads.

Those bastards at the GRU had infiltrated Palma Ceia, the suburb of southern Tampa where Dennison had been living for the past few years. The bungalow she had once called a sanctuary was midway between the international airport and MacDill Air Force Base, where the Joint Strike Force had established one of its many command posts adjacent to United States Special Operations Command (USSOC). Palma Ceia, she kept reminding herself, was a highly desirable neighborhood, and she lived on a private canal, with access to Tampa Bay and the Gulf beyond. Maybe Doletskaya's men had slipped in by boat to bypass her security system and wire her house for sound and video.

But she had yet to locate any of his devices, and that was driving her even more insane.

Maybe they'd already been removed.

Or maybe he was getting his information from another source. But who? The only friends she had were her colleagues, and they, like her, were so plugged into the work that there was barely any free time. Sleep, eat, get back to work, back to the war . . . She couldn't remember how many nights she had spent at the command post, stealing four hours on a cot, putting in a twenty-hour day.

She grabbed her .45 from the kitchen counter, chambered a round, then started toward the door, not daring to get close enough to stare through the peephole, already imagining an assailant firing through the wooden door.

"Who is it?"

"It's me, Alice, open up."

Oh, God. She almost collapsed as the tension washed down into her legs. She threw the dead bolt, removed the chain, and opened the door—

To find her father, shock of gray hair and gray mustache, holding a brightly wrapped present in his hands. He smiled and said, "Happy Birthday, sweetheart! I know I'm a couple of days early, but I'm going to be out of town and I wanted to surprise you before I left. That Charlie down at the gate is a good guy, let the old man have a little fun."

His gaze finally found the gun in her hand, and he frowned.

"I wasn't expecting company, Dad."

"Well, Jesus, put that piece away. But I guess I should be glad you're not taking any chances, especially in times like these."

She moved aside, shut the door after him—but not before stealing a furtive glance at the porch and front yard.

"You should have called, Dad."

"Holy . . . what happened?" He gaped at the place. "Were you robbed? Oh, my God. Did you call the police?"

"I wasn't robbed. I did this."

"You? What the hell?" He shifted over to the bar counter, set down his gift, which looked like a hardcover book, and came to her, gripping her shoulders. "Alice, what's going on. Are you all right? Are you . . . angry?"

She opened her mouth once, closed it, stammered, "I-I'm . . . tired."

His gaze reached the ceiling, the unscrewed fixtures; that did it for him. "You think you've been under surveillance."

"I know I have been. Dad, I feel like I've been raped."

"Come here."

"I'm too old for a hug."

"I don't care, you're still my kid. Give the senior citizen a hug."

She did, and it felt good, reminded her of all those times as a child when she had fallen asleep in his lap, feeling utterly protected. And maybe she hung on now a little too tightly.

"If you're worried about surveillance, I want you to move. You think they're watching now?"

"I don't know." She wanted to whirl around, as she'd done earlier, flipping off the Russians.

"Why don't you get a team in here to do a professional sweep?"

"I'm too embarrassed. When I'm off the base, I never talk about anything anyway. Everything he learned about me was personal, not professional."

"You want to go sit in my car?"

"No. I'm okay."

"Alice, what can I do to help?"

She shrugged. "Give me my birthday present."

He fetched the gift, handed it to her.

"It's a book, and you know I don't have any time to read," she began.

"This one you might find interesting."

She peeled away the wrapper to reveal the title: *Russian Myths and Folklore.*

"Dad?"

He nodded. "Yesterday, the general and I played eighteen holes, and when I asked him how my daughter was doing, his reply was, 'Excellent, though she's obsessed with Russian folklore at the moment.' I didn't know what he meant, but for the daughter who has everything, I thought what the hell, you might like this, if you don't have it already."

"No, I don't," she said, thumbing through the pages.

"So, is this a new hobby, or does it have something to do with . . ." He trailed off, gesturing to the disaster that was her living room. "Or do you not want to talk here."

"Maybe we will take a walk outside."

She tucked the book under her arm, and they headed out, into the backyard, and moved down to the dock and the shimmering, still waters of the canal.

"And sweetheart, the book isn't your only gift. I've

placed a little something in the card. And I want you to use them, all right?"

"More plane tickets? Dad, I can't take the time off right now. I mean, the entire world is—"

"Not your responsibility. We all need downtime— and it looks like you do more than ever now."

"I'll be all right. Soon as I find out who Snegurochka is." She rapped a knuckle on the book. "Snegurochka is the snow maiden in Russian fairy tales. In one story, she's the daughter of Spring and Frost. She falls in love with a shepherd, but when her heart warms, she melts. In another story, falling in love turns her into a mortal human who will die. And then there's another one where she's the daughter of an old couple who make her out of snow. She hangs out with some girlfriends, leaps over a fire, and melts."

Her father snickered. "The Russkies love their happy endings, huh?"

"Well, she's known to kids now as the granddaughter and helper of the Russian Santa."

"So you've already read the book."

"Not this one. Thank you."

"Well, it seems to me you already know who the snow maiden is." He was implying she should let it go. She'd heard that tone a thousand times before.

"I think Snegurochka is the code name for a Russian operative working for the GRU. And that operative must be a woman."

"So how many women do they have at that level? There can't be many."

"Exactly eleven."

"So narrow it down."

"I already have."

"And?"

"And I shouldn't be telling you this, but the most likely candidate is a Colonel Viktoria Antsyforov."

"So study her. See if she's the one."

"I found out yesterday that she's dead."

"You're sure?"

Dennison sighed in frustration. "Pretty damned sure."

"So maybe that's a loose end the Russians took care of. Don't pursue that anymore."

"Or maybe they want us to think that. You know what's really crazy, Dad? I've been obsessing on this so hard that I'm beginning to believe that *I'm* the snow maiden."

"What? The cold career bitch who never got married because she'd melt? Come on, Alice."

"I know. We don't feel sorry for ourselves. Never have before, even after Mom died. We're strong. I guess it's just the stress. You know, thinking that someone's been watching me all this time."

"I want a team in there to sweep the place, and then if you want to put the house on the market, let's do it. You'll get another place."

"No, I won't let them win. I'll get the sweep."

"Good."

"Dad, thanks for coming. Sorry I dumped all this on you."

He grinned, moved in for another hug. "That's what fathers are for."

On the way back into the house, her cell phone rang. She reached into her robe's pocket, answered. They needed her back at the command post.

TEN

The USS *Florida*'s sonar team had quickly switched from the BQQ-10's broadband to narrowband and had isolated two of the Russian ship *Varyag*'s SSTGs (ship's service turbo generators).

Identifying, isolating, and tracking "tonals"—pure sound sources—was the equivalent of an acoustic fingerprint.

And thanks to Andreas's skilled men, the enemy command and control ship could now be identified by any U.S. sub, anywhere in the world, solely by those two discreet frequencies.

By filtering out extraneous noise, it was now possible to trail the surface group at a comfortable five-mile distance using *Varyag*'s SSTGs as a homing beacon.

The ship and her consorts transited the Dolphin and

Union Strait, entered the Coronation Gulf, and set a course toward Hepburn Island, situated in the gulf's southeastern corner; all the while, the *Florida* followed, undetected as it sliced through the icy cold waters.

The Russians passed the southwestern tip of Hepburn, spread out, then proceeded to anchor in the shallow waters.

Andreas and his men watched as the combatants spaced themselves two miles apart, pointed their bows seaward, and dropped stern and bow anchors.

"Keeps them from swinging around on the bow hook and interfering with each other when the tide shifts," Andreas said aloud in the control room.

The oiler and the ammunition ship anchored three miles away to the east.

"Let's move in and get some good beam-on shots for the Harpoons to use—assuming we get that OPORDER," said Andreas. "And, navigator, get an exact—and I do mean *exact*—GPS fix on *Varyag*, *Ulyanovsk*, and *Rogov*'s anchorage position."

"What about the oiler and the ammo ship, Captain?" queried the navigation officer.

"They don't represent a threat like the combatants, although I do plan to take them out with the Mark 48s." Andreas wriggled his brows. "The pyrotechnics should be spectacular, don't you think?"

His navigation officer smiled.

Once the beam-on digital photographs were taken,

and it was apparent the Russians were settled in, Andreas took his boat northeast into the Dease Strait and then continued on as far as the ten-mile gap between the northeast tip of Kent Peninsula and Victoria Island.

Global warming had produced huge areas of open water nearly year-round, but there in the narrow gap, the ice had accumulated. A combination of snow, reduced seawater salinity, and the natural choke point had allowed the ice to become nearly fourteen feet thick. The submarine could handily pass under it, but there was no way the two icebreakers could plow through to the open waters of the Queen Maud Gulf beyond.

Andreas began to draw some conclusions, and he voiced them to his men. "That admiral's just a taxi driver."

"What makes you say that, sir?" asked the XO.

"This is that GRU general's show. No self-respecting northern fleet admiral would box himself in this way."

"Ah, I see."

"What do you think they're up to?" asked the navigation officer.

"Oh, we'll find out. Trust me."

In the back of Andreas's mind sat an important fact: they were long overdue for a position check to update the SINS (ship's inertial navigation system) and a GPS check. Above the Arctic Circle, SINS was often unreliable. Fortunately, GPS solved the problem of getting a reliable corroborating fix.

Once back in the Coronation Gulf, Andreas brought

the sub to periscope depth and raised one of the photonic masts, which was followed immediately by the BRA-34 antenna mast. He forced himself to wait a full sixty seconds, allowing the BRA-34 antenna to dry, hoping to improve the reception of any "burst" broadcast traffic from the satellite.

An ELF message would precede specific operational orders. While anxious to engage the Russians, Andreas knew his initial SITREP to the Commander of the Pacific Fleet (COMPACFLT) had to move up to the National Command Center and then back down to CENTCOM, SOCOM, and finally the JSF. He just needed to be patient.

"That's strange," he said to the XO.

"I know. No broadcast traffic. Absolutely nothing."

"Check the antenna."

"Aye-aye, sir."

The broadcast provided routine administrative notices such as promotions, personnel transfers, and, more important, personal e-mails for the crewmembers. Andreas knew Petty Officer Second-Class Ramirez was waiting to hear from his wife about the birth of their first child. As the ship's morale officer, Andreas was acutely aware of how much these broadcasts contributed to the smooth functioning of his submarine. He regretted that the upgrade to the new OE-538 multifunction mast got pushed back during the *Florida*'s last overhaul.

"The antenna looks fine," reported the XO. "And the GPS signal came through five by five, but I'll have them check all the gear again. What do you think?"

Andreas was about to venture a few guesses when the ECM operator called out, "Sir? I have encrypted UHF chatter and shipboard air-search radar emissions originating from the Russian task force."

With a nod, Andreas answered, "Well, well, well. They've finally broken radio silence. As soon as we get a match between the SINS and GPS we'll swing back down there and take a look."

"It's a Top Plate, Captain," added the operator.

"Are you kidding me?"

"No, sir."

Top Plate was the old NATO designation for a Russian MR-710 Fregat-M, 3D air search radar, a model normally found onboard Slava class cruisers.

"Well, then either the Russian Army's hogging all those petrodollars or somebody in the Navy's skimming big-time. They're cannibalizing their ships."

By now, a steady stream of Kamov Ka-29 helicopters with one to three crew members and hold capacities of up to sixteen troops were beginning to leave the *Ulyanovsk*, landing on the *Ivan Rogov*'s flight deck, onloading troops, then taking off, heading south into the Canadian interior.

"Gentlemen, I'm stumped," Andreas said with a snort. "If this is a Russian invasion, it's analogous to a flea crawling up an elephant's leg with intentions of rape."

"Well, this can't be some kind of exercise," the XO said. "This must be part of —"

"Sir," the officer of the deck interrupted. "Flashing light between the *Varyag* and the oiler, and it's plain language: FROM VARYAG TO KALOVSK: MAKE MY PORT SIDE 0500 HOURS TOMORROW FOR REFUELING."

"We can take out two ships with one missile," Andreas said. "XO, set up another slot buoy. Admiral Stanton needs to see this . . ."

ELEVEN

President Becerra listened intently to Chief of Staff Hellenberg, who was briefing him regarding the recent Motorola-Iridium deal.

Iridium Satellite of Bethesda, Maryland, had established a LEO (low earth orbit) communication satellite network consisting of sixty birds, some in polar orbit, at an altitude of five hundred miles.

The system provided cell phone—voice and data— communication anywhere in the world. It did this by building in satellite-to-satellite transfer capability among all of its birds.

General Rudolph McDaniel, United States Air Force and vice chairman of the Joint Chiefs of Staff, had recommended that Becerra contact the CEOs of Motorola and Iridium and ask them for total control of the network in the name of national security. McDaniel had confirmed with the Navy that the USS *Florida* did have at least six Iridium 9505A satellite phones on-board.

"Well, the network is ours," said Hellenberg.

"Have they made contact with the sub yet?"

"Not yet."

"What's the holdup now?"

"Sir, when the Navy tried to reactivate the Michigan ELF transmitter, the only site capable of communicating under the polar cap, they found that two of the underground diesel fuel tanks had rusted out and ruptured. The fuel in a third tank was contaminated and unusable. Remember, that equipment has been sitting there for more than ten years, unused."

"What now?"

"The Navy says they need all six diesel generators on-line to produce enough power to push an ELF signal down through the underlying bedrock. Right now they have four eighteen-wheeler fuel tankers heading to that transmitter site in the middle of the wilderness. They'll implement a direct hookup between the trucks and the diesel generators."

"Let me know when we've reestablished."

"Yes, sir. And right now it looks like General Kennedy is on three."

"Route it to my screen."

After a second, the monitor before Becerra flickered

into the image of the chairman of the Joint Chiefs of Staff, General Laura Kennedy, United States Army, her blond hair pulled into a tight bun, her expression grave. "Hello, again, Mr. President." She immediately glanced down at her notes.

Here it comes, Becerra thought. He'd never asked for a war during his presidency. But this . . . he could have never imagined this . . .

"The Joint Chiefs have reviewed the data we've gathered from the ISS and from the satellite debris fields, as collected by NASA and the ESA, along with real-time, long-range imagery. It's our conclusion that the ISS is, in fact, under Russian control, that they've violated the 2019 treaty regarding use of the station, and that a portable, tactical high energy laser-based weapon was fired from that platform. The station is now maneuvering again."

"I understand."

"We recommend that this threat to national security be eliminated immediately. General McDaniel informs us that he can shift one of our live-fire prototype AN-GELS satellites to within striking distance."

Autonomous Nanosatellite Guardian Evaluating Local Space (ANGELS) were cylindrical devices no larger than a wastepaper basket used primarily to monitor other satellites. However, during the last four years the JSF had piggybacked at least a dozen new ones aboard other communication satellites with the future mission of converting those ANGELS into low-power laser weapons and orbiting bombs.

"General, I'm wondering if there's a way we can neutralize the threat without destroying the station."

"Sir, we've considered every possibility. We could cut off their life support, force them to go to the suits. But they might reach their next target before exhausting their oxygen. We can't send up astronauts in time. And if you open this up to debate with the other nations involved, the Russians will achieve their goals before the representatives even sit down."

"Oh, I'm well aware of that, General."

"Mr. President, I will say this. If the weapon is clearly identifiable on the station, perhaps attached to one of the Russian modules, we'll make every attempt to destroy it first, then see how they react. They might decide to take the ISS on a suicide run to destroy other orbital platforms, maybe even Freedom Star—in which case we'll have the ANGEL attach itself to the station and self-destruct."

"General, stand by for one moment please." Becerra put her on hold, then tapped another screen, bringing up Roberta Santiago, his national security advisor. "Roberta, you've been listening in."

"Yes, sir. And my God, sir. They want you to authorize the destruction of the ISS."

"Do we have a choice? They will attempt to take out the weapon first."

"I do have another thought." Santiago's tone darkened. "Why do we need to take full responsibility? Why can't we turn this situation around? We're the victims here and we should remain victims. Striking back, killing those two innocent researchers . . . that's—"

"Roberta, what are you saying?"

"I'm saying that within an hour I can have video released to the media. The Green Brigade Transnational will take full responsibility for the ISS's destruction. And the ironic part is, Green Vox won't dispute the lie. It'll surprise him, but he'll be happy to take full credit. He'd blow up the ISS himself if he could. That's a fact."

An icy feeling crept into Becerra's spine as he considered how cunning and clever such a ploy might be—

And how it might backfire. This could be his Watergate, his Monica Lewinsky, his war in Iraq.

He leaned forward and steeled his gaze. "Roberta, I won't do that. I'm going to authorize the destruction attempt and I'm going to stand behind it. The ISS is an ongoing threat to national security. There is collateral damage in every war, and that's terrible and unfortunate. But as president, my first responsibility is the defense of the United Sates of America. This will be an unpopular decision—but we have to make it. And we have to be willing to take the international heat. Roberta, are we absolutely clear on this?"

She pursed her lips. "Yes, Mr. President. I understand."

He switched back to the chairman's line. "General Kennedy, you have my authorization to take whatever steps are necessary to neutralize the threat."

"Yes, Mr. President. We'll act immediately. And I'll update you as soon as we know anything."

Becerra tapped off the call, closed his eyes, and imagined the news stories to follow, pretty graphics beside the words BECERRA ORDERS DESTRUCTION OF ISS.

TWELVE

The Commander of the Pacific Fleet, Admiral Donald Stanton, called Admiral Charles "Chuck" Harrison, Commander Submarine Forces Pacific, regarding a most intriguing loss of communication up in the Arctic.

Stanton was in his office at COMPACFLT Headquarters in Pearl Harbor, Hawaii, staring at a computer screen showing him the bio and military service record of the USS *Florida*'s current commander.

The communications screen indicated they had a link, and Chuck appeared, his silver hair expertly razored into a crew cut, his face barely wrinkled for a man pushing sixty. Stanton had already broken that barrier, and he wanted to believe he looked as good as Chuck. Aw, hell, who was he kidding?

"Hey, Donny."

"Hey, Chuck. Listen, I just got an e-mail from American Eagle telling me we've got total control of the Iridium cell phone system. He wants us to reach out to your boy up north. I was just reading his record."

"Andreas is a pretty clever lad. Once he figures out the satellite is bent, he just might poke up his sail long enough to check for a text message. But how can I help?"

"My techies tell me they need the phone numbers for every Iridium 9505A onboard *Florida*, plus we need something—something personal—that will convince Andreas that our text message is legit. I know how serious you guys are about the *silent* in silent service."

"I'll get the squadron commander on the horn. Smitty keeps a roster of all the allocated 9505As, and next I'll give Andreas's wife a buzz. I'll bet she can come up with something personal to authenticate with."

"Sounds like a plan, Chuck. My best to Jamie. Fifteen minutes?"

"Back in fifteen, Admiral."

"Captain, we've covered—"

"Hold on," Commander Jonathan Andreas said, cutting off his communications officer. "Right now I want to hear Senior Chief Radioman Sheldon's assessment of the situation."

"Captain, I've been over every inch of that gear. I

even got Chief Electronics Technician Burgess to look over my shoulder. I swear that the ELF and satellite receivers are good to go." His tone grew ominous. "There's just no signal."

Andreas couldn't estimate how much pride calling in another chief for help had cost his senior chief radioman.

Andreas nodded, "Sheldon, that's good enough for me."

Andreas returned to his quarters and sat on his bunk for almost ten minutes, allowing himself to work through the mystery, taking in each piece of evidence, examining it, probing it, trying to reach conclusions. Then he started down a new path, one in which they took action to get answers.

He came up with two plans.

Finally, he stood and purposefully stepped through the doorway into the head separating his stateroom from the XO's. He knocked twice on the door in the opposite bulkhead, then stepped through to where the XO was reading something at his desk. He glanced up. "Sir?"

Without preamble, Andreas said, "XO, I'm about to break a cardinal rule, and I want you to hear it."

"Skipper, are you sure?"

"Yes, I am." The first plan sounded even more logical to him as he voiced it rapid-fire. "I'm going to go deep, sprint thirty miles northwest, stick up the antenna, and ping the transponder on the satellite. The problem could still be ours, but right now it's the next-to-last action we can take. What do you think?"

"Skipper, with the shrouded propulsor, and at a depth of, say, eight hundred feet, we can do that."

"I just can't wait around any longer."

"No doubt. We sprint at nearly thirty knots and find us a nice lonely spot out in the middle of the gulf."

"So it's worth a try?"

"It is, but I have to play devil's advocate—what happens if we don't trigger an answering ping from the transponder?"

"I said this was my next-to-last plan, XO. If this doesn't work, you won't believe what I'll do next."

THIRTEEN

"Ghost Hawk, this is Siren. Contact is now three minutes out, over."

Major Stephanie Halverson, dressed like a praying mantis in her pressure suit and alien-like helmet with attached O_2 line, took a deep breath and adjusted her grip on the stick.

The F-35B Joint Strike Fighter's electro-optical targeting system (EOTS) continued to feed her up-to-the-nanosecond images and data on the approaching targets, and her helmet-mounted display system had some of the best head-tracking hardware and software she had ever fielded, along with all the usual requirements like a binocular-wide field of view, day/night capability with sensor fusion, and a digital image source for helmet-displayed symbology—all of which was engineer-speak for some wicked cool battlefield capability.

After an unusually long delay, her wingman, Captain Jake Boyd, finally replied with a curt "Roger that," his own F-35B streaking over the frozen tundra just off Halverson's right wing, its tail glowing faintly in the night.

"Ghost Hawk, do you have a problem, over?"

"Negative, Siren. Just shaking my head."

They had nearly forty Russian Ka-29s on the AN/APG-81 AESA radar, the helos on a bearing due south across the Northwest Territories, maintaining an altitude of just one thousand feet.

To say that Halverson and Boyd were surprised was an understatement.

Operating out of a small JSF training base located approximately two hundred miles north of Yellowknife, the capital of the NWT, she and Boyd were on their third scheduled night flight of the F-35B Short Take-Off and Vertical Landing (STOVL) fighter used primarily by the United States Marine Corps and the Royal Navy.

As JSF pilots and members of the Air Force, they were being cross-trained in the fighter so that its features could be exploited in non–carrier based operations located far inland and in more rugged terrain. The JSF had struck a deal with the commissioner of the NWT to use the largely unpopulated areas for tests.

Halverson and Boyd had both hoped that after the fourteen-day training mission, they'd get a chance to take their state-of-the-art killing machines into Russia and show those vodka-soaked wolves what they could do.

That the Russians would help by dropping in themselves was as exciting as it was troubling.

Halverson maintained a video blog, Femme Fatale Fighter Pilot, and she couldn't wait to share this with her readers, though she'd carefully dance around the classified details, and her face was always hidden behind her helmet.

"All right, Ghost Hawk, two minutes now," she reported. "Let's hit the gas and ascend before they spot us."

"Roger that."

"Igloo Base, this is Siren, we're climbing to fourteen thousand to hover and observe contact, over."

"Roger that, Siren. Igloo Base standing by."

She and Boyd climbed to fourteen thousand, then, with the targets about to pass below in thirty seconds, they prepared to hover.

All right, baby, show me what you got.

Instead of utilizing lift engines or rotating nozzles on the engine fan and exhaust like the old Harriers, Halverson's F-35B employed a shift-driven lift fan, patented by Lockheed Martin and developed by Rolls-Royce.

The contra-rotating fan was like a turboprop set into

the fuselage, just behind the cockpit. Engine shaft power could be sent forward to it while bypass air from the cruise engine was sent to nozzles in the wings as the cruise nozzle at the tail vectored downward.

Thus, under her command, panels opened over the lift fan behind her, and a column of cool air providing 20,000 pounds of lifting power vented from the bottom of the aircraft, holding her steady, a fighter plane seemingly locked in the air by an invisible tractor beam.

Boyd was at Halverson's wing, hovering as well.

"Siren, this is Igloo Base."

"Go ahead, Igloo."

"We've received no response from your contact. You have authorization to fly by those helos, attempt once more to make contact yourselves. Instruct them to turn around—but do not engage unless fired upon, over."

"Roger that, Igloo Base. If they fail to comply, we'd like authorization to engage, over."

"Understood, Siren. Just let 'em know we're here first."

"Roger that, Igloo Base, descending to intercept those helos. Ghost Hawk, you ready?"

"Oh, yeah, Siren."

"Just follow me. This'll be . . . interesting."

With that, she broke from her hover, jamming the

stick forward and diving, the Pratt & Whitney engine thundering behind her with a force that crept into her gut, energized her, made her feel powerful beyond measure.

There was no darkness. Infrared peeled back the night to reveal the helicopters, flying in two clusters about three choppers abreast, spread far enough apart to be engaged individually.

Halverson took her bird straight down toward the lead three helos, diving directly in front of them, just fifty meters ahead.

She could only imagine the looks on those Russian pilots' faces as their radars went wild, their canopies lit up, and they were suddenly buffeted by her jet wash—

Only to be hit again two seconds later by Boyd's exhaust.

Screaming toward the mottled carpet of snow and trees below, Halverson pulled up and banked right, while instructing Boyd to bank left. They both came up, then suddenly went back to hover mode, floating there at one thousand feet, on either side of the column of Ka-29s as they advanced.

"Russian helos, this is Joint Strike Force Fighter Siren, do you copy, over?

Halverson's pulse raced.

"Here they come," said Boyd.

Tactical data links transmitted every reading from

the instruments onboard their fighters back to Igloo Base and to every JSF tactical and strategic command post on the planet via the satellite links. At any time, any operations XO could tap in to her cockpit to see what she was doing.

That Mr. Network-Centric Big Brother was always watching did unnerve Halverson, and there had been lots of talk among pilots of deliberately switching off certain systems at certain times. Since the war had broken out, the concept of network-centric operations (NCO) had proven a first step at dissipating some instances of the "fog of war," in which communication breakdowns and poor information handling resulted in heavy losses. However, when misinformation *did* get into the system, it flowed like a virus and was hard to stop.

For now, though, the information coming at Halverson was pretty damned obvious and accurate. The Russians had no intentions of stopping.

"Russian helos, this is Joint Strike Force Fighter Siren. You have crossed into Canadian airspace and are instructed to turn back, over."

Halverson waited a moment, then repeated the same instructions in Russian. Her language skills weren't great, but her pronunciation was clear enough for them to understand—if they were willing to listen.

She also wondered about the Canadian response.

They had adamantly maintained their neutrality in the war, though it wasn't beyond imagination that they might court the Russians for some "diplomatic" purpose.

For all Halverson knew, these helos could be en route to a southern location at the invitation of the Canadian government; if that were the case, it would have been nice to inform the JSF of their little visit.

But what kind of drinking party were the Canadians throwing that required the Russians to come in forty helos? If crates of vodka and droves of loose women weren't on the list, Halverson doubted they would attend.

"Igloo Base, this is Siren, over."

"Go ahead, Siren."

"We buzzed the helos and are hovering at one thousand as they approach. No response to our requests, over."

"Roger that, Siren. Just maintain—"

"Siren!" cried Boyd. "Rockets incoming. Jesus—"

Out of the corner of her eye, Halverson caught the flash of a bright light, and just as she throttled up—

More unguided rockets fired from the lead choppers tore through her wake.

"Siren, this is Ghost Hawk! Jesus, damn it, I'm hit! I'm hit! Got a fire. Electrical failures. Damage to left wing. I saw the radar warning, and I just didn't believe it! Losing control!"

"Eject! Eject!"

Halverson climbed over the swarm of choppers to look down upon the scene, spotting Boyd's fighter beginning to drop like a rock, nose tipping down.

"Boyd, get out of there!"

He was at about one hundred and fifty knots when a tiny flash erupted, and the canopy tumbled away. Then the ejection seat fired, and out came Boyd, with approximately eight hundred feet between himself and the ground below.

Halverson wished she had time to see if he was okay, but the rage inside—awakened by the audacity of these Russians—launched her into action. She wheeled around, brought the jet into another hover, pivoted toward the helos.

Speed and maneuver. Speed and maneuver . . .

She had missile lock. There was no thinking it over or calling to base for authorization. And there were no second thoughts.

The two wingtip-mounted AIM-9X Sidewinder missiles exploded away from her jet, using a passive IR target acquisition system to home in on infrared emissions. They each raced toward a chopper in the lead group, leaving glowing white tendrils of smoke in their wake.

"Igloo Base, this is Siren. Ghost Hawk has ejected! Can't see if he's on the ground yet! I've engaged the helos, over!"

"Roger that, Siren."

Twin booms shone in her display, the fireballs expanding then plummeting toward the icy deck.

Two Ka-29s down.

Thirty-five? Thirty-six to go?

She'd exhaust everything she had, she didn't care.

But first she had to find Boyd, see if he made it, and if he did, be sure those bastards weren't trying to finish the job.

His beacon shone in one of her displays, as the choppers below scattered like bees being swatted, spreading out, gaining altitude, while a few pilots descended even lower.

Two of the choppers banked hard, coming around to engage her as she hovered above them.

Rockets flashed from their underwing pods. She rolled to her left, even as she engaged her four-barreled GAU-22/A gun mounted in a teardrop pod along the jet's aft center pylon, the four barrels bound in one spinning cylinder.

Armor-piercing discarding sabot with tracer rounds leapt out ahead of her fighter at a rate of forty-two hundred per minute, chewing into the first chopper's canopy amid a flurry of sparks and the laser-like streaks drawn by the tracers.

She shifted fire to the next helo, more rounds drumming along its side as the pilot attempted to evade.

The first chopper began to fall away, out of control,

smoke pouring from the shattered cockpit. And suddenly, the second one joined the first, rolling away, trailing more smoke.

She carried only two hundred and twenty rounds of ammo for the gun despite its cyclic rate of fire, and she had already blown through half. Damn it. The cost of being trigger-happy.

There were two more Sidewinders in her internal bays, along with two AGM-154 Joint Standoff Weapons for hitting hardened surface targets. She also had a pair of five-hundred-pound JDAM bombs under the wings, but they wouldn't help unless those helos put down. Finally, she had a pair of laser-guided training rounds they were supposed to use in a couple of days.

Boyd's fighter had crashed just ahead, the flames still soaring skyward; he had drifted downwind about a half kilometer farther south.

"Ghost Hawk, this is Siren, you copy, over?"

No response.

"Igloo Base, this is Siren. No contact from Ghost Hawk on the ground. Four choppers engaged and destroyed, over."

"Roger that, Siren. You're ordered to return to base, over."

"Negative, Igloo Base. I'm not leaving until I can confirm if Ghost Hawk made it or not, over."

"Stand by, Siren . . ."

Well, she'd stand by, all right, but not without unleashing her last two Sidewinders.

The helos, now much more spread apart, maintained their southerly course, a speckled field of potential targets glowing on her display.

"Here you go," she whispered. "Eat this."

Dinner was, in fact, served, a late-night course of explosives delivered with blinding efficiency.

The bay doors swung open, and the rockets spat from the warplane's belly, arrowing through the night.

She throttled up once more, dove, and came in for a final run with guns—

Even as the two Sidewinders slammed into their targets, sending debris and flaming bodies hurtling outward in all directions.

Not liking her current angle, she drove the stick left, banking hard, the fighter riding the cold air as though racing on rails. She came back around, diving once more, and squeezed the trigger, targeting another chopper from behind until its engine flared and died.

Then she ceased fire, lined up on the next bird and squeezed the trigger, more rounds streaking away.

But in a few seconds, the gun went dead, out of ammo, and the chopper was still flying.

"JSF fighter plane, this is American Eagle, over."

Halverson gasped. She knew that call sign but could

hardly believe it. The President of the United States was on the radio.

"American Eagle, this is Siren, go ahead, over."

"Major, what am I looking at here?"

"Sir, those blips on the screen are approximately thirty to thirty-five Russian Ka-29 troop transport helos on a southerly heading. I've taken out seven of them, damaged an eighth, but I've exhausted my ammo. They fired upon us first, sir. I lost my wingman, who ejected, and I want to fly over the crash site and see if he made it."

"Can you do that without losing your bird?"

"Yes, sir."

"Then you've got my permission. Major, you're looking at them. What do you think they're up to?"

"Sir, I honestly have no idea. But I'd recommend calling the Canadians to get some people up here ASAP."

"Roger that, Major. Good work. I hope your wingman made it."

"Thank you, sir, Siren out."

She shuddered as she realized she had just had a conversation with the president! Damn, whatever was happening had to be huge.

With a hard blink, she brought herself back to the moment. The enemy helos passed over the crash site and continued on as she descended behind them, homing in on Boyd's beacon.

She slowed as she got on top of the signal, spotted

one chute, tangled and whipping in the breeze, still attached to the ejection seat. She wheeled around once more and slowed to a complete hover, keeping a wary eye on the radar while searching for Boyd and his chute.

"Ghost Hawk, this is Siren, over."

Come on, Jake. Be there . . .

FOURTEEN

After President Becerra finished speaking with that fighter pilot up in the Northwest Territories, he took a video call from the Canadian prime minister, Robert Emerson. He'd met Emerson on several occasions, an elder statesman who was about as low-key and conservative as they came.

Which was why Becerra was taken aback by Emerson's immediate hostility. "Just what the hell is going on up there, Mr. President!"

"I don't have all the details yet. What I do know is that thirty to forty Russian helos are moving south toward Yellowknife. They fired on two of our fighters training up there. In the meantime, they knocked out a couple of our satellites over the Arctic, and I've lost contact with one of my subs up there."

"I warned you what would happen if this war came to Canada."

"Prime Minister, it's not a coincidence that they're moving toward Alberta. I told you this day would come," Becerra reminded him.

"And I told you they wouldn't dare," Emerson snapped.

"Four years ago, on the day the Saudis and Iranians exchanged nuclear weapons, Canada became the home of the world's largest oil reserve."

"Our bitumen is still more expensive to produce, and the Russians have exploited the European markets far better than we have."

"But they know we're not entirely dependent upon them anymore. And they know what will happen if we're allowed to continue exploiting this reserve."

"I don't believe it."

"Prime Minister, how long did you think the Russians would let you control the supply? If this is the prelude to a major invasion, then you've got a very important decision to make. But I'll say this: it is in the best interests of the United States to have you in charge of those reserves. If the Russians attempt to take that power from you, I'll have no choice but to send in my troops. Join us," Becerra urged.

"We can't support this war. We don't believe in it. Our economy cannot suffer that kind of blow."

"Then watch from the sidelines, as you have been.

But when the time comes, don't stop us. Turning on each other is exactly what the Russians want us to do. It's exactly what they tried to do between us and the Euros."

"If I allow you on my soil, they'll consider that aiding and abetting."

"And if you don't?"

Emerson sighed explosively. The Prime Minister raked fingers through his thinning white hair. "Mr. President, please keep me informed the minute you know more."

"Of course. And if you want to mobilize your military for a training exercise, I'm sure no one would stop you."

"One more thing, Mr. President. If the Russians are coming in by helicopter, they had to have used carriers or some other ships."

"That's why I'm trying to reestablish contact with my submarine. They might be able to confirm that."

"Meaning your submarine was operating illegally in our waters."

"Let's not go there. The debate whether the Northwest Passage waters are international or Canadian is irrelevant right now. There are only four words that are important to us: the Russians are coming."

"Mr. President," called Chief of Staff Hellenberg from across the aisle. "Sorry to interrupt you, but General Kennedy is on the line." Hellenberg's expression said it all.

"Mr. Prime Minister, I have to go, but myself or a member of my staff will update you as soon as we know more."

With that, Becerra, ended the call and switched to the other video line. "You don't look happy, General."

"No, sir. It seems we're backed into a corner on this one. We've attempted several different scenarios, but at this point, the ANGELS satellite has attached itself to the ISS. No communication at all from the crew inside. We suspect that the Russians have already killed the Japanese and Brazilian crew members. The ISS will be within range of one of our kinetic energy platforms in approximately fifteen minutes. The Russians could destroy that platform," she pointed out. Unnecessarily.

"Understood."

"All I need is authorization from you."

Becerra rubbed the corners of his eyes, took a deep breath. "You have it, General. Take out the station."

"Yes, sir. I'll connect you in to the platform's cameras."

Hellenberg came over and stood behind Becerra. "I'm sorry, Mr. President."

"For what?"

"For this difficult decision you've had to make."

"It's cut-and-dried now, Mark."

Voices of the ANGELS satellite controllers sounded in the background as an image of the ISS, floating over the blue globe of Earth, dominated the screen. They had a spectacular view of the station and listened as one controller, in a cool, even voice finished his sentence with the words, ". . . and detonate . . ."

A small flash came from the underside of the station, followed by a much larger, more orange explosion haloed in white-hot specks.

The station's long, rectangular arrays, perhaps its most prominent and memorable feature, suddenly broke away and began tumbling end over end, as the rest of the laboratories and connecting modules began their own strangely graceful ballet, moving with underwater slowness in the vacuum of space.

General Kennedy returned to the screen. "Sir, the threat has been eliminated. Now I suggest we turn our attention to the next one."

"Those helos up in Canada."

"That's right. But sir, we count more than sixty heavy Russian transport aircraft with fighter escorts lifting off from every air base along the east coast of the country. Could be one or more brigades, with accompanying vehicles. We believe they'll put down just north of Alberta."

"Let's get some fighters up there to stop them."

"There are far too many aircraft, and many of our units in Alaska have been deployed to Europe. The squadrons we do have are already in the air."

Becerra held back a curse. "Kapalkin has been working on this one for a long time, carefully weakening us, spreading us out too far."

"Well, as we like to say, Mr. President, the balloon is going up. At the very least, we'd like to get boys from the Tenth Mountain up there, along with some Marines from Pendleton. And we have a Stryker Brigade in Alaska we'll bring down, along with another one we'll bring up from Fort Lewis, so long as you can work out a deal with the prime minister."

"What about air strikes?"

"They'll have limited effect, because if we're right, the Russians will be attempting to seize key infrastructure, pipelines, refineries, and so on, intact. We can't risk damaging those facilities, so for the most part, we'll be on the ground, with close air support at our shoulders. We'll need to hold back on the bombers and kinetic energy weapons as our very last resorts."

"I think the prime minster would agree."

She smiled crookedly. "Mr. President, I also have to point out that the Russians could cut off their noses to spite their faces."

"You mean if they can't control the Alberta reserves—"

"They'll destroy them. In fact, if those inbound Russian aircraft were bombers, we'd assume that's the mission. Still could be."

"General, can we do this? Can we fight this war on multiple fronts and put more people up in Canada?"

"We think so, sir. And remember, the Russians are further dividing their own forces to continue their push. But the key is the prime minister. If you can get him to commit his forces, we'll be in a lot better shape."

"I don't think that's going to happen, not in any official capacity anyway. There will always be some Canadian units that'll fight if attacked, no matter what the prime minister says."

"So in that regard, the Russians might be doing us a favor."

"Yes, sir. In the meantime, we'll get what fighters we can in the air to disrupt those incoming aircraft."

"Good. You know, I just spoke to an F-35 pilot operating out of a little base north of Yellowknife. She took out more than half a dozen of those Russian helos. I want her up there."

"I'll make sure of that, sir."

FIFTEEN

Major Stephanie Halverson spotted Boyd lying in the snow, not far from the ejection seat, half covered by the drogue chute. He'd unbuckled, crawled a few meters in the snow, and collapsed. He wasn't moving.

Now she wouldn't just fly over, trying to figure out if he was alive or dead. And she wouldn't tell Igloo Base what she was doing. With the Russian helos still not far off, they would never authorize such an action. They had just ordered her back to refuel and rearm.

Of course she would comply (eventually), but she couldn't live with herself if she abandoned Jake. She'd rather take the risk, which was, damn it, risking everything.

And God help her, she set down on the snow, landed

the multimillion dollar bird, leaving her entirely vulnerable to air attack.

It took her another minute to detach herself from the cockpit, remove her helmet, and finally get down to the snow.

The icy wind stung her cheek, and it smelled as though a storm was coming.

"Jake!" She jogged toward him, the top layer of snow breaking into glistening puzzle pieces that rose to her ankles.

She reached him, slowly rolled him over, and worked on getting off his helmet. Finally, it gave. His nose had been bleeding and his left cheek was beginning to swell.

"Jake, can you hear me? It's Steph."

His eyes flickered open. "I want to puke."

"It's good to see you, too."

He swallowed. "I'm so embarrassed. I don't know what happened. It was like a dream . . . they fired rockets!"

"I know, Jake."

"Wait a minute. What the hell? You landed?" He suddenly sat up, looked to her plane, the engine still humming.

"Jesus, Major!"

The ejection seat had a built-in survival kit that was now connected to his chute. Ignoring him, she fetched it, brought it back over. "Can you move?"

"I'm just banged up. I don't think anything's broken."

"Think you can fly?"

"What the hell you talking about?"

"I want you to take her back. Rescue helo is already on the way. I'll catch it."

"Steph, you're not thinking right. You don't put an injured pilot back in the cockpit."

She looked at him, thought about how wired to panic she was, how full of rage, the tremors still working into her hands.

"Okay, yeah. You'll be all right?"

"I'm okay." He glanced over to the still-burning wreckage of his fighter. "My flying career just went up in flames, but I'm okay . . ."

"You're not done yet. Not if I have anything to say about it. Just hang tight." She pulled out her sidearm, handed it to him. "Now you got two."

"If they come back, this won't matter."

She knew that, too, but pushed back his hand, forcing him to take the weapon. "Rescue will be here soon." She started back toward her fighter.

And once she was strapped in and lifting off, the news that came in from Igloo Base took her breath away.

The USS *Florida*'s radio room, immediately aft, starboard side of the submarine's command, control, communications, and intelligence (C3I) space, made it easy for the radioman on watch to stick his head into the passageway and announce, "ELF traffic," even as Commander Jonathan Andreas watched the extremely low frequency (ELF) call light start to blink incessantly on his Q-70 display console, accompanied by a steady beeping. "The first character is in, and it matches our first call letter," continued the radioman.

"Finally," Andreas said through a deep sigh. He pressed the Acknowledge button, stopping both beep and flash, then stepped across to the port side of C3I and placed his hand on the sonar operator's shoulder. "Give me a careful three-hundred-and-sixty-degree listening sweep." Catching the officer of the deck's eye, he continued, "If we're all clear, take us up to periscope depth."

"Aye-aye, sir," responded the OOD.

Andreas had done as he and the XO had discussed. They had sprinted out of the immediate area, pinged the satellite's transponder—and had received no response for their effort.

And that had left Andreas standing there in the control room wanting to pummel someone.

In the time it took for them to complete the acoustic sweep, rise to periscope depth, and extend their mast to visually confirm no surface contacts in the immediate vicinity, the second character of the ELF message had arrived on board. It matched the second of the *Florida*'s three assigned ELF call letters.

"Captain, there's still no operational traffic from that satellite," said the senior chief radioman. "GPS is coming through okay. The clincher for me, sir, is that ELF data rate. That's about the speed of the old Michigan ELF transmitter. Their big bird in the sky is dead. I'll stake a promotion to Master Chief on that, sir."

"Roger that, Senior Chief. XO, round up all the Iridium satellite phones and make sure they're fully charged. We're going to execute my last plan, the one I didn't tell you about."

"Sir, are you serious? We're going to call on the satellite phones?"

"Well, it ain't pretty, but it's all I got. It's time to phone home."

Andreas stepped aft to the Radio Room, poked his head inside and said, "Senior Chief, I'll bet you a shiny new set of silver eagles for *my* collar that you'll continue to get ELF transmissions until we figure out how to talk to COMPACFLT."

Admiral Donald Stanton glanced up as his aide appeared in the little window on his computer screen. "Admiral Harrison for you, sir."

Stanton accepted the call, and the window switched to Harrison in his office. "Chuck, what have you got?"

"Well, even though Michigan's up, Andreas will be

extremely cautious about breaking radio silence. It goes against everything he's been taught. But when that silence becomes deafening, as it is now, he'll run through his options."

"We put the same four-line text message on every satellite phone on board."

"And Andreas's wife assures me he'll understand the message."

"All right. He just needs to receive it. Thanks, Chuck. We've run it up the flagpole, let's see who wants to salute it. All we can do now is wait."

Back on the *Florida*, Andreas reminded his XO that they needed just enough speed to maintain steerageway but no more. They didn't want the sail to create a visible wake by agitating the bioluminescent organisms in the water.

Andreas then turned and regarded his communications officer. "Dan, you take two sat phones, and I'll carry two. We turn all four on just before we open the hatch in the sail, then we head up to get a signal. We're looking for a text message—that's all. We aren't ready to transmit anything. Got it?"

"Yes, sir."

Andreas looked intently at the young lieutenant. "Do you remember what else I told you?"

"Yes, sir. Whatever I see on the display, write it down."

"Good man, let's go."

Nine minutes later, the *Florida* was completely submerged, banked to starboard, preparing to level off at five hundred and thirty-eight feet, and coming to course one-six-zero.

All four cell phone text messages read the same:

URGENT-CALL COMPACFLT/8085553956/3672

Any submarine crewmember home-ported in Pearl Harbor would recognize the 808 prefix as the Honolulu area code. The COMPACFLT acronym didn't need any explanation.

"But sir, how do we verify?" asked the XO.

"Oh, the message is authentic," replied Andreas. "See those last four digits? Only my wife and the Honolulu National Bank know that's my PIN number. Good thing she picked that and not our anniversary date."

"I hear that, Skipper."

Andreas's expression and tone grew more serious. "Now, XO, let's surface again and make the call."

"Aye-aye, sir."

SIXTEEN

General Sergei Izotov sat in the back of his armored Mercedes, the driver returning him to GRU headquarters after an earlier evacuation due to a bomb threat.

Izotov was about to access the GRU tactical database for the latest report when Major Alexei Noskov called via satellite video phone. Izotov tapped a key on his notebook computer to take the call.

Noskov had been reassigned to their latest battlefront, his rosy cheeks and red nose showing clearly on the screen.

"The first transports are on the ground," he began, raising his voice, his breath heavy in the frigid air.

"Excellent, Major."

Behind him, in the darkness, Izotov could barely make out some BMP-3s, their 100 mm guns making them resemble tanks, rolling down the ramps of two AN-130s, the Motherland's latest fleet of huge cargo aircraft capable of landing on unprepared airfields—like the frozen, snow-covered ground of the Northwest Territories. Dozens of soldiers scrambled to prepare each vehicle once it was on the ground under the steady hum and wash of the cargo plane's colossal engines.

Noskov grinned. "I have more good news. Our helos have landed in Behchoko, and operations have begun there."

Izotov tapped the screen and brought up the maps.

Behchoko was located on the northwest tip of Great Slave Lake, about seventy-six kilometers from the much larger town of Yellowknife. The road between them was Highway 3, which ran south from Behchoko, then became Highway 1 until it crossed the territorial line of Alberta, where it changed to Highway 35 and ran into the town of High Level.

Because of the winter weather conditions, Noskov's ground forces were forced to use the main roads; thus, controlling them and the small towns between was imperative.

"I'm told that our men will secure the refinery and avgas depot before sunrise. They're already setting up the first roadblock. Have a look."

The night-vision images piped in to Izotov's screen came from the helmet cameras of Spetsnaz infantry and were grainy and shifting quickly, but it was clear they'd used one of the Ka-29s to block the road, along with a confiscated civilian SUV and a pickup truck. Shouts and gunfire echoed from somewhere behind the roadblock.

"There are only about fifteen hundred there, and they're mostly aboriginal people, poorly armed as we noted. I expect no complications."

"Don't get too cocky, Major. You haven't confronted the Americans yet, and I see here that only a small number of transports have landed. The others will soon be engaged by American fighters."

"What do the Americans say? I am cautiously optimistic?" Noskov chuckled loudly. "I predict much blood will flow. I predict we will be drinking vodka in the bars of Edmonton and Calgary within a week and that the reserves will be ours!" His laugh now bordered on a cackle.

Izotov sighed. Major Noskov was an unconventional operations specialist at best, a cocky thug at worst.

Yes, he was a keen analyst of battles, able to spot and exploit an enemy's weaknesses with speed and proficiency, but he always seemed slightly unhinged, a little mad, even. He rarely referred to superior officers by rank and seemed suspicious of them, especially Izotov.

That Noskov had joined the Russian Army at seventeen to avoid imprisonment for manslaughter was unsurprising. That he had led forces in the Second Chechen War from 1990 to 2005 and celebrated several key victories was admirable. That he'd had his left leg blown off by a rocket-propelled grenade, which had rendered him ineligible for active combat duty, was unfortunate.

However, his talent for planning and directing operations remotely was as unexpected as it was valuable, and Doletskaya had insisted that Noskov be sent to Canada to coordinate operations in the northern areas of Alberta, especially seizing the town of High Level.

But the man had a temper, and his dangerous instability caused him to be passed over for promotions. Although forty, he was still as brash as an eighteen-year-old at times, and Izotov found himself repeatedly cautioning the man, as he did now.

"Major, continue your good and *cautious* work for the Motherland."

"Of course. What else would you have me do?"

"And know we will be *carefully* monitoring your progress."

Noskov nodded, then, sans any good-bye, he whirled away from the camera and limped off on his artificial leg, shouting to the men unloading the BMP-3s that they weren't fast enough and that he would shoot them if they didn't hurry.

Well, so far, the operation was unfolding as planned, and based upon the enemy's initial response, it seemed Colonel Pavel Doletskaya had somehow managed to keep silent.

Izotov could not understand that—unless, of course, the Americans had accidentally killed the colonel, for

Izotov refused to believe that one man's force of will could be that strong.

Or could it?

Soldiers at Fort Lewis were pumped with adrenaline, and Special Forces Team Sergeant Nathan Vatz was no exception. He was about to leave his barracks and head to Robert Gray Army Airfield, his load-out bag slung over his shoulders.

In the hall outside his room, he spotted Staff Sergeant Marc Rakken rushing toward him. "Yo, Nate, I just heard, man!"

"Yeah, I know, it's crazy."

"Why couldn't they invade someplace warm?"

"The Russians can't take the heat."

Rakken nodded then raised his brows. "Maybe we'll bump into some snow bunnies up there, eh?"

"So you're going, too?"

"The brigade's already got a quartering party heading up to start RSOI base ops."

Establishing a reception, staging, onward movement and integration base, which included all the support facilities the brigade would need to operate, was the first step of moving 3,900 folks riding in more than 300 Stryker vehicles up to Canada. Once those facilities were established and artillery had arrived, the infantry would roll in and begin operations.

Rakken added, "I just heard they've called up the Fourth in Alaska, so those Strykers will be rolling down. I heard another rumor that a brigade from the Tenth Mountain Division is heading up in about sixty sorties of C-17s. They'll establish the first blocking positions."

"And what are the Canadians doing about all this?" Vatz flashed a crooked grin.

Rakken pretended to think hard. "Trying to duck."

"I thought so. Well, good hunting then, huh?"

Rakken slapped a palm on Vatz's shoulder. "I just wanted to give you this before you go."

"Oh, man, don't do that."

Vatz stared down at the closed knife in Rakken's other hand; it was a balisong, or Filipino "butterfly knife," with two handles that counter-rotated around the tang and concealed the blade within them when not in use.

Only this wasn't an ordinary balisong. This was Rakken's prized possession: a custom Venturi made of intricately patterned Damascus steel with black lip pearl inlays in the handles. It was as much a piece of art as it was a functional cutting tool, and it had been designed and crafted by famed knife maker Darrel Ralph.

"Nate, I'm giving this to you for two reasons: first, if one of us is going to make it, it's going to be you. I believe that. And second, I'm just tired of carrying it."

Vatz shook his head. He didn't believe a word of it. And in a world full of high-tech toys, it was ironic that they should be standing there, discussing the exchange of a knife. Nevertheless, he took the balisong and slid it into one of his hip pockets. "You're too much, Marc. I'll borrow it. Give it to you when we get back, if we're not all frostbitten by then."

"All right, you got a deal. Good luck up there. And if you SF boys need any real men to come bail out your sorry asses, just give me or Appleman a call on the cell, 'kay?"

Vatz snorted, raised his fist to meet Rakken's for a pound. Then he muttered a quick, "See ya," and jogged off.

Captain Jake Boyd spotted the rescue chopper's searchlight sweeping across the snow, so he sat up and began to wave them in. He wouldn't miss the unforgiving cold or the sight of his beautiful fighter plane burning in the distance.

The blood had frozen on his lips and chin, and he could barely feel his cheeks. He slowly, carefully, got up as the chopper turned and pitched its nose for the landing.

Boyd's heart sank.

The searchlight had blinded him, and he'd only seen a vague silhouette in the sky.

Now he saw it, a Ka-29, setting down with heavily armed infantrymen hopping down from the bay door.

Boyd had both pistols now, one in each hand; he charged back to the ejection seat and threw himself down behind it, then came back up and began firing at the oncoming troops.

He struck one soldier in the leg, caught another in the thigh, as they suddenly raked his position with so much fire that he could no long hear the whomping of rotors, only the echoing bang and subsequent ricocheting of rounds off metal.

He keyed the mike of his emergency radio. "This is Ghost Hawk on the ground! I'm being engaged by Russian infantry! What's the ETA on that rescue bird?"

A sudden and nearby thump made him whirl.

Grenade. Right there.

He sprang up, knew that if he ran backward, they'd simply gun him down.

So he did what any other red-blooded American fighter pilot would do: he ran directly at the troops, screaming and firing.

The grenade exploded behind him, knocking him to his chest. That was when the first stabs of pain came, when he realized he'd been shot—and not just once.

He glanced up at the Russians, cursed as one came over, raised his pistol.

Stephanie's voice was coming from the radio. He should have told her how he felt, should have told her what she meant to him.

But at least now, at the end, he had that music, that sweet music of her crying out.

As Major Stephanie Halverson lifted off, her eyes burned with the knowledge that Jake was dead.

She'd been monitoring the radio, had listened to his last transmission. She wanted more than anything to streak back there and finish off the men who had killed him. But it was too late now.

The skies above the Northwest Territories were alive with incoming transports and fighters, and Halverson and the other three pilots training at Igloo Base had been tasked with getting up there and intercepting as many as possible, all while attempting to evade detection from those fighters.

There would be no dogfight—just a standoff surgical removal of those lumbering AN-130s.

But she could barely keep her thoughts focused on the task. She kept telling herself that she shouldn't have been so distant from him, that she could sense how he'd felt about her, that she, too, had felt the same.

She raced into the heavens, going supersonic, moving into her standoff position to begin launching missiles at the cargo planes, now at 28,450 feet and descending rapidly.

A check of the 130s' range revealed they were about fifteen kilometers away, within the Sidewinder's killing zone. Her electronic countermeasures—including the jamming of enemy radar systems—were fully engaged.

And her first two missiles were locked on.

Her wingman, Captain Lisa Johansson, call sign Sapphire, announced that she, too, was locked up and ready to fire. The other two JSF fighters were already engaging the enemy.

Halverson opened her mouth to give the order—

Just as the alarms went off in her cockpit.

Incoming enemy missiles launched from Sukhoi SU-35 long-range interceptors. She already had the angle of arrival.

The computer identified the missiles as Vympel R-84s, the latest incarnation of Russia's short-range, air-to-air missile, considered by most combat pilots to be one of the world's most formidable weapons.

"Sapphire, abort missile launch! We got incoming. Check countermeasures. IR flares and chaff! Evade!"

SEVENTEEN

In February 2006, the Marine Corps Special Operation Command (MARSOC) was activated, which in
effect made Force Recon Marines an official part of the
U.S. Special Operations Command (SOCOM) team
along with the other special operations units—SEALS,
Rangers, Army Special Forces, and Special Tactics
teams. MARSOC was fully constituted in 2010 and
became part of the Joint Strike Force at that time as
well.

Consequently, when the Russians began their move
into Canada, MARSOC was among the first to get the
call.

And that particular call had funneled down through
command to one Staff Sergeant Raymond McAllen, who
was now sprinting back to his two-story barracks to get

packed up and get the hell out of Southern California, bound for the Northwest Territories, more than two thousand miles away.

Elements of the 13th Marine Corps Expeditionary Unit (MEU) were being deployed from Marine Corps Base Camp Pendleton up to Alberta. They were pumped full of lightning and ready to crack and boom onto the scene. The only thing missing from all the excitement was Jonesy.

And his absence was sorely felt by the five remaining members of the Force Recon team: McAllen, Palladino, Szymanski, Friskis, and Gutierrez.

Five minutes prior, McAllen and the rest of the Outlaws had been listening to their company commander, Colonel Stack, going over the warning order; the CO singled out McAllen's team to spearhead the company's reconnaissance operations.

Marine Corps brass, along with the JSF, believed that the Russians would move a large ground force, maybe even a couple of brigades, into several areas of Alberta. They would take the town of High Level and use it as a staging area, and would also move down Highway 63 in the eastern part of Alberta toward Fort McMurray and the Athabasca Oil Sands north of "Fort Mac."

Much to McAllen's chagrin, his new assistant team leader, Sergeant Scott Rule, had to open his dumb-ass mouth and ask what was meant by "oil sands." The CO loved to hear himself talk and loved to impress everyone with his attention to details, whether they put you to sleep or not. That he didn't have a PowerPoint presentation was the only saving grace.

So they got the one-minute lecture about oil sands, a mixture of crude bitumen (a semisolid form of crude oil), silica sand, clay minerals, and water. The CO even knew that the bitumen was used by the aboriginals back in the day to waterproof their canoes.

Point was, the oil sands could be turned into real, usable oil, and the Russians wanted control of all the reserves.

But they wouldn't get them—not if United States Marines stood in their path.

Once McAllen and his boys arrived in Alberta, they would chopper way up Highway 63, establish a reconnaissance post, deploy two robo-soldiers that would be controlled by human operators, and confirm where lead elements of the enemy force were heading.

They were a small piece of a much larger defensive dubbed Operation Slay the Dragon by the JSF, an operation that included all branches of the U.S. and European Federation armed forces, with the Euros focusing on the major city of Edmonton.

Now, back in his barracks, a shirtless Sergeant Rule approached McAllen, cocked a brow, all pierced nipples and twenty tattoos. "Hey, Ray, you got a minute?"

"If this is about what we discussed earlier—"

"Look, man, you set me straight. I'm so squared away that if you brush against me, my corners will cut you."

"Nice."

"But I'll never be Jonesy. Nobody will. Just want you to know that I'm giving you a hundred and ten percent. Always."

"We'll see how long it takes for you to create your own shadow. And I hope it's a pretty long one. The other thing is, I got about eight, nine years on you. In my book, that makes me old school." McAllen reached out and flicked one of Rule's nipple rings. "Maybe the Corps's gotten a little soft on this crap since you hide them under your shirt, but I haven't."

"I'll remove them, Sergeant—if they bother you that much."

"I just want to be sure we're on the same page."

"We are. Good. Now don't forget to pack an extra sock."

"Huh?"

"Our suits have all those fancy micro-climate conditioning subsystems, but if the suit fails, you and your family jewels will be glad you got that sock. Trust me."

Rule grinned. "I hear that, Sergeant."

McAllen turned and looked the man straight in the eye, then proffered his hand. "The last time I met the Russians, they couldn't help but fall to their knees and bleed."

"I hope I have the same effect on them."

They shook firmly, then Rule rushed off to pack.

McAllen returned to inventorying his gear. He fetched a picture of himself and Jonesy from his footlocker and slipped it into his ruck. They'd been pretty drunk that night, and Jonesy had been the one to get McAllen home. He was like that. Dependable beyond belief. And McAllen had to get it into his head that though no one could replace Jonesy, he had to give Sergeant Rule, nipple rings and all, a chance.

At least the spirit of Jonesy would be heading up into the Great White North, along with the spirit of the Corps.

Whenever they went into battle, every man who had ever been a Marine went with them.

With white-hot chaff flashing beside her wings, Major Stephanie Halverson took her F-35B fighter into another dive, rolling as she did so, then banked sharply to the right, cutting a deep chamfer in the air.

Her pressure suit compensated for what would've been excruciating g-forces, keeping the blood from pooling in her legs, yet still she felt the usual and sometimes even welcome discomfort.

One missile took the bait and exploded somewhere above her; she didn't waste time to check its exact location because the other one was still locked on.

Utilizing all of the jet's sensors and the helmet-mounted display, Halverson was able to look down through her knees, through the actual structure of the aircraft, and spot the missile coming up from below.

She punched the chaff again.

Then killed the engine and let the fighter drop away like an unlucky mallard during hunting season.

The only problem was, the missile had been designed to "see" whole images rather than just single points of infrared radiation like the heat from her engine.

So that Vympel R-84 with its "potato masher" fins had a decision to make: detonate its thirty kilograms of high explosive in the chaff or continue on to Halverson.

With her breath held, she watched as the missile penetrated the chaff cloud—

And kept on coming.

She cursed, fired up the engine, then started straight for the cargo planes still glowing in her multifunction display.

Okay, steady. Okay.

She pressed a finger against the touch screen, viewing a much clearer, close-up image of the nearest aircraft. She tapped another button, and target designation and weapons status imagery appeared in her HMD. She closed in, the target now being automatically tracked, the crosshairs in her visor locking on the AN-130.

If I get taken out of the fight, I'm bringing a couple of you with me.

She tightened her fist, pressed the button.

Missile away. She pressed again. Missile #2 streaked off a second behind the first.

The radar alarm was still going off.

And there it was, a glowing dot. You didn't need a key to the display's symbols to know what that one meant: death.

"Sapphire, this is Siren, can't shake my last missile, over."

"Yes, you can, Siren! Chaff again! Come on!"

Aw, what the hell. She popped more chaff then broke into a diving roll that would have left most nuggets barfing in their helmets.

And what kind of miracle was that? The damned missile took the bait and exploded in a beautiful conflagration, the dark clouds traced by flickering light.

"Sister, I'm listening to you next time," Halverson cried. "And here comes another pair of 130s. Let's get 'em. I want to head back to Igloo empty, refuel, rearm, and do it all over again!"

"Roger that!"

Halverson shut her eyes for just a second.

Jake, if you can hear me, then you know what I'm thinking . . .

Major Alice Dennison couldn't afford to leave her JSF command post in Tampa and was closely monitoring the data coming in to her from Alaska, where the 11th Air Force and 3rd Wing from Elmendorf and the 354th Fighter Wing from Eielson had scrambled to intercept the Russian transports, along with that handful of JSF fighters whose pilots had been training in the Northwest Territories.

She couldn't leave, but she shuddered with the desire to do so, to travel back to Gitmo and question Doletskaya again.

However, she had arranged the next best thing—a video conference with the prisoner.

And, despite her better judgment, she stole away to a private conference room for ten minutes to speak one last time with Colonel Pavel Doletskaya.

She thought maybe she could put the demons to rest and begin to actually sleep.

The colonel looked even more haggard than the last time she had seen him, gray stubble creeping across his chin, and it seemed an effort for him to keep his head upright. His eyes failed to focus, then finally he blinked and leaned forward, too close to the camera, then threw his head back and suddenly laughed.

"Colonel, stop it."

After another few seconds, he composed himself and said, "I'm sorry, Major. I just . . . I can see that look in your eyes. So, are we happy with the information I gave you? Because you don't look very happy."

"No, we're perfectly fine with it."

His expression grew serious. "You're bluffing."

"You cried like a baby, Colonel. I know exactly what Operation 2659 is and exactly who Snegurochka aka the snow maiden is, all right?"

"So then, why have you interrupted my vacation?"

Dennison took a deep breath. Yep, she was bluffing. She hadn't learned a damned thing—the bastard was the most highly skilled and resistant prisoner the interrogators had ever encountered. In fact, at this point, they swore he knew nothing . . .

But Dennison refused to believe that. "I just thought it would be in your best interests to formally defect. That way, you would enjoy the benefits of such a decision."

"You don't know anything, do you. You ran 2659 through every database in the world, compared the number to other operations, thought it might be an address, a date, a model number for the memory chip of a computer. You've had experts from every government agency looking at it, people trained to study ciphers, even that agent from the CIA who swears he decrypted the messages on that statue outside the office in Langley. What's it called? Kryptos? Yes . . . But you know nothing—or rather, you know that I know everything about you."

"Colonel, this is not a game. Do you have any idea how many innocent people are about to die?"

"I do—even more so than you."

"Is it worth it?"

"Oh, those kinds of questions give me a headache, Major. I want to know if you have redecorated your apartment recently. Maybe you have pulled up the rugs, decided to buy some new lights for the ceiling? Or maybe some new paintings?"

"Operation 2659 is the invasion of Alberta. The snow maiden is the code name for an operative, a female operative who is part of or perhaps leading the mission."

"Yes, you knew that before we ever met. The Euros fed you that on a spoon. And since then, you've spent all your time reading fairy tales . . ."

"This is your last chance, Colonel. Otherwise, you're going to rot in prison for the rest of your life. You could defect, tell us what we need to know. You could work with us to bring a peaceful solution to this conflict."

"Do you want to be president of the United States? Because you sound so convincing."

"Did you murder Viktoria Antsyforov?"

"No, she killed me."

"Colonel . . ."

"This I will tell you. She was my mistress, a brilliant officer, but her ego and ambition got in the way. I did not kill her, but she made many enemies in the GRU."

"She was the snow maiden."

"Of course not, Colonel. You are."

Dennison snickered. "How am I part of your invasion plan?"

"You are the one with the cold heart who is trying to stop it. You are the one we worried about most of all."

"I'm a JSF operations officer. I'm not chairman of the Joint Chiefs. I don't wield that kind of power."

"You are more powerful than you know."

"Colonel, will you defect?"

He took a deep breath, closed his eyes. "Good-bye, Major."

EIGHTEEN

The USS *Florida* had surfaced once more, and Commander Jonathan Andreas stood in the sail, shuddering against the cold wind and holding the satellite phone to his ear, waiting for someone to answer.

"Hello, Commander Andreas, this is COMPACFLT Duty Officer. Please hold for Admiral Stanton."

She already knew he was calling?

He waited about twenty seconds, then a familiar voice jolted him. "Good morning, Jon. It's Donald Stanton."

"Uh, good morning," he responded tentatively.

"How much time can you give me?"

Andreas glanced around at the black waves crashing against the equally black skin of his boat. "I'm comfortable with five to ten minutes, Admiral."

"Very well, then—"

"But, uh, with all due respect, sir, can you tell me the title of that speech you gave in the old sub base auditorium last fourth of July?"

"Oh, that one," Stanton said with a slight chuckle. "That would be '101 Ways Chief Petty Officers Trick Admirals into Believing We Run the Navy.'"

"Thank you, sir."

"Good man. Now I'll talk fast. The Russians shot down the ELF and Comsat satellite, Michigan's back online, and we have one SITREP from you that's two days old. News doesn't get any better. The Russians have begun moving a large force, perhaps two brigades, into the Northwest Territories, most likely headed for Alberta, for the cities, the oil reserves, the whole she-bang. I've heard they're running more sorties than they did in Paris. On top of that, the president ordered the destruction of the International Space Station, since the Russkies used it to shoot down our satellites and were preparing to strike other targets. Now you talk, Jon, I'll listen."

Andreas's mouth fell open, and it took a few seconds before he could launch into a capsule summary of his observations regarding the Russian task force, concluding with, "Sir, request permission to destroy those ships."

"Permission granted."

"There's an opportunity at 0500, when they'll engage in refueling ops. I'm going to seize it."

"Excellent. For now, though, get back under, stay safe, and make this your last voice call. We'll start sending you traffic via the sat phone data link so you don't need to transmit anything. I'm sure you've already surmised this phone is manned 24/7, and right now it's the *only* working number on the Iridium system."

That explained how the duty officer knew who was calling when she answered the phone.

"Aye-aye, sir. I'll try to poke my nose up every two hours starting from the termination of this call."

"Good."

"Oh, and one personal item, Admiral: please have someone call my wife and tell her to change our PIN."

"Right. I'll call her myself. Good hunting, Captain."

"Thank you, sir."

Andreas thumbed off the phone, his thoughts still whirling as he barked out the orders to dive, dive, dive!

It was at Army Airborne School in Fort Benning, Georgia, that Team Sergeant Nathan Vatz had been taught how to wear a parachute harness and had stood near the mock door, waiting for his turn to learn the proper method of exiting an aircraft.

The parachute landing fall platform had allowed him to develop the proper landings, while the lateral drift apparatus had helped him acquire the proper technique for controlling the chute during descent.

Then there was the good old thirty-four-foot tower, which let you experience a jump into nothingness. And once you got to the 250-foot tower, you were feeling good about yourself—until you saw someone make a mistake.

Still, Vatz had survived, made his qualification jumps, and had kept current by jumping at least once every three months.

Yes, it seemed like yesterday. Felt like yesterday, too. He still got the jitters every time he jumped, despite the hundreds of hours in other training courses he'd attended at Fort Bragg, the ones that had really kicked his butt.

Now that butt was firmly planted on the bright red web seat of a C-130's vibrating hold with the rest of his new twelve-man ODA team.

Vatz had barely gotten to know these guys, and he still mixed up a few names. That was all right. There'd be plenty of time to get to know one another, after they finished their work.

And thanks to the Russians, the best way to get to work was to engage in HALO operations, an SF specialty.

What you did was you jumped from your perfectly good aircraft at a high altitude, in their case 25,000 feet, allowed yourself to freefall for a while at terminal velocity, then engaged in a low opening of your parachute so you could glide in clandestinely on your target from miles away, the target in this case being the sleepy little town of High Level, population: less than five thousand.

In order to perform such a miracle, Vatz and his fellow operators had to don their heavier helmets and oxygen masks. Their high-speed downward fall, coupled with their forward airspeed and the fact that they wore a minimal amount of metal, would allow them to defeat Russian radars.

A report from the pilot came in: winds were at twelve knots and holding. That was good. If they got up over eighteen knots, they'd have to abort the jump.

Thirty minutes prior they had all been breathing one hundred percent oxygen to flush the nitrogen from their bloodstreams, and the flight psychologist was making sure no one flipped out before the ramp opened.

Breathing in all that pure oxygen was a huge deal because hypoxia was a huge enemy. Without enough air, you could lose consciousness, fail to open your chute, and literally dig your own grave.

Vatz had seen it happen. Twice. And both times the problem had occurred when changing over from the pre-breather to the oxygen bottle. Those guys had allowed nitrogen to slip back into their bloodstreams. At least neither had felt the impact. They'd just blacked out, dropped, hit the ground.

He shuddered. A dozen other things could go wrong, too, stuff he couldn't even imagine. They had to jump in a tight-knit formation, and one bad move by himself or a fellow operator could result in a fatal midair collision. No, Vatz had never seen anyone die from that, but he'd seen a lot of guys slam into each other.

At their stage of the game, though, those things shouldn't be issues. But if your name was Nathan Vatz, you always thought about them in the minutes before the jump.

And there wasn't much else to think about. If he didn't focus on that, he'd be back to Doletskaya or Green Vox, imagining himself exacting revenge on those bastards.

Or he'd be back to that night in the chopper, watching his brothers die before his eyes—

And asking the same damned question over and over: Twelve good men went into Moscow, and only one came out. Why me?

The jumpmaster gave them the twenty-minute warning, which they all acknowledged with a great cheer: it'd been nearly four hours since they'd lifted off from Gray Army Airfield.

Then the jumpmaster went through his checklist. Helmets and oxygen mask, check. CDS switches, load marker lights, anchor cable stops, ramp ADS arms, cargo compartment lights, all good for him.

"Complete!" he boomed.

And as all safety-minded paratroopers did, they checked the gear of the men ahead of them. Again. And again. Perhaps four, five, maybe six times.

Some said the last twenty minutes before a jump were the longest of their lives. Not for Vatz.

He blinked.

And they were on their feet, the ramp open and locked, the navigator coming over the radio to say, "Ten seconds."

They were nearly on top of the CARP—the computerized airborne release point—which accounted for all the data coming in from the aircraft's systems and the current weather conditions. Vatz was glad neither he nor anyone else in the company had to figure out those calculations. They'd thrown some of that math at him back at Fort Bragg, and he'd spent most of the time ducking.

All right, the time had finally come.

The eight officers, seven warrant officers, and sixty-seven enlisted soldiers of Vatz's Special Forces company were about to go for a little walk.

But then the pilot cursed, and the navigator screamed over the radio: "We got a missile locked on! Get 'em out! Get 'em all out!"

Vatz's mouth went to cotton. He now knew those pilots had discovered they'd been probed by enemy radars a while ago, but they hadn't said anything. No need to cause a plane full of SF guys to get unraveled.

The Russians had poured so much money into new technology that they'd been routinely defeating JSF electronic countermeasures, and wasn't it Vatz's luck that his ride up to Canada had a bull's-eye painted on its nose?

Nevertheless, the reaction of the men inside the cargo hold was a testament to the professionalism of Special Forces operators everywhere.

There was no frantic rush to the ramp, no mob scene of helmeted troopers stampeding to get out.

They began the jump as they ordinarily did—just ten times faster, the jumpmaster hidden behind his visor and waving them on. Vatz's helmet was equipped with the latest, greatest, and smallest generation of night-vision goggles attached over the visor. A host of other readings, including data from his wrist-mounted altimeter and parachute automatic activation device (AAD), were fed to him via a head's-up display in the visor itself. The unit automatically switched on as he left the ramp, among the first twenty or so to exit, along with their heavy equipment/ordnance crates.

Down below, lights shone like phosphorescent stitching on a black quilt, but those stitches were few and far between. This part of Canada was scarcely populated.

Also somewhere down there was the railroad, and the river, but he couldn't see them just yet.

No one said a word over the intra-team radio.

They were all holding their breaths, Vatz knew.

A slight flash came from the corner of his eye, and he craned his head, just as the missile struck the C-130 in the tail, impacting right above the open ramp—even as operators were still bailing out.

He couldn't even say *Oh my God*.

He was shocked into silence. The aircraft exploded in a fluctuating cloud of flames that swallowed the operators floating away from the tail.

Vatz deliberately rolled onto his back and watched as the roiling sphere of death grew even larger, pieces of flaming debris extending away from it, trailing tendrils of smoke.

And it was all delivered to Vatz in the grainy green of night vision as operators suddenly appeared from the cloud, on fire and tumbling hopelessly toward the earth.

The voices finally came over the radio, burred with anger, tight with exertion, high-pitched in agony. He listened to his brothers try to save each other, listened to some gasp their last breaths . . .

As he floated there with a front-row seat, his pulse increasing, his breath growing shallow, every muscle in his body beginning to tense.

Until suddenly someone struck him with a terrible thud, knocking him around into an uncontrollable barrel roll.

Flames flashed by.

He'd been hit by one of the dead guys.

He had to recover and fast. The longer he rolled, the longer it'd take to recover.

He arched his back, extended his arms, but kept rolling. Someone called his name.

Part of him thought it was no good. He should've died back in Moscow with the rest of them. He'd been living on borrowed time.

Then he heard Rakken telling him how lucky he was, having escaped death twice. Why not make it a hat trick?

Hell, he could've been blown up with the plane. Giving up now would be a terrible waste.

And then he thought about his dead brothers. They needed him to carry on. He remembered the last few lines of the Special Forces Creed:

I am a member of my nation's chosen soldiery. God grant that I may not be found wanting, that I will not fail this sacred trust.

A sacred trust.

Damn it, he would not let them down.

He arched his back again, thrust out his arms, and screamed to regain control.

The roll slowed, and he was disoriented, the altimeter's digital readout ticking off his descent, the ground still spinning a little, but he was on his belly, and his detachment commander was calling him on the radio.

He took a deep breath, about to answer, when he spotted the long column of smoke in the distance . . .

Where the C-130 had once been.

NINETEEN

Rearmed and refueled, Major Stephanie Halverson streaked down the runway, engine roaring, her gear just leaving the ground as dozens of Russian bombs finally hit Igloo Base.

She pulled up and away, banked left, and came around to witness a chilling sight.

The snow-covered Quonset huts housing the enlisted soldiers' bunks, the offices, and the officers' quarters burst apart, ragged pieces of metal flying everywhere as chutes of fire swept through them and ignited the stands of lodgepole pines behind the base.

Barely two seconds later, the refueling trucks went up like dominoes, their crews trying to evacuate in HMMWVs but caught in the blast.

Those explosions triggered several more among the

smaller vehicles parked nearby, just outside the two hangar facilities that stood only a moment more before two bombs suddenly obliterated them.

Inevitably, the small, five-story tower and adjacent command center took one, two, three direct hits from thousand-pound bombs and were lost in mushroom clouds that rose and collided with each other, throwing up a black wall of fire-filled smoke.

Halverson was exhausted, overtired, her thoughts consumed by horror and disbelief.

From her vantage point, the devastation below was silent and seemingly less significant.

But she'd met nearly everyone at that base, and she realized now that there would be no survivors.

"Oh, God, Siren, you see that?" asked Sapphire.

She could barely answer. "Yeah."

They had one job left, one last sortie.

There was nowhere to refuel. Nowhere to rearm. And the last orders they'd received from Igloo were to engage the enemy.

So they would.

She and Lisa Johansson were the only two left. Had their refueling gone a minute longer, they, of course, would already be dead.

Dozens of Russian cargo ships soared through the sky, their escort fighters engaging the squadrons from Alaska.

"Where are the Canadians?" Sapphire asked.

"I don't know, but I have a feeling they won't watch this happen for very long."

"Roger that."

Halverson took a long breath to steady her nerves. "This is it, girl. You ready?"

"Ready."

"Let's go get 'em!" With that, she engaged the afterburner, accelerating with a force that was hard to describe to someone who'd never sat in a cockpit.

Just as she hit Mach 1, the Prandtl-Glauert singularity occurred, a vapor cone caused by a sudden drop in air pressure that extended from the wings to her tail. She left the cone behind in her exhaust trail.

They held their steady course, ascending over the enemy aircraft, bound for coordinates seventy-five kilometers northwest of Behchoko, where dozens of AN-130s had landed and were off-loading their BMP-3s.

The five-hundred-pound JDAMs under Halverson's wings were accurate to within thirteen meters, and she and Sapphire could launch those precision-guided bombs from up to twenty-four kilometers away during a low-altitude launch or up to sixty-four kilometers during a high-altitude launch. You plugged in the coordinates, delivered the munitions—

Barring of course, angry swarms of Russian fighters whose pilots thought otherwise.

The AGM-154 Joint Standoff Weapons in the F-35B's internal bays were the "C" variant developed for the Navy. The weapon utilized a combination of an imaging infrared (IIR) terminal seeker and a two-way data link to achieve point accuracy and was designed to attack point targets. It was a thousand pounds of general purpose destruction.

And it was most definitely time for her and Sapphire to flash their fangs and lighten their loads.

"Two minutes," Halverson warned her wingman.

"Roger that. I have two targets on the ground on the east side of their staging area, over."

"I see them," Halverson said, checking her own display. "I've got two more 130s on the west side. Christ, you see all those BMPs?"

"I do. Two bad we weren't packing more punch."

Sapphire was right. Thousand-pound JDAMs instead of five hundred would have really done the job.

"One minute," Halverson announced.

That's all we need is one minute, thought Halverson. She glanced up through the canopy, where the first streaks of dawn turned the sky a light purple on the horizon.

Just thirty seconds now. Give me thirty seconds.

Sapphire cursed into the radio. "Four bogeys at our eleven o'clock, closing in."

Halverson swore under her breath as she checked her own radar. "They ain't ours."

"Nope. Got ID: Su-98s. Countermeasures seem ineffective. I think they have us. We better launch before they do!"

The Sukhoi S-98 was Russia's latest single-seat fighter, deemed by most JSF pilots as the most deadly in its arsenal and capable of carrying up to 18,000 pounds of ordnance.

"Just keep course. Fifteen seconds."

"They're going to get missile lock!"

Halverson's voice turned strangely calm as her years of training kicked in, like muscle memory. "Sapphire, let's make it all worth it. We're almost there."

"Oh my God," gasped Sapphire. "We won't make it!"

"Hang on! Five, four, three, two . . . Bombs away! Flares, chaff, evade!" Halverson cried.

The two JDAMs fell away from her wings as behind her, the chaff and flares ignited.

Sapphire did likewise, and Halverson lost sight of her as they both rolled inverted and dove away in a split S, the oldest trick in the book, hoping the sudden maneuver would prevent those Su-98 pilots from getting missile lock.

As she came upright, flying in the Russians' direction about two thousand feet below, the bad news flashed: missiles locked.

And her wingman confirmed the next inescapable fact: "Siren, they've fired!"

Halverson longed for the days of good old dogfighting, when maybe she and Sapphire could've pulled out the old Thach Weave, one of them baiting an enemy pilot while the other waxed him from the side.

Though they would occasionally get to tangle with the enemy, it was mostly distant and faceless now, missiles launched from kilometers away from jets you never saw—

And those missiles you'd only glimpse for a second, your last.

Halverson reacted out of pure instinct, jamming the stick forward and plunging straight down, even as she hit the afterburner.

Her first thought was to outrun the incoming missiles, get her fighter up near Mach 2, practically melt off the wings. She imagined the missiles running out of fuel behind her and simply dropping away.

But that was a fantasy.

The Vympel R-84 had a range of at least one hundred kilometers, and everything Halverson knew about missiles and evading them told her that if these Vympels didn't take the flares or chaff, then she was in their no-escape zone.

She blasted through the clouds and checked her screens.

Twelve seconds to impact.

"Oh, God, Siren, I don't think I can—"

Sapphire's transmission broke off, and her fighter vanished from Halverson's display.

Her wingman hadn't even ejected.

Halverson blinked hard. *Is this how it'll be, then? Give me more time. I'm not finished yet.*

No barrel roll, split S, break turn, chandelle, or wingover would save her now.

No maneuver in the world.

No amount of thrust from her engines.

She cut the afterburner, hit the damned brakes. Hard.

Below lay the haphazard rows of Russian cargo planes, and Halverson's AGM-154s were locked on a pair of targets.

So, with seven seconds left, she cut loose both bombs—

Then tugged the black-and-yellow striped handle between her legs.

The canopy blew off with a violent shudder.

Nearly at the same time, the Martin-Baker Mk. 16 ejection seat rocketed her out and away, the straps and padded cuffs of the leg restraint system pinning her shins to the seat, even as the wind struck her squarely and sent her rushing back and away, long flames extending from her boots.

An explosion lit in her helmet, but it turned into a streak as she continued back a second more.

Then the seat's drogue chute caught the wind, abruptly yanking her down, and she pendulummed toward the earth; the main chute, stowed behind her headrest, deployed while the seat dropped away, yanked up by its own chute.

Just then she caught sight of the lines of AN-130s below, where her second two bombs had impacted. Fires raged everywhere, with massive wings lying detached from fuselages.

At that moment, another AN-130 came in for a landing and crashed into debris lying in its path. The plane spun sideways, sliding wildly across the snow until it impacted with several others in a chain reaction that left Halverson wanting to cheer, but she felt too sick.

She was glad she hadn't had time to eat. She had practiced ejections before, but this one . . . she thought for a moment she might pass out.

Her comm system had automatically switched over to the helmet's transmitter, and while she knew her ejection had automatically been sent to every JSF command post in the world, she knew it was imperative that she confirm she was alive.

Yes, her flight suit would also transmit her bio readings, but a voice on the end of an encrypted transmission carried a whole lot more weight.

Protocol dictated that she get on the tactical channel to contact the nearest command post, but she said screw it and broadcast over the emergency channel reserved for strategic operations. Better to ring the louder bell.

"This is JSF Fighter Siren out of Igloo Base, North-west Territories. I've ejected north of Behchoko." She rattled off the last coordinates she'd read on her display. "I'm descending toward a heavily wooded area, GPS coordinates to follow once I'm on the ground, over."

After about ten seconds, a voice came over the radio: "JSF Fighter Siren, this is Hammer, Tampa Five Bravo. Received your transmission. We'll see if we can get some help up to you. Send GPS coordinates once you're on the ground."

"Roger that, Hammer. And here's hoping our boys get to me before they do."

"We'll do everything we can. And you do the same. Standing by . . ."

All right, she'd survived the ejection.

Would she survive the landing?

The forest unfurled below for kilometer after kilometer, dense, snow-covered, a bone-breaking gauntlet.

She imagined herself plunging through the heavy canopy and getting impaled by a limb.

Wouldn't that be her luck?

Some training mission. The fighters were gone, the base was gone, her colleagues were dead.

Jake, are you there?

Yeah, why didn't you say anything?

Because it would've been too complicated.

You're wrong.

I know. I've been lying to myself.

Just don't panic. It'll be all right. I'll be with you every step of the way. You know what to do now. Get your mind off of it. Calm down.

Halverson took a deep breath.

The ground came up faster.

With a vengeance.

TWENTY

Commander Jonathan Andreas glanced down at his watch: 0513 hours.

You would need a hell of a lot more than a knife to cut the tension in the *Florida*'s control room.

A plasma torch might not even do it—because the moment had come, and Andreas and his crew were a pack of artic wolves, poised before their prey, still and silent in the dim red light.

The AGM-84 Harpoon antishipping missiles were loaded in tubes one, two, and three.

And presently, the *Varyag,* the converted aircraft carrier now serving as the Russian task force's command and control ship, had the oiler *Kalovsk* tied up alongside, with lines fore and aft, separated by evenly spaced fenders between them to cushion any accidental impact between the ships. Now, with the first pale ribbons of dawn wandering along the horizon, refueling operations were well under way.

This was it.

Two ships. One missile.

Andreas held his breath a moment more, and then turned his key, granting the weapons control console permission to launch. The reaction of three thousand psi jettisoning more than fifteen hundred pounds out the torpedo tube rumbled through the control room.

The submarine variant of the AGM-84 Harpoon antishipping missile was housed in a blunt-nosed, torpedo-like capsule called an ENCAP, which had positive buoyancy and burst away from the *Florida*, while a lanyard caused fins to pop out as it glided to the surface without power.

Once the ENCAP breached the surface, Andreas watched as it blew off its tail and cap, then fired the Harpoon on its solid-fuel booster.

His pulse leapt as the glowing orb shot off.

The missile was directed by an INS (inertial navigation system), where it conducted an autonomous search for a specific preprogrammed target image. A number of different search patterns could be programmed into the Harpoon, which not only increased its probability of detecting the target but made it harder to trace the missile's flight path back to its launcher.

Now the Harpoon dropped down to wave height as it homed in, skimming along the icy spray.

Andreas checked his watch once more, then glanced up at the image on the flat panel.

The Harpoon's WDU-18/B—an innocuous description for a 488-pound, penetrating, blast-fragmentation warhead—pierced the *Kalovsk*'s port beam.

A heartbeat . . . then 297,000 gallons of aviation and ship fuel ignited.

The *Kalovsk*'s crew was vaporized before her aft superstructure fractured into five pieces and hurtled skyward. Her port side spewed molten, fragmented steel more than two miles out into Gray's Bay.

Then, in less than thirty milliseconds, molten fragmented steel—formerly the *Kalovsk*'s *starboard* side—bridged the twenty-five-foot gap separating the oiler from the port side of the *Varyag*.

Andreas gasped as the *Varyag*'s partially filled fuel tanks immediately exploded, peeling back and curling 150 feet of her main deck like a sardine can.

The enormous holes at the *Varyag*'s waterline brought icy arctic water in direct contact with the 1,200-psi superheated steam in both boiler rooms. The resulting explosions shattered *Varyag*'s keel in three separate locations.

Andreas beat a fist into his palm, and the crew saw that as a sign to cut loose and cheer.

Her spine broken, *Varyag* took nine minutes to join

Kalovsk at the bottom of Gray's Bay. There were no survivors from either vessel.

Two down, two to go. The *Ulyanovsk* and the *Ivan Rogov* . . .

Half his company had been killed in the C-130 explosion, leaving Sergeant Nathan Vatz in a state of shock as he gathered his chute with the other operators who had managed to bail out before the missile had struck.

He'd shut down the oxygen, popped off his helmet, and was panting in the frigid morning air, occasionally glancing across the broad, snow-covered field toward several buildings, lumber mills maybe, and the dense forests toward the east and west.

With the chute gathered, he charged toward the embankment along a snow-covered road, probably dirt, where the rest of the operators were gathering and burying their chutes in the snow.

There, Vatz crouched down with twenty-six other men, noting immediately that every operator of ODA-888 had made it, along with most of the operators from ODA-887, though one guy was lying on his back, looking pale as two medics attended to him.

"Everybody else, all right?" asked Detachment Commander Captain Mike Godfrey. He was Vatz's CO, bearded and barely thirty, and wise enough to lean on Vatz for advice. "This mission is not over. Captain

Rodriguez and I have decided we're carrying on and have put in the request for another company to be sent up. Of course that's going to take time. Meanwhile, we get to work."

Captain Manny Rodriguez, big eyes and a Fu Manchu mustache, nodded and added, "Me and my boys from Zodiac Team will hit the Chevy dealership and secure some SUVs, while you guys from Berserker hit the sporting goods store and pick up the gear in our crates. Same game plan. We all dress up like hunters. But it'll be Captain Godfrey, Warrant Officer Samson, and Sergeant Vatz who'll meet with the mayor and the RCMPs here."

The Royal Canadian Mounted Police would be one of the keys in securing and preparing the town for the Russian invasion, but Vatz had a sneaking suspicion that their support wouldn't be easily won. And with the area's small population, Vatz figured if they found a dozen Mounties to help, that'd be a lot.

"All right, gentlemen. We rally on the police station no later than oh-six-thirty hours," said Godfrey. "The Russians are already on the ground and on the move. No time to waste!"

"Okay, let's move!" hollered Vatz.

And with that, all of them took off running across the field, shouldering their heavy packs.

Vatz couldn't wait to see the look on the Mounties'

faces when he, Godfrey, and Samson walked into the station.

That would be an interesting conversation.

Major Stephanie Halverson crashed through the tree limbs with a horrible cracking noise. She was jolted left, then right, her helmet scraping against the trees, then suddenly she—

Stopped short.

Her entire body tugged hard against the straps, and her neck snapped back as she lost her breath.

It took a few seconds for her to get her bearings.

The snow lay about twenty feet below. She glanced up, saw that the chute had tangled in the limbs and she now dangled in midair.

After ditching the ejection seat, she'd done her best to steer herself into the widest gap between trees, and that had probably saved her life, but it had also left her hanging, literally, between the big pines.

Detaching the chute line and jumping meant risking a fracture.

She undid her helmet, let it drop to the snow, *thud*. No, she wasn't jumping.

"Oh," she said aloud, breathing in the cold, crisp air. In the distance came the muffled drone of props, and she wondered how long it would take before they sent out a squad of Spetsnaz troops for her. They couldn't have missed her chute.

The thought sent her into motion, swinging from side to side, trying to get close to the nearest trunk, where she might grab on and attempt to secure herself.

After five or six swings, she built up enough momentum to strike the trunk, bark flying as she wrapped an arm around and came to a sudden halt, her grip already faltering.

She detached the chute, let the twenty-two-pound survival kit fall away to the ground, where it broke open, scattering its contents.

Nice, Major.

Then she threw herself forward, wrapped both arms around the tree, then both legs, as lines fell away.

Repressing the morbid desire to look down, she slowly loosed arms, just a bit, and began to slide—

Just as a shattered limb from above decided to drop, missing by only six inches.

The sudden shock caused her to loose her grip even more, and she slid much too fast down the tree, bark ripping her across the legs, which were beginning to warm behind the flight suit.

She wasn't sure if she screamed or not as she suddenly hit the ground, lost her balance, and collapsed onto her rump, sending up clouds of snow.

For just a few seconds she sat there, gingerly testing her legs, making sure she hadn't broken or sprained anything. Then the internal voice took over, the training: *All right, all right, get the gear and get the hell out!*

She had a couple of meals ready to eat (MREs), a couple liters of water, a .45 with two spare magazines, a survival guide for exciting reading in case she got bored fleeing from the Russians, a fixed-blade survival knife in nylon sheath, a radio beacon (which she checked to be sure was *off*), a pair of high-powered binoculars with integrated digital camera, and a small emergency blanket.

She tried her helmet's radio. Dead. Damn, it'd been smashed up in the trees on the way down. She also had her wrist-mounted GPS and a satellite phone in her breast pocket, which she now fished out, switched on.

No signal.

"Are you kidding me? The entire network's down?"

Well, wasn't that a bitch? She'd have to find the ejection seat, which had recently been equipped with a secondary transmitter.

But breaking radio silence would mean giving up her location, the same way the survival kit's satellite beacon could.

Damned if you do, damned if you don't.

It wouldn't hurt to at least track down the seat, and let them know in which direction she was headed, which was—

She spun around.

If the Russians were heading south, any direction but south might be good. Then again, the farther north, east, or west she traveled, the farther her rescuers would have to come—if they were planning to rescue her.

It would be all too easy to write off one pilot in an operation as massive as this would be. Did they even have the resources?

She vowed to stop feeling sorry for herself. She would find the ejection seat, send off the last transmission, then take it from there.

The sound of jet engines sent her gaze skyward, where the stars were beginning to fade, where she should be right now.

After slinging the survival kit over her shoulder, the two .45 magazines in her left hip pocket, the pistol in her gloved hand, she took one last look around to make sure she'd hadn't left anything. Then, remembering she had been gliding northwest when she'd dumped the seat, she jogged off and headed southeast through the forest.

She got no more than a thousand yards from her landing site when she heard the sounds of multiple, somewhat high-pitched engines. The sounds left her puzzled. She crouched down, then dug through her kit, produced her binoculars.

In a clearing off to her left, a half dozen black snowmobiles had come to a halt. Climbing off them were heavily armed Spetsnaz troops.

Lowering the binoculars and placing them back into the kit, ever so gently, as though the tiniest sound might be heard by the enemy, Halverson glanced up, saw how the forest dipped down ahead, and figured there might be better cover there.

She rose, started off, wouldn't look back, wouldn't do a damned thing except focus on the next position.

One of the Spetsnaz cried out in Russian, loud enough for her to hear, and she understood the words: "I found the chute!"

And now they knew she was alive.

TWENTY-ONE

A weatherworn man in his early sixties whom the computer identified as Ivan Golova, commander of the helicopter assault ship *Ulyanovsk*, was standing on the main deck, midships, inspecting his vessel for debris damage.

Andreas's men had just intercepted and decrypted communications between him and the skipper of the amphibious assault ship *Ivan Rogov*. Both men agreed that the destruction of the *Varyag* and *Kalovsk* was the worst refueling accident in the history of the Russian Navy.

And both men were unaware of the wolf at their door.

Andreas tensed as Golova looked up, a half second before the Harpoon struck his ship broadside.

The incredible amount of energy directed upward into the main deck instantly blasted the commander apart—

Just as the flooded engineering spaces exploded in a magnificent conflagration that, seconds later, split *Ulyanovsk* in half.

The helicopter assault ship's stern section sank within a minute, but the bow section remained afloat, and crewmembers scrambled to get into lifeboats. The dozens in the water would die within minutes from hypothermia induced by the unforgiving arctic sea.

Those lucky men in the lifeboats, about twenty-five by Andreas's count, paddled furiously for the *Ivan Rogov* as they watched the bow section finally join the *Varyag* and *Kalovsk* at the bottom of Gray's Bay.

This time there was no cheering in Andreas's control room. The odd thing was—and every man serving on his boat would attest to this—if there wasn't a war going on, they and the Russians sailors would probably buy each other drinks. They were all proud Navy men and women. There was a kinship there that extended beyond politics and culture.

But, as always, when push came to shove, they would kill each other without hesitation, and often without remorse. So, yes, there was no cheering this time while the tortured faces appeared on the *Florida*'s screens.

For a few minutes more, everyone in the control room

watched as the *Ulyanovsk*'s survivors struggled to reach a ship that was already doomed.

Andreas, unwilling to subject himself and his crew to any more, gave the order to fire.

The *Florida*'s third Harpoon struck the *Ivan Rogov*'s forward fuel tank. The enormous blast instantaneously consumed the first hundred feet of the ship, including the *Ulyanovsk*'s overloaded lifeboats.

As long columns of fire and smoke billowed from the vessel, wave action and shifting tides swung her 180 degrees on her stern anchor, causing her to dislodge the flukes. Dragging a useless anchor and powerless to stop, *Ivan Rogov*'s broken hulk foundered against the rocky shore.

The handful of survivors who began making their way to the rails would face the hostile Northwest Territories. Andreas doubted that they'd last more than a week.

Throughout the Harpoon attack, he had stood with his right hip pressed against the plotting table and suddenly realized his right leg had gone to sleep. The realization carried him back to his boyhood and Melville's Captain Ahab. He shuddered free the memory and got back to work.

The task force's icebreakers had left, leaving the ammunition ship, which had already lifted an anchor and was on the run.

Andreas spoke softly. "Let her pass. I want to see her plimsoll line and draught markings. I'd also like to get her name before we kill her—for the log."

The ammo ship's angle on the bow was currently port thirty, making it impossible to see her stern and name. However, she had been zigzagging and was just about due for another course change.

Andreas got his wish when she turned right seventy degrees. He let her pass then slowly fell in behind to read her transom:

МОЛНИЯ

"Anybody. Translate that for me," he said.

"It means lightning, sir," replied the SpecOps communications technician.

"How apropos." He glanced sidelong at the XO. "Her draught markings indicate she's drawing forty-two feet. Set up the Mark 48 accordingly and let her open out to ten thousand yards—we don't want her coming down on us when she blows. Load up tube one. You have the honors."

"Aye-aye, sir."

The Mk-48 ADCAP (advanced capability) was a wire-guided, active/passive homing torpedo, nineteen feet long and twenty-one inches in diameter. Thrust from its pumpjet propulsor was developed by an air turbine pump discharge (ATPD) system, and liquid fuel powered the swash-plate piston engine.

Once the XO confirmed that the torpedo was loaded, Andreas paused a moment more, thinking about all the men and women about to lose their lives. War was a terrible thing.

After a barely discernable nod from Andreas, the XO gave the order.

As the torpedo shot through the launch tube, a thin wire spun out, electronically linking it with the submarine. This enabled the operator of the submarine's sensitive sonar systems to guide the torpedo toward the target.

The ammo ship *Lightning* had deployed several decoys and jamming devices, but the operator would avoid those as the torpedo reached seventy-five knots.

A few seconds later, the wire cut free, and the torpedo's high-powered active/passive sonar steered it during the final attack.

The Mk-48's warhead contained the explosive power of about 1,200 pounds of TNT, and both Andreas and the XO knew that that power could be maximized when the warhead detonated below the keel of a target ship.

"Three seconds," said the XO, monitoring his console's timer. "Two, one."

The warhead exploded exactly as planned. The resulting pressure wave of the blast lifted the *Lightning*, and while Andreas couldn't see it, he felt certain that her keel had been broken in the process.

As she settled, the second detonation occurred, tearing her apart and igniting her huge cache of ammunition. Long plumes of water and fragments shot nearly two hundred meters skyward. Dozens more explosions joined the first in a rainbow of colors that lit waves pockmarked by splashing debris.

When the smoke cleared a bit, Andreas confirmed that they had broken the ship into several pieces. The larger bow and stern sections were taking on water fast, while still more ammunition began to cook off.

Again, more silence in the control room, until—

"Should we close and search for survivors, sir?" asked the XO.

Andreas thought a moment. "No." He took a deep breath, then called, "Navigator? Give me a course to the mouth of the Dolphin and Union Strait. With the east end of the gulf iced in, that strait is a perfect choke point—and we get to say who comes through there."

"Hello, Prime Minister," said President Vsevolod Vsevolodovich Kapalkin. "I'm glad you could take my call. I know it's early there."

Prime Minister Robert Emerson of Canada had dark circles under his bloodshot eyes. He had loosened his tie, and he barely opened his mouth when he said quite curtly, "Get out of my country."

"I'm afraid, Prime Minister, that it is far too late for that. But what I have to tell you is quite urgent and will benefit you greatly, if you are willing to negotiate."

"Kapalkin, you're a creature of realpolitik, coercive and amoral. There are no negotiations here. Get out of my country."

"Prime Minister, I understand how you feel, and I know how important it is for you and your people to remain neutral in this conflict. I can guarantee that Canada will not become involved, if we work together."

"We are already involved. You've invaded the Northwest Territories and are heading for Alberta."

"That's not all. As we speak our Spetsnaz forces are heading toward Edmonton and Calgary. They will parachute into those cities and seize control of power and communications uplinks, as well as those early warning radar systems for the JSF's missile defense shield. It is winter. Very cold. And we will shut down the power. But we don't have to do that."

"If we hand over control of Alberta?" Emerson guessed.

Kapalkin spread his hands in a gesture of bon homie. "What is politics, Prime Minister? It is simply the pursuit, possession, and application of power. Let us share that power."

Prime Minister Emerson closed his eyes and massaged his temples, then suddenly blurted, "You know the Americans want to . . .'share power' with us as well."

"And we know you've already failed to stop them from crossing your borders. But we'll forgive that. All we need from you now is a promise not to interfere. And once we control Alberta, you will continue production—even increase it—with our assistance."

"And of course, the Russian Federation will receive a substantial portion of our profits. Come on, you were a smuggler. And this sounds like a proposition put forth by the Russian mafia, not the Federation."

That remark stung, and Kapalkin sharpened his tone. "Prime Minister, if you'll recall, I was also co-owner and chairman of one of Russia's largest oil and gas companies. I know this business. I know how together we can continue production and force the Americans and Euros to pay dearly for that oil. Let Canada become richer—with our help."

"Mr. President, I must be frank with you. I don't believe a goddamn word."

"I'm sorry you feel that way."

"Get out of my country."

"It's too late for that." Kapalkin raised his index finger. "Let me add this: If your government decides to offer military assistance to the Americans, you will suffer the full military might of the Russian Federation."

"Don't threaten me."

"Mr. Prime Minister, at this point you are far better off doing nothing. Remain neutral. We will respect that. We will do everything we can to limit the number of casualties and preserve your infrastructure. Take some time to think it over. You will come to see that what I'm offering is far more attractive and will allow Canada to step out from the shadow of those American cowboys. You could take it to your people, but I understand a cabinet revolt would bring you down quickly, and that your parliament is quite anemic, with several members vying for your position. Sit on your hands for now, if that is your wish. But do not help the Americans or the Euros. I will call you again in a day or two. And we will see how you feel then."

Emerson just stared blankly at him, a man still unwilling to admit defeat. He would. In time.

"Good-bye, Mr. Prime Minister." Kapalkin suppressed his smile.

The large, touch-screen map table showing the Northwest Territories and Alberta flickered with "Blue" and "Red" force activity as Major Alice Dennison shifted past it on her way back to her desk to take a call.

When she sat down and saw the origination, she nearly fell out of her chair. She swallowed hard and smoothed back her hair, then adjusted the collar of her uniform to buy some time and calm herself a bit. After another deep breath, she reached out with a trembling finger and touched the screen.

President Becerra was seated aboard Air Force One. His brows raised. "Hello, Major Dennison."

"Uh, hi. I mean, hello, Mr. President. This is, uh, I'm sorry," she stammered.

"Relax, Major. I just need a little favor."

The President of the United States was asking *her* for a favor?

"Actually two things."

He could ask for ten. "Uh, yes, Mr. President?"

"It's my understanding that you've been in direct contact with an F-35 pilot forced to eject up in the Northwest Territories, Major Stephanie Halverson, call sign Siren."

"Yes, sir. We lost all those fighters. She was the last one to hang on. She put a hell of a dent in their operations."

"I know. And it's also my understanding that no one's been assigned the TRAP mission to get her out of there."

"No, sir, we tried. I was hoping we could split up one of the ODA teams we dropped into High Level, but their C-130 got hit before the whole company got out. We only have a couple dozen operators on the ground, with no air support yet, so I can't spare them. And even if I could, I doubt I could get them up there in time. The first sorties carrying the brigade from the

Tenth Mountain won't reach Grand Prairie for a couple of hours now, and they'll be even farther south."

"I want that pilot recovered."

"Of course, sir, but she's way behind enemy lines."

"Major, I talked to her myself. She was the tip of our spear, and I won't write her off. Now before you even think it, this isn't some PR stunt to create a 'feel-good' story. That pilot is a valuable asset. And she's worth the risk."

"Yes, sir. Getting a team up there could also provide us with some boots-on-the-ground intel of their staging area."

"Exactly."

"Sir, I'll do everything I can."

He nodded. "And the second thing. I know you've been trying to crack Doletskaya. Keep at it. The GRU rarely engages in straightforward ops like this."

"I know, sir. We've got that number, that code name, then we just hit the wall."

"Dig more into his past. Maybe the key is there. And also . . . consider the source of that information."

"Sir?"

"The Euros tipped us off, handed over that intel. There's nothing to say that the intel isn't corrupt, or that the intel will point to the Euros being directly in-volved."

"I'll expand my search. Anything else, sir?"

"Oh, that'll keep you busy. Thank you, Major."

Someone beckoned him. He smiled politely and ended the call.

Dennison sat there, just breathing. Then she bolted from her chair and cried, "Where are those Marines from Pendleton? Are they still in the air?"

TWENTY-TWO

Were it not for the arrival of those Spetsnaz troops in their snowmobiles, Major Stephanie Halverson would not have located her ejection seat.

She wouldn't have looked up, considering that maybe her best hiding place would be in a tree, carefully hidden among those thick, snow-laden limbs. While she had been scanning the trees, her gaze had lighted upon an irregular shape, and as she approached for a better look, she realized the damned seat had lodged itself some twenty feet above, the chute tangled in the limbs. So much for calling Hammer again. At least for now.

With the troops still behind her, she forged on, darting between trees, leaving a terribly clear trail in the snow.

After ducking around the next trunk, she paused to catch her breath.

All right, think. Can't keep running. Need a direction. Something.

A glance back revealed more forest to the southeast. Her GPS showed nothing but more of the same. However, if she went directly west, she'd run into a small road and an open field. Might even be a farm or two out there.

The reckless and basically suicidal thought to confront the troops did cross her mind. Shelly would have said, "Go for it." Her sister had taken on some bullies when they'd been in middle school, literally beating all three girls to the ground, earning her a suspension for a month and summer school for two years.

But no one bothered Stephanie after that.

Unsurprisingly, it had been Shelly who had urged Stephanie to join the military, to take life by the horns, to recognize the warrior inside. She had cheered Stephanie on through the Air Force Academy and beyond—

Until the cancer had struck.

Sorry, Shell, I can't take them on this time. I think I'll beat them by running, not shooting. I've never been a great shot anyway.

When Sergeant Nathan Vatz, Captain Godfrey, and Warrant Officer Samson walked into the RCMP station, they were confronted by an empty front desk. On the walls behind hung photos of Mounties wearing their

Stetsons and scarlet tunics with lanyards slung across their chests.

"I see they got things under control," quipped Godfrey. "They're at DEFCON One."

Vatz laughed under his breath.

"It's early," Samson reminded them.

"Hello, anyone home?" Vatz called.

A woman, probably in her late fifties and dressed in a gray-and-blue RCMP uniform, appeared from behind a closed door, looking as though she had just risen from a deep sleep.

She took one look at their Nomex jumpsuits and frowned. "Can I help you?"

Vatz smiled inwardly over her accent.

"Ma'am? I'm Captain Godfrey. This is Warrant Officer Samson, and Sergeant Vatz. We're Special Forces troops from the United States Army. We need to speak to the police chief or detachment commander, whatever you call him. And we need the mayor here immediately."

"What's going on? I saw something on the news about some Russian planes up north. Then we started getting weird military broadcasts by guys with Russian accents. We thought the satellite dish was messed up."

"Ma'am, if you could just get those people here, we'll fill you all in A-SAP."

Vatz stepped away as one of his weapons sergeants called on the radio to say they'd used their plasma knives to gain entrance into the local sporting goods store and were securing clothing and more gear.

"Roger that. Zodiac Six's team will be around to pick you up, then rally on us."

It took ten precious minutes for the local detachment commander and mayor to arrive. Both were overweight men in their late fifties whose cholesterol levels had to be skyrocketing, Vatz mused.

But Vatz appreciated the mayor's candor and easygoing demeanor when the man drawled, "What the hell's going on, boys?"

Captain Godfrey spelled it out for him, and Vatz had never seen two men grow pale so quickly.

"You need to evacuate the entire town right now," added Godfrey. "Get all the women and children in their cars, get on Highway 35, and get them down to Grand Prairie. That's where our brigade from the Tenth Mountain Division will be coming in. We'll set up camps for IDPs there."

"IDPs?" asked the mayor.

"Internally displaced persons," answered Godfrey. "Trust me, in the next few days, there will be tens of thousands of them."

"All right, let me get everybody I have out there," said the detachment commander.

"Just get those Suburbans rolling through those neighborhoods. Get on the bullhorn. Get 'em out."

"You said only the women and children," repeated the mayor.

"Vatz?" said Captain Godfrey. "Why don't you explain it to him."

Vatz cleared his throat. "Sir, the Russians will send recon elements first, by land and air. If we can hold them off until the Tenth arrives, we'll have control of Highways 35 and 58. That's what we need to do. The Russians can't move their ground troops across the frozen lakes or through all the snow. It's just too damned slow. They'll stick to the roads. They'll come to take the oil and gas fields at Rainbow Lake and Zama City west of here. And they'll need control of this town if they're going to push farther south. We can't let that happen. Sir, we're just two teams here, about twenty-five operators. We need every man willing to fight."

The mayor's jaw dropped. For a moment, he couldn't speak; then he managed, "Are you kidding me?"

"No, sir. And there's no time for a debate. They're coming to take your town. If you own a rifle, I suggest you get it."

"But this is Canada! We're not in the war. We're neutral, for God's sake."

Warrant Officer Samson drew an unlit cigar from his breast pocket, shoved it in his mouth. "Tell that to the Russians."

* * *

McAllen and his Marines marched down the C-130's loading ramp, ready to set foot on the tarmac of Fort McMurray Airport.

But before they could reach said tarmac, Colonel Stack accosted them. "Sergeant McAllen?"

"Uh, yes, sir?"

"This your team?" The colonel's gaze played over the five men standing on the ramp behind McAllen.

"Yes, sir."

"You boys feel like taking a little ride?"

They all boomed: "Sir, yes, sir!"

"I'm talking way up north, behind enemy lines."

McAllen smiled. "That's the way we roll, sir."

"Very well. Seems there's a pilot who got shot down. It seems the president has taken a liking to her. So this comes down from The Man himself."

"Sir, begging your pardon, sir, but it's obvious why you picked us. We're the best, of course, but—"

"Slow down, Sergeant. And stow that ego before you hurt someone with it. Truth is, I didn't pick you for this. I wanted your green Marine asses up on Highway 63, but apparently there's a major in Tampa who took orders from The Man, and she personally requested you boys."

"You hear that, Sergeant?" cried McAllen's new assistant, Scott Rule. "We haven't even dropped a Russian and we're already famous."

McAllen grinned crookedly, then silenced the man with a look.

The colonel went on, "So this major heard you were the first team at that crash site in Cuba. She must've figured you're doing something right. Bad news is, best I got to get you up there is a civilian chopper. It's a Bell LongRanger III. Company's called Highland. Might be a blessing. The Russians might not take a potshot at a tourist bird. But that's only your ride up. I'm still working on your ride home. There's an HMMWV coming off one of the other 130s. You'll hop on and take that up to Highland's hangar. Official warning orders to follow. Questions?"

"I assume we have the last known GPS coordinates of this pilot?"

"We do. She's northwest of Behchoko, though she hasn't activated her survival kit's beacon."

"Sat phone?"

"Iridium is down."

"So there's no guarantee she's even still alive."

"Sergeant, you come back with the woman or her body. That's what The Man wants."

"Yes, sir."

Stack glanced off in the distance, shielding his eyes from the morning sun. "There's your ride now."

Staff Sergeant Marc Rakken sat inside the Stryker with the rest of his rifle squad. It would be at least another six hours before they reached the outskirts of Calgary, and the ride east on Interstate 90 had taken forever because of the patches of ice and civilians getting in the way to gape at the brigade rumbling east. They finally had turned onto 95 to head north.

The Stryker's driver, Private First Class Penny Hassa, was a spunky, freckle-faced twenty-one-year-old who kept Rakken entertained with her sarcastic remarks regarding the traffic, the weather, and anything else that struck her.

She'd assume a general's deep drawl and announce into the intercom, "Gentlemen, the rules are different in this Stryker. We have a strict sexual harassment policy—we believe in it!"

And that'd inspire Rakken into a fit of laughter. In point of fact, Hassa didn't take any crap from anyone, but she loved to tease.

The vehicle's commander, Sergeant Timothy Appleman, who was also wired into the intercom, allowed Hassa her indulgences, and Rakken certainly appreciated that.

Rakken and his troops sat knee-to-knee, facing one another, their heavy packs and boxes of ammo, along with a half dozen AT-4s, jammed into the storage areas above and behind their seats. Since it was too loud to converse, they slept, read, or listened to music or watched videos on their iPods.

The squad was divided into two teams, A and B. A team had a team leader, a grenadier (GREN) who carried a rifle with attached M203 grenade launcher, an automatic rifleman (AR) with an M249 SAW (Squad Automatic Weapon), and a rifleman with the AT-4 antitank weapon (RMAT). B team had all of the same, except the RMAT was replaced by a DM—a designated marksman equipped with an M16A4 with a heavy barrel and improved optics.

While the Force Recon Marines, SEALs, and Army Special Forces were already fielding a lot of the new future force warrior gear, budget restrictions along with heavy pressure from liberal antiwar lobbyists had forced the Army to push back implementation of most of that high-tech equipment to the general infantry to at least 2032, war notwithstanding.

The unnerving thing was, while Rakken and his people were headed into urban terrain with outdated weapons, the Russian Spetsnaz had dropped in with state-of-the-art firepower. Rakken's squad could be facing anything from directed energy weapons to the microwave weapons made famous by the Euros to Electrodarts delivering fifty thousand volts.

And of course, the threat of biological and chemical weapons always loomed.

"You guys are awful quiet," said PFC Hassa.

"Just thinking, Hassa," said Rakken. "I got a buddy who got sent up to High Level."

"Where the hell is that?"

"Way up in Alberta. I'm just hoping he's okay."

"Aw, you believe that?" she asked, interrupting him.

"What?"

"Bunch of kids in a pickup truck just drove by and flipped us the bird!"

"Call in some air support."

"I'll give them air support, all right."

"So, you guys want the good news or the bad news?" said Appleman.

Rakken was about to answer when Hassa cursed and cut the wheel, the Stryker rumbling as they tipped sideways and left the road, bouncing onto the embankment.

"Oh, my God!" she cried.

TWENTY-THREE

Almost every vehicle in the brigade possessed a built-in GPS to pinpoint their exact location. All you had to do was click on a blue icon to learn exactly which unit that was. If you saw an enemy, you could e-mail in the report, and red icons would appear on every display in the brigade.

But when Private Hassa shouted and Sergeant Appleman added, "The screen's showing nothing. No enemy contacts," Sergeant Marc Rakken knew better and sprang into action. "We have to get out!"

"Hassa, stop!" hollered Appleman.

"Let's move, let's move!" Rakken ordered.

Before the ramp had fully lowered, Rakken's squad was out on the embankment, up to their ankles in slush and snow.

Smoke billowed from two of the four Strykers in Rakken's rifle platoon. Pieces of the road were gone. The stench of gasoline hung heavily in the air. With a whine, ramps opened on the two smoldering vehicles, and the squads stumbled out, coughing and disoriented. A few guys fell to their knees.

The vehicle commanders were already screaming for medics as still more troops leapt from the backs of the Strykers behind them, fanning out to sweep the area, a broad section of the interstate with literally no place to hide.

And above, fighter planes sliced through the clouds, engines echoing.

"Russian jets all the way down here? No way!" shouted Appleman.

"They're ours!" hollered Rakken. "That's a flight of Raptors."

"Did they fire on us?" asked Appleman.

"I don't think so. They're covering." Rakken bit back a curse and jogged to the front of the Stryker, where Hassa was in her driver's hatch. "What'd you see?"

"They just lit up, one after another."

"Nothing dropped?"

"No. And we went over our vehicles with a fine-toothed comb, like we always do."

"Sergeant?" Rakken called to Appleman. "Better send up word. Those Green Vox bastards didn't stop at the mess hall."

"Oh, man. They must've planted them on the vehicles."

"Think about it. The Russians planned their attack. They knew in advance we'd be called up. The Brigade hit the mess hall, now they hit us again. That's too much of a coincidence. I think they're back to working for the Russians."

"Maybe you're right."

Rakken sighed. "All right. A Team? You got security." He cocked his thumb toward the still-burning Strykers. "B Team, go help 'em out!"

About a quarter mile back, another explosion suddenly rocked the convoy. Then, six vehicles up, yet another series of booms.

"I'm getting out," shouted Hassa, quickly dismounting from the vehicle and jogging away, as though it, too, might explode.

This was exactly what the Russians wanted, thought Rakken. Delays and paranoia.

Sergeant Raymond McAllen and his frozen little band of Force Recon Marines piled onboard the Longranger III helicopter, barely able to squeeze themselves and their gear inside.

The pilot, a rugged-looking blond in his forties nicknamed Khaki, was an ex–Canadian Special Forces guy who had a lot to say about his country's unwillingness to take up arms against the Russians (he was pissed). He had a lot to say about his willingness to fly them into hell and back, too—not because he was pro America or pro Canada, but because he was pro saving a fighter pilot's life.

He'd been there, done that himself. So Colonel Stack had lucked out when he'd made that call to Highland to rent them a bird on American taxpayers' dollars.

The bad news was that the helo only had a range of about three hundred miles, so they'd have to put down in High Level to refuel before heading up into the Northwest Territories. The company's own hangar there was empty, since they'd already assisted in the evacuation, but there was a full fuel truck waiting for them.

McAllen recalled that two ODA teams from the Army's Special Forces were up there. And he learned via the network that at nearly the same time they reached the town, High Level might be paid an unexpected visit from some Ka-29s inbound from Behchoko, part of a Spetsnaz combat and reconnaissance patrol (CRP) that would no doubt have mechanized forces on its heels.

Not wanting Khaki to get too excited if they rubbed shoulders with a few Russkies, McAllen carefully filled him in over the intercom.

Surprisingly, the pilot said, "Well, if the Russians are en route, let's get to the gas before they do. And hey, you like Subway? Quiznos? They even got a Kentucky Fried."

McAllen laughed a little. "We won't have time for lunch."

Khaki smiled. "They got drive-through."

The RCMP had gone through the town of High Level ordering everyone to evacuate to Highway 35, and Sergeant Nathan Vatz was getting reports from his team that the citizens were indeed complying. One of his commo guys did say that he spotted quite a few men driving their families off; if Vatz were married with children, he wondered whether he'd do the same.

At the police station, members of the local chamber of commerce, along with the local fire chief and mayor, were engaged in a huge debate over whether they should defend themselves or simply surrender to the Russians in order to preserve the town and save lives.

Captain Mike Godfrey and Warrant Officer Samson had walked out of that meeting, telling the townsfolk that they welcomed help but had no intentions of surrendering. A lot of the local men had told the mayor to kiss off. They were fighting to protect their town. Period. And their numbers were growing.

Meanwhile, Vatz worked with about twenty guys to set up the main roadblock north of town. Fortunately, demolition derbies were a big pastime in High Level, and with the drivers' help, they were able to create a nice little wall of vehicles, even adding a couple of tractor trailers from the local lumber mill. This wall would channel oncoming mechanized forces to the left or right, into the embankments—

Where Vatz and his men had set up a little high-tech surprise that, when they were finished, left all of them wearing evil grins.

The roadblocks on 58 to the east and west were hardly as reinforced, containing just four cars each but manned by another twenty riflemen that Vatz had organized into two teams. Nice thing was, quite a few of those guys were hunters who owned high-powered rifles with scopes—one of the benefits of working with a more rural community.

The final roadblock on the south side of the town was not yet in place, since there was still a steady flow of evacuees. But they had another 18-wheeler whose driver claimed he could flip the thing onto its side so that the entire trailer would lie across the road. He seemed eager to try that. At least thirty more guys would help hold that exit.

Finally, half of Vatz's team had staked out the local airport, six miles southeast, with its single five-thousand-foot runway and small air terminal building. It seemed highly likely that at least some of the air recon forces would land there, the crews refueling while the troops dismounted. Vatz's boys had negotiated a little something special for that party.

Vatz figured that a few more helos would land in the downtown area, near the RCMP station, town hall, fire station, and the local hotel and motels. So that's where he and his half of the team were now positioned, strung out along the rooftops in sniper positions. Vatz had found himself a nice perch above the town hall, near a large stone balustrade. He was in one corner of the rooftop, while Captain Godfrey was in the other.

In some respects, this was a classic foreign internal defense (FID) mission, often an exclusive task of Special Forces operators. The training of the resistance in occupied France during World War II was one of the more famous FID missions that Vatz had studied. However, most teams had a lot more time to train and organize the citizens. Still, Vatz was proud of the work they'd accomplished in such a short time.

Though dressed like locals, Vatz's team wore their camera-equipped Artisent ballistic assault helmets with laser target designator; the headgear subsystems' 180-degree emissive visors provided them with maps, routes, and other networked data in the cross com monocle below their left eyes. High bandwidth wireless communications, along with a microelectronic/optics sensor suite, provided 360-degree situational awareness and small arms protection.

At the moment, Vatz worked the system's handheld controller, not unlike the ones used for video games. He studied a radar image being piped in to both ODA teams. Twelve glowing blips were superimposed over a local map. The blips morphed into the glowing silhouettes of inbound Ka-29s with an ETA of about twenty-two minutes.

After muttering a faint, "Whoa," he pulled up the camera images from every man on his team, silently making sure that each operator was in place.

ODA 888, call sign Berserker, and ODA 887, call sign Zodiac, lay in wait.

Many ODA team members liked to pick radio call signs based upon the first letter of the team's name, with the detachment commander always being the team's name followed by the number six, for command. Vatz's old team used "Victor," and he'd picked Vortex, which in his humble opinion sounded cool.

But when he'd been reassigned to Berserker, a "B" name had eluded him. The depression hadn't helped. It was Marc Rakken who had suggested "Bali," short for balisong, referencing the knives they both collected and reminding Vatz once more of the Venturi in his pocket.

Thus Nathan Vatz, call sign "Bali," was reborn.

Captain Godfrey got on the radio: "Berserker team, this is Berserker Six. Enemy force inbound on your screens. Start with the plan. And when it goes to hell, you think. Adapt. Shoot. Move. Communicate. Are we clear?"

"HOOAH!" they all boomed over the channel.

"Hey, up there! Hey!"

The voice had come from below, and Vatz peered over the rooftop to spy the mayor on the sidewalk below, shielding his eyes from the glare.

"Mr. Mayor!" shouted Captain Godfrey. "They'll be here soon. Stay inside!"

"We've made a decision. It's the best for everyone. Now I need you people to come down. We're not going to offer any resistance when they arrive. We don't want any bloodshed."

The mayor was joined by the fire chief and the RCMP commander.

Before Captain Godfrey could reply—and Vatz could shake his head in disbelief—Warrant Officer Samson's voice boomed over the radio: "Berserker Six, this is Black Bear. We got an inbound helo on radar, coming in from the southeast. Lone aircraft, could be a civilian. Trying to establish comm with that pilot now, over."

"Roger that," said Godfrey. "We need him on the ground A-SAP!"

"I hear you, Six. Working on it."

The captain then lifted his voice. "Mr. Mayor, get inside. It's too late now."

"I won't. We need to wave our white flag, damn it. You're going to get us all killed!"

"They're going to kill you anyway," cried Vatz, unable to contain himself.

"Sergeant, I got this," said Godfrey, who winked and hollered, "He's right. You don't get inside, you're dead."

The mayor dismissed them with a wave. "We'll see about that!"

TWENTY-FOUR

Colonel Pavel Doletskaya had convinced them to remove the straitjacket. He had no intention of hurting himself, and it was ridiculous for him to summon a guard every time he needed to use the small toilet in the corner of his cell.

Besides, they had four cameras inside and two guards outside. If he so much as held his breath, they would be on him in seconds.

They had even given him a small metal cot with a thin mattress and a military-issue blanket. His requests for reading material—for anything, really, to occupy his time—had been ignored. Moreover, it had been several hours since his last visit from the interrogators.

So he lay there, staring up at the ceiling, burping up the remnants of MRE #07, meat loaf and gravy. It was no wonder the American soldiers so often retreated during combat; they were all running to the bathroom after consuming 1,200 calories of pure indigestion.

Doletskaya draped an arm over his head and closed his eyes, longing to clear his mind . . .

They were back at her apartment now after a remarkable first meal together, and he looked into her eyes as she straddled him.

"Colonel," he began softly. "I didn't expect this."

"Neither did I."

Viktoria Antsyforov was even more beautiful in the shadows of her bedroom, her long hair, usually bound in a tight bun, fluttering like dark flames.

Following that fateful meeting at Kupol, they became lovers and spent the next few months working out the logistics of her plan. She foisted her ideas upon her colleagues and summarily crushed those who challenged her in their meetings.

On several occasions, Doletskaya had watched as she caught the eye of Izotov himself. Soon, the rumors that she was sleeping with the general circulated. Doletskaya only grinned them away.

On the last night he had seen her alive, they'd returned to Kupol for an elegant dinner at his suggestion.

She'd been quiet throughout the meal.

And when he asked what was wrong, she snapped at him, "I want you to leave your wife. Does that make me a bad person?"

"No. But you know that's not possible. Not for a man in my position."

"Why not? You can't bear a few scars? All my life I've been the snow maiden, afraid my heart would melt me. But it is warm now. For you. And I'm not melting. I'm asking you to do something for me."

"And I'm telling you I can't."

She rose, stormed away from the table.

"Viktoria, please . . ."

He sat there for a few more minutes, paid the check, then went to a local bar for a drink. It was there he decided that he would leave his wife for her, no matter the cost. He did love her.

As he left, he felt lighter, half his age, and suddenly very, very happy.

But when he returned to her apartment building, the entire floor was engulfed in flames, and he couldn't get anywhere near the area. He stood there in the street, the snow falling on his head and shoulders, watching the firemen, the flames bending in the high wind, the people covering their mouths and crying.

Two days later they identified her body. They said the fire had originated in her apartment and had been deliberately set. Arson. A suicide.

And Doletskaya had been left wondering why.

Meanwhile, he continued to push forward with her plan. There was too much momentum, too much at stake.

It was what she would have wanted.

But he just could not believe what she had done. And there was still no extinguishing the fire in his own heart.

For her.

He lay there in the cell, wishing he had been strong enough to tell her yes at that last moment. *Yes, I will leave her. Yes, I want you.*

Now he had lost the only thing that had mattered to him—more than the war, his career, everything.

He bolted up from the cot, faced one of the cameras. "Get me Major Dennison. I'm ready to talk!"

Khaki was speaking to one of the Special Forces commo guys on the ground at the airport, and all Sergeant Raymond McAllen could think was, *Damn, I was right. We got no luck.*

"He wants to talk to you," said Khaki, lifting his chin.

"This is Outlaw One, go ahead over," McAllen said.

"Outlaw One, this is Beast, team Berserker, on the ground. Need you to put down A-SAP. Incoming enemy helos. ETA ten minutes, over."

"Roger that, Beast. We plan to refuel and get the hell out of there, over."

"Negative, Outlaw One. You will remain on the ground until further notice, over."

"Beast, let me talk to your CO, over."

"Roger that, stand by."

After ten or so seconds, a voice crackled over the radio, "Outlaw One, this is Bali, over."

"Roger, Bali, I want to speak to the CO."

"Uh, sorry, he's got a little situation right here, asked me to talk to you, over."

"Bali, listen to me, we're going to refuel and try to get out before those inbound helos arrive, over."

"Negative."

"Bali, maybe you're not hearing me—"

"Outlaw One, you are instructed to land, begin your refueling ops. We'll let you know when you can take off."

McAllen lost it. "Sergeant, we have orders from American Eagle himself! Do you read me?"

After a moment's silence, Bali returned: "Outlaw One, I understand, but we have incoming enemy helos and a party planned. You can't ruin it. And to be honest with *you*, Sergeant, we could use your help."

"Roger that, Bali. We got orders that say otherwise, but, uh, we don't want to ruin your party plans. When we're on the ground, we'll see what we can do, understood?"

"Roger, Outlaw One. Link up with Black Bear at the main terminal. Bali, out."

McAllen spoke into the intercom: "Listen up, guys. The Russians will reach the town about ten minutes after we do, maybe less. Sucks for us, but we'll be in the process of refueling when they arrive. But we're also accidentally crashing a little party the SF boys have set up for them. So . . . the second the skids hit, we're out the door. We might need to lend these boys a hand before we get back in the air."

"It's just like that time my cousin went to fill up his boat before fishing, and the station was being robbed at the same time," said Sergeant Rule.

"You think if your cousin knew the place was being hit he would've stopped for gas?"

"No way."

"Well, Rule, we're stopping anyway."

When Captain Godfrey returned to the roof, he told Vatz that he'd managed to calm down the mayor and that he, a few RCMPs, and the fire chief had persuaded the politician to suck it up, take responsibility, and defend his home.

After all, there was no stopping the nearly five hundred citizens from High Level who had volunteered to remain and defend their homes. They were scattered throughout the town, some hiding in their own homes, poised to attack; others, like the Special Forces, lining the rooftops or crouching in doorways. They were just ordinary folks, caught in an extraordinary situation. One woman in her late fifties whose kids were already grown up carried a big hunting knife and a shotgun.

She'd told Vatz that the first Russian to cross her doorstep would be shot, wrapped in Hefty bags, and buried out in her backyard without a funeral. The second one, if he hadn't learned his lesson, wouldn't even get the burial.

The people of High Level were not giving up without a fight, no matter the mayor's reservations.

As Vatz crouched down once more, raising his binoculars to study the plains north of the town, Big Bear's voice sounded over the radio: "Outlaw team is just setting down."

McAllen had instructed Khaki to land near a thick stand of trees adjacent to the terminal. The wooded area would provide them with marginal cover, so the incoming Russian pilots might miss them.

However, it was a cool, crisp morning, with lots of sunshine and visibility—painfully good visibility.

Such a pretty day for a battle.

The Longranger III hit the dirt, and McAllen put his mouth to work, sending off recon scouts Palladino and Szymanski to secure the fuel truck, while commo guy Friskis and medic Gutierrez guarded the helo.

Khaki said he would stay with the helo to supervise refueling, but if the Russians started firing, he was out of there to get some action for himself. He carried a couple of rifles and pistols whose magazines he intended to empty. He also had four illegally procured fragmentation grenades. You had to love an ex–Special Forces guy.

Meanwhile, McAllen and Rule jogged across the parking lot toward the terminal, where a thick-necked guy in flannel with an unlit cigar jutting from his mouth was walking out the glass doors.

"You Black Bear?" asked McAllen.

"Yep, Warrant Officer Samson, ODA-888 out of Fort Lewis." He proffered a gloved hand

McAllen shook firmly. "Sergeant Ray McAllen, Force Recon, Thirteenth MEU out of Pendleton. This is Sergeant Rule, my assistant team leader. Well, we just came to fill her up and clean the windshield. Do we need a key for the bathroom?"

"Funny guy. Why don't you boys get up on the roof? Keep low so they don't see your uniforms. We want them to think we're all locals for now, good old Canadians with hunting rifles, not much of a threat."

McAllen grimaced. "We'll stick with our bird, get the fuel, and get the hell out. We're headed up north on a TRAP mission."

"We don't stop those incoming helos, you're not going anywhere." Black Bear removed the cigar from his mouth. "Tell you what. You take up positions along the west wall, close to your bird. Stay out of sight. Get on our channel. You wait for us. All I'm going to say is 'Outlaw Team,' and you cut loose."

"Good enough. Good luck."

Black Bear nodded. "Good luck to us all."

Major Stephanie Halverson ran along the wooden fence, keeping within a meter of it, hoping the poles might break up the vertical line that was a United States Air Force pilot shot down and fleeing.

The farmhouse was just a thousand yards ahead, with a couple of barns in the back, a few horses, and another long building. The place stood postcard still.

Almost there. Fight for it.

Nearly out of breath, her nose running, her legs on fire, she repeatedly glanced over her shoulder; there were no Spetsnaz troops in sight.

But as she left the fence to make a final mad dash to the main house, whose front door looked more inviting than anything in the world, the terrible whining of those engines drew near, and a glance back triggered a wave of panic.

She mounted the front stoop, wrenched open the screen door, tried the knob.

Open. Open? Well, what did she expect? She was in the middle of nowhere Canada, crime rate: zero.

Bursting into the house, she cried, "Hello? Hello? Is anyone home?"

It was a weekday morning, and a middle-aged woman in jeans and sweatshirt appeared from the kitchen beyond. "Who are you? What are you doing in our house?" she demanded.

A middle-aged man with a graying beard came rushing forward, along with a long-haired teenage boy, wearing a ball cap.

"Dad, there's a crazy lady with a gun in our living room," said the boy, strangely calm. "And she's wearing a costume."

Halverson spoke a million miles a minute: "I'm Major Stephanie Halverson, U.S. Air Force. I got shot down. Russians are here. On snowmobiles. They're coming. Do you have a car?"

The father glanced down at the pistol in her grip and raised his hands. "If this is some kind of sick joke . . ."

"It's not a joke! Do you have a TV? Do you watch the news? The Russians are invading!" Halverson nearly screamed at the family.

"They were talking about some kind of military maneuver on the morning show," said the mother. "And now there's some weird news program on every channel."

As the snowmobile engines grew louder, the teenager, unfazed by Halverson's pistol, darted to the front window, peeked past the curtain. "She's not lying. Looks like soldiers out there. They're coming!"

"I'll get my rifle," said the father. "Joey, you take her and your mom to the basement."

"We can't stay. We have to go!" Halverson said.

"Well, Major, you picked the wrong address, because my pickup's battery is dead, and the one tractor I have would never outrun them. I was supposed to drive my boy to school."

Halverson waved the pistol, tipped her head toward the window. "Those are Spetsnaz troops. Do you know what that means?"

"It means you'd better get in the basement!" cried the father.

Without time to think, Halverson followed the boy and his mother through the kitchen, past an open door, and down a flight of rickety wooden steps. It was a full cellar, the entire footprint of the house, cluttered with boxes, machinery, a washing machine and dryer, and clothes hanging from lines spanning the room.

The boy, Joey, switched the light off, but a dim shaft filtered in through the single window, up near the ceiling. Then he headed toward the back, where he wanted to hide between sheets of plywood leaning against the wall.

"No," said Halverson. "You and your mom stay here. I'm under the steps. Go."

Even as she spoke, a crash resounded from upstairs, and a man shouted in a thick Russian accent, "Come out, Yankee pilot!"

TWENTY-FIVE

President Becerra leaned forward in his seat aboard Air Force One and sharpened his tone. "Prime Minister, Spetsnaz forces are in the streets of Edmonton and Calgary."

Emerson's tone turned equally sharp. "I'm well aware of that, Mr. President."

"They've captured your communications uplinks and early warning radar, and they've hacked in to and now control your power grid."

"Yes, they have."

"And my advisors tell me they've already begun psychological operations using their new 130X electronic warfare planes. The Euros took out their first two, but two more are in the air. They're taking control of your radio, TV, Internet, even military communications channels."

"I know that."

"My SEALs and Special Forces have infiltrated those areas, but they're only gathering intel. They tell me some of your local fire and police are fighting back, but they need help. They need you to take official military action, otherwise I'll be watching executions on CNN."

"Mr. President—"

"They'll move your women and children to holding areas, to separate families and sow terror. This is what they do, Prime Minister. This is how they control cities—through fear and intimidation."

Becerra glanced over at Hellenberg. The White House Chief of Staff shook his head from the other side of the table. He was off camera, but that didn't matter. Becerra displayed enough disgust for both of them.

Emerson thought a moment. "I spoke with Kapalkin. If I make a move, the hammer will come down. I won't do this."

"He's bluffing. He doesn't have the resources. And he knows the Euros will be in Edmonton soon."

"I think he's right. I think we have less to lose if we do nothing. And if we play the victim of two evil superpowers, we might actually gain something: the world's sympathy."

"Prime Minister, you're making a terrible mistake. This is your Pearl Harbor. It's your time."

"No. Not yet."

"If not now, then when?"

"The situation is being carefully evaluated."

"That's a line for the media, not for me. Come on, Prime Minister! Together we can shut them down. Otherwise, it'll take time, resources, and your people will suffer the consequences."

"I understand."

"I hope so. Because at this time I'm informing you that one of our Stryker Combat Brigade Teams is en route to Calgary to help evacuate your civilians. They also have orders to take out enemy positions designated by our SEALs and Special Forces. I'm not asking for your permission, Prime Minister. If you won't save your own people, we will, because doing so is in the best interests of the United States."

Emerson slammed a fist on his desk, "Damn you, Becerra, you have no idea what a position I'm in! No idea!"

"It'll only get worse, Prime Minister."

"Look, we won't stop you from helping. But I can't take the risk. Not now."

"I'll check in again, once my brigade reaches Calgary. The Euros will be calling. Good-bye, Mr. Prime Minister." The second Becerra ended the call, he huffed and added, "What a fool. What a waste of time."

"General Kennedy's waiting to give you an update," said Hellenberg.

"Before I take that, let me ask you something, Mark. We've known each other for a long time."

"A lot of years."

"You think there's anything I could've said to that man?"

The chief of staff frowned. "As an old attorney, I'd say you made a good argument. You hit him with the facts and appealed to his emotions. But they're afraid to commit. Do you know how much money is resting on Emerson's decision?"

"Yes, like he said, the *position* he's in. The Canadians ally with us, and their remaining overseas oil markets could crumble. The Chinese have already gobbled up most of their oil firms operating abroad. Sure, they know they'll never lose us as customers, so they can take the gamble, hold out, see what they can get."

"These are games for the academics to figure out. Right now there's a battle to fight."

Becerra nodded, tapped the screen, and there she was, Chairman of the Joint Chiefs of Staff Laura Kennedy, looking slightly less rankled than the last time they'd spoken. "General, sorry to keep you waiting," he began.

"That's all right, Mr. President. We have intelligence coming in from multiple command posts. As always, it's information overload, but here are the highlights. The company of Special Forces up in High Level is about to engage a Russian recon patrol from Behchoko. Unfortunately, that TRAP mission you asked for is being conducted by a Force Recon team who just landed in High Level to refuel. They could get caught up in the fighting there."

"Damn, I hope not."

"Good news from the *Florida* up in Coronation Gulf. Her skipper says they wiped out that Russian task force and have moved to the mouth of the Dolphin and Union Strait, a natural choke point. He's got us covered up there."

As the general spoke, Becerra watched images of the sinking ships captured by the sub. The sight left him awestruck.

"The first sorties carrying our brigade from the Tenth Mountain Division have landed without incident in Grand Prairie, and the Marines from Pendleton have begun their deep reconnaissance up Highway 63, north of Fort McMurray. They'll be reinforced by at least one follow-on Euro battalion, I'm told. No ETA on the Euros arrival yet."

"I'll contact General Bankolé to see what's holding them up."

"Mr. President, I hate to use this phrase, but it's been bandied about in the past few hours. What we're seeing so far from the Russians is an invasion plan, but one with a real failure of imagination."

"Well, you've made me wince, so now you'd better explain."

"The Russians are using all available avenues of approach, initiating the operation with basically no surprises. We expected them to seize those key towns up north to keep avenues open, which they are doing. We know they'll push down 63 and 35. We've already seen them drop in a separate battalion augmented with petroleum specialists to help gain control of the fields and refineries up near Fort McMurray. And we know they're using the avgas up in Behchoko to refuel their 130s. They sent some of those refueled planes farther south. The first flight passed Edmonton, so we believe they're either bound for Calgary or maybe they'll put down in Red Deer, right between the two cities. There's a regional airport there that they might use as a staging area, sending infantry both north and south to the cities. Initially, they'll need at least a battalion to fully secure each city until their reinforcements arrive."

"How are we doing in the air?"

"So far the space backbone layer remains clear since the destruction of the ISS. Euro lasers and the Rods from God are fully online. We've managed to disrupt the Russians' airborne network layer with Euro lasers, taking out those first surveillance and 130X craft, but that won't last for long, since their fuel cells will need recharging. The tactical and terminal layers are where it's all happening. We can take out their transports, but, as always, collateral damage is a primary concern, especially once they get near the cities."

"Yes, and the joint chiefs know very well how I feel about that."

She nodded. "You shoot a missile at one of the largest transport planes in the world and it crash-lands in downtown Edmonton, suddenly we're the terrorists, invasion or not."

"We won't let that happen."

"No, sir." She regarded her notes. "The fighters from Alaska have had only limited success up in the Northwest Territories, given the Russian fighter escorts, but with the infrastructure concerns, the joint chiefs continue to assert that this will be a ground battle with close air support. The Russians seem to agree. We've seen no evidence that they're readying strategic bombers. If they take Alberta, they'll want to take it intact. Again, no surprises. The Rules of Engagement seem remarkably clear. The only unexpected thing they did was launch this attack during winter, making ground movement all the more difficult—but that goes for both sides."

"You seem bothered by all of this."

She hesitated. "Given our dealings with the GRU in the past year, sir, it would be foolish to assume this is all they have planned."

"For all our sakes, I hope those fools in Moscow know where to stop."

"Me, too. But while it's perfectly logical for them to

want control over the reserves in Alberta, you always wonder: is this just a diversion to keep eyes on Canada while they slip one under the table?"

"So we keep one eye on Canada and one on the rest of the world."

"Yes, sir. And, oh yes, one more smaller matter. Green Vox and his cronies are back at it. They've delayed the Stryker brigade heading to Calgary."

"What happened?"

"Not sure. Reports indicate they might have planted IEDs. But these weren't roadside bombs. They might have been planted on the vehicles before they even left Fort Lewis. If that's the case, it was definitely an inside job. Those crews are trained to go over their vehicles very carefully."

"If a bomb is made to resemble a component that's already there, how do you check for that?" asked Becerra.

"Exactly."

"Are they moving again?"

"Just in the last hour."

"Good."

"But here's what bothers me, sir. For the past eight years, the Green Brigade has hit targets all over the world, significant targets."

"And you're wondering why they'd attack Fort Lewis, then disrupt the convoy?"

"Two smaller bombs just went off at Fort McMurray

Airport, where our Marines have landed. No one was hurt."

"So the Russians have Vox back on their payroll. Another failure of imagination, eh?"

"Maybe so. I'm sure time will tell. Well, that's all for now, Mr. President."

"Thank you. And General, when that Russian recon force hits High Level, I'd like to monitor those channels."

"Absolutely. Should be any minute now."

"Where's everyone else? Where are they?"

The captain shook his head.

Barnes and the medic were no longer moving, and the engineer was clutching his leg, shot in the femoral artery and bleeding all over the bay floor.

Just then Gerard pulled open his bloody jacket and lifted his shirt, revealing a pair of dark holes in his chest. He wouldn't make it, and neither would the engineer.

"We need help!" Vatz cried to one of the door gunners.

The guy ignored him, tending to his own shoulder wound.

Gritting his teeth, Vatz pushed himself over to the Russian, wrenched up the man's visor, and grabbed him by the neck. "Are you worth it, you bastard?"

The Russian stared up with vacant eyes.

Vatz glanced back at the remains of his team, then glared at the colonel once more and screamed, "Are you worth it?"

"They're splitting up now," said Black Bear over the radio.

Sergeant Nathan Vatz shivered. Looking down, he saw his gloved hands had formed into fists and felt the sweat pouring down his face, despite the cold wind blowing across the town hall's rooftop.

Don't do that again, he ordered himself. *This isn't about revenge. Stick to the plan, the mission.*

"Looks like a couple heading toward downtown. Two more holding back, probably scouts. Four breaking off, coming for us at the airport. The other four? Not sure where they're going yet. Looks like the scouts see the roadblock, over."

Captain Godfrey, still off to Vatz's right, was working his Cross Com, studying the imagery coming in from Black Bear's men at the airport. Suddenly he cried, "They're jamming us!"

Vatz checked his own channel: static. No voice, data, imagery.

Didn't matter. They'd hoped for the best, prepared for the worst, as always.

Every operator knew his role.

They just needed the Russians to be good enemy soldiers and die according to the plan.

The two Ka-29s, painted in camouflage patterns, swooped down into the middle of the broad intersection, their rotors echoing so loudly off the buildings that Vatz wished he'd shoved in his earplugs. They had no tail rotors, he noticed, just a large main rotor with a smaller rotor beneath it. The tail sections had horizontal wings with vertical fins attached to the ends, like the dorsal fins on sharks. Each fin was emblazoned with a bright red star.

A close look through his binoculars yielded more of the expected: Spetsnaz infantrymen visible behind the two crew members. Vatz assumed the hold was jammed to capacity: sixteen troops. Their landing gear unfolded, their noses pitched up, and they set down, one after the other.

Vatz didn't need to give the order. His weapons sergeants knew exactly what to do next. All of them did.

He took in a long breath—

And the battle began.

TWENTY-SIX

Still crouched beneath the cellar staircase and not moving a muscle, Major Stephanie Halverson listened to the commotion going on upstairs:

"Where is she?"

"Who?" asked the father.

"The Yankee pilot!"

"I don't know!"

A gunshot boomed, causing the mother to cry out, and Halverson thought, *This is it. It's over.*

They had killed the husband. They would come down and finish the job.

Suddenly, the mother bolted from her hiding place in the back and charged toward the stairs, where a Spetsnaz soldier was just coming down.

"Don't shoot!" she screamed.

He did.

Put a bullet in her chest.

But a half second after he fired, so did Halverson, carefully aiming between the slots of the wooden stairs, her round coming up between his legs and into his torso.

He tumbled forward, his rifle dropping to the concrete. Before Halverson could come out and grab it, the boy was there, snatching up the rifle. He panted as he looked at his mother slumped across the floor—

Then a creak from the stairs seized his attention. He cut loose a dozen rounds.

Yet another troop slumped.

Halverson darted across the room, got up on a chair, broke out the window with the butt of her pistol, then hoisted herself up and squeezed through the hole. "Come on!" she cried, reaching out to the boy.

He raced over and took her hand, just as a metallic thump sounded, followed by a loud hissing: gas.

They'd killed two. Had the father shot one? Maybe. There'd only be three left, then, she thought.

Out in the snow, she and the boy ran straight for the barn, about a hundred yards away.

Gunfire boomed behind them.

She hazarded a look back. One troop, who had come out the back door, had just spotted them.

"Run!" she screamed.

* * *

Sergeant Raymond McAllen wasn't shaking in fear but in frustration. His men had the fuel truck pulled up beside the Longranger III, the hose attached to the bird. However, filling the tanks took time. Too much damned time.

Come on, come on.

The Russian helos were twenty meters above the tarmac, ten, five . . .

He tightened up against the wall, his helmet and combat subsystems fully activated, his Heckler & Koch XM9 assault rifle at the ready.

Each operator on the team handpicked his own weapons, sometimes purchasing a few fancy toys themselves, and McAllen had recently been experimenting with the XM9, a weapon whose earlier version, the XM8, had been abandoned by the military.

Like the XM8, the 9 was a modular weapon with four variants: a baseline carbine, a compact carbine, a sharpshooter, and a heavy-barreled automatic. McAllen carried the baseline carbine with attached XM322 grenade launcher.

McAllen glanced off to his left, where Palladino lay prone beneath a tree, eye pressed to the scope of his M82A1 sniper rifle with its bipod dug deep in the snow. He'd taken the big girl along for this ride, and her .50 caliber rounds would easily penetrate the fuselages of those helos, the booming alone enough to strike fear in the hearts of the enemy.

Gutierrez had positioned himself a couple meters farther south, near another tree, his SAW balanced on its bipod. Radio operator Friskis and assistant team leader Rule were closer to the chopper, each armed with an MR-C—Modular Rifle Caseless—which fired 6.8 mm caseless ammo at a rate of nine hundred rounds per minute. Both weapons were also equipped with rail-mounted 40 mm grenade launchers.

All of which was to say the boys from Force Recon were good to go and waiting for showtime.

But the order to fire would never come, McAllen realized. The Russians were jamming all communications. He would let the SF boys take the first shots, as they had indicated. His years of experience would tell him when to engage his men.

The first two helos touched down, the third and fourth only seconds behind.

From somewhere on the other side of the terminal came a boom and hiss, followed by a white streak that spanned the tarmac in the blink of an eye, reached the lead helo—

And detonated directly over the canopy.

After the initial explosion, two more quickly followed, knocking the chopper onto its side, rotors digging into the ice and asphalt, while another burst sent flames shooting from shattered windows.

Those Special Forces guys must've brought an AT4 from their cache back home. They had some very nice toys.

Jagged pieces of fuselage and engine components from the first chopper flew into the second, striking its rotors just as a side door popped open and the first infantryman tried to get out. Meanwhile, the third and fourth choppers began to lift off.

McAllen craned his head toward the forest. "Outlaw Team, fire!" Even as he issued the order, he burst from his position and launched a grenade at the open door of the second chopper.

That first infantryman was already cut down by Gutierrez's machine gun—and as he slumped, McAllen's grenade flew into the helo's crew compartment.

What a shot!

With a slightly dampened boom, the grenade exploded, shredding the men inside and blanketing the chopper in thick, gray smoke.

The thumping of more helos from behind sent McAllen's gaze skyward. For a moment, his heart sank as he assumed more enemy troops were inbound.

But no. He had to blink to be sure he was seeing them: a pair of civilian choppers with riflemen strapped in and leaning out their open bay doors, already opening fire on the two Russian helos below.

McAllen had to hand it to the SF guys, who'd

managed to recruit those pilots and get some shooters up there. Sure, it was amateur close air support, but he'd take it.

Palladino let his first round fly, the rifle emitting a crack of thunder that rattled the buildings. He was targeting the crew members of the third helo. His round punched a gaping hole in the canopy and blew the pilot to pieces.

That bird wasn't going anywhere now. It dropped back toward the tarmac, hit hard, then began to bank erratically over the grass, as Gutierrez raked it with more fire.

The bay door popped, and a few Spetsnaz infantry leapt out, hit the ground, and came up firing—

But they were quickly cut down by the riflemen in the air, helos sweeping over them, rounds sparking as they ricocheted off the street.

McAllen was ready to call it day. Khaki was giving him the high sign: the tank's full, let's boogie.

"All right, Outlaw Team," McAllen began.

The sudden hissing and sparking of new fire on the wall behind him, on the ground, the snow, and over his head sent him diving onto his gut.

And just beyond the chopper, in the forest, came at least a dozen Spetsnaz infantry, probably two full squads, with one guy dropping to his knees, balancing a tube-like weapon on his shoulder.

McAllen's mouth fell open. He recognized an RPO-A

Shmel, or "Bumblebee," when he saw one. The weapon fired a thermobaric projectile utilizing advanced fuel-air explosive techniques. Some described the weapon as a flamethrower, but it was more like a rocket with a flamethrower's aftereffects, burning for a very long time.

The guy aimed at the fully fueled Longranger.

"Get out of there!" McAllen hollered to Khaki, Rule, and Friskis. "Get out!" At the same time, he cut loose with his XM9, directing all of his fire on the guy with the Bumblebee.

Squinting against the smoke from his barrel wafting into his eyes, McAllen watched the guy fall forward and drop the rocket, just as Khaki, Rule, and Friskis came racing toward him, gunfire raking their paths.

Gutierrez swung his rifle around and began to suppress the oncoming troops, but McAllen already saw they couldn't hold them back for long.

And yet another Spetsnaz troop picked up the Bumblebee and was leveling it on his shoulder.

McAllen fired at that guy, dropped him, then another salvo sent him rolling to the left, out of the bead. He felt a dull pressure on his shoulders as a few rounds struck his Crye integrated body armor, but he was okay.

"God *damn*, Jonesy, you would've loved this," he grunted, wishing his old assistant were here in the fray.

Then he cried, "Outlaws, fall back to the front of the terminal. NOW!"

As his men continued, still returning fire, McAllen got to his feet and did likewise. He chanced a look back, saw yet another guy shouldering the Bumblebee.

There was no one to stop him now.

McAllen sprinted forward, reached the corner, and ducked around to his left, just as a massive explosion struck like thunder from a hundred rain clouds.

A gasp later, the concussion wave struck, lifting him a meter into the air, then knocking him flat onto his belly.

With the whoosh and roar of flames still resounding, accompanied by an unbearable gasoline stench that seemed to clog the hot air, McAllen felt a hand latch onto his wrist and pull him to his feet.

"They blew up my goddamned chopper!" shouted Khaki, releasing him. "They blew it up!"

Just then the two civilian birds swooped down, riflemen ready to strafe the oncoming infantry behind them.

"Forget the bird. I'll buy you another one!" cried McAllen. "Let's get some cover!"

Ahead lay a garage, home of the airport's fire crew. They swept along the main terminal, headed for that—

One of the terminal doors opened, and Black Bear appeared. "Marines, get in here now!"

"Do what he says," hollered McAllen.

They filed into the terminal, stealing a moment to catch their breaths.

Black Bear smiled, removed his cigar. "Guess you boys will be staying awhile."

TWENTY-SEVEN

While they usually packed light, Sergeant Nathan Vatz's team, along with the rest of the company, had opted to haul some of the bigger gear up to High Level, especially when faced with a cold weather operation against a numerically superior force.

Fortunately for them, some of that equipment had made it out of the C-130 before the missile had struck. Their AT4 and Javelin had survived, along with a couple of other surprises still waiting for the Russians.

The boys at the airport had taken the AT4. Vatz's team had the Javelin, and he tensed now as the missile, fired from the other side of town, dropped like Thor's hammer on top of the Russian helo.

Well, the U.S. government would have to make some reparations to the townsfolk of High Level, Alberta—

Because the helo burst apart, raining ragged pieces of metal, tubes, and wires onto the surrounding buildings. Doors folded in, and large glass windows shattered into the road. Still more brick facades crumbled, and a steel street sign was cut down like a blade of grass.

More shrapnel and other debris hurtled into the second chopper, whose troops were already jumping down, a couple immediately succumbing to the blast.

Vatz firmly gripped his pistol-like combat weapon, nicknamed Lethality Central, LC for short.

The first 15 mm, cold-launched, intelligent-seeker round streaked away from one of the weapon's five tubes, homed in on that chopper's open door, and punched through several infantry.

Vatz triggered two more rounds, saving the 4.6 mm projectiles in tube number five for close encounters of the final kind.

One of the locals down below ran out in the street and rolled a grenade beneath the chopper. The pilot couldn't achieve liftoff in time, and the blast sent him banking sideways. With a grinding, crunching, glass-shattering racket, the bird chewed its way into the local courthouse. The rotors snapped off and spun away like knives thrown in a circus act as the helo's nose vanished inside the building.

Another grenade, this one launched by Vatz's engineer, dropped beside the helo, the detonation opening up the bird's fuel tanks, and the fires quickly rose, triggering several more explosions.

Wind-whipped smoke appeared in the distant north. Vatz seized his binoculars and swore as one of the Russian helos fired rockets on the main roadblock. He'd been hoping they'd leave that obstacle to the mechanized infantry, but sometimes luck—and bullets—ran out.

Those local guys manning the roadblock couldn't do much against that bird, and they wouldn't last long. Vatz already felt the pang of their loss.

"Bali, this is Black Bear, over."

The voice surprised Vatz, and he switched his Cross Com to an image piped in from Samson's helmet camera. "Bear, this is Bali, go ahead, over."

"Communications are back. Go figure. Anyway, we've taken out four enemy helos, but we got twenty, thirty Spetsnaz guys on the ground from at least two we didn't get, moving toward the terminal, over."

"Roger that. We destroyed our two helos. Still got one out by the northern roadblock. No location for the rest, over."

"Yeah, I see the smoke."

"Black Bear, hold them there. If we don't get any more visitors, we'll rally at your position, over."

"Sounds good, Black Bear, out."

Captain Godfrey, who was coordinating operations with Captain Rodriguez from 887, said those guys were sending a truck out to the roadblock to see if they could assist with fires on that helo.

Meanwhile, the thumping of more rotors drove Vatz to the opposite side of the roof. Down below, in the side street, a Ka-29 had just landed, and troops began pouring out.

He cursed, got back on the radio, told his boys to expect dismounts in the area.

Then he express-delivered another pair of guided munitions down on the helo through its canopy. He slipped the LC into his Blackhawk SERPA holster, took up his MR-C rifle, and fired down on the still-exiting infantry.

The Spetsnaz rushed around the chopper and began returning fire, rounds tearing up the stone balustrade as Vatz rolled back for cover.

"We have to get down," he shouted to Godfrey, who was still speaking to Rodriguez. "They're getting inside! They'll come up and cut us off!"

"All right," cried the captain.

Automatic weapons fire was already drumming from somewhere below as Vatz wrenched open the door leading to the dark stairwell.

He rushed down to the first landing, turned—

And locked gazes with a Spetsnaz troop below whose rifle was still pointed down.

While Vatz's first reaction should've been to lift his rifle and fire, adrenaline had already taken over.

And muscle memory.

And a rage simmering deep down.

He launched himself from the landing and crashed down onto the guy before the enemy soldier could react. They fell onto the floor, the Russian's rifle knocked free, Vatz's weapon having dropped somewhere behind him.

The guy's left hand was going for the pistol holstered at his waist. Vatz seized that wrist with his right hand, now unable to draw his own LC from the SERPA holster.

"Sergeant, get him!" shouted Godfrey, who had just reached the landing above.

But Vatz couldn't stop the guy's right hand from coming up to unsheathe a small neck knife dangling from a chain.

The troop thrust upward with the three-inch blade, and Vatz took hold of the guy's wrist with the blade tip poised a few inches from his cheek.

The guy raged aloud, fighting against Vatz's grip, as the captain yelled, "Move, I can't get a shot!"

Drawing in a quick breath, Vatz did three things: released his grip on the trooper, threw his head back away from the blade, then forced himself onto his rump while drawing his LC.

He fired.

Nothing. *What the* . . .

Vatz realized in that horrible moment that he'd failed

to switch the pistol from the guided munitions to the stacked 4.6 mm rounds for close quarters, which was why she clicked empty.

Another shot rang out from above: Godfrey.

But it was dark, and that round punched the wall beside the soldier.

The Russian went for his pistol.

Vatz thought of the Blackhawk caracara blade he always packed for those up-close and personal moments, but it was buried deep in one of his hip pockets.

The seven-inch fixed blade he carried, the Masters of Defense Mark V, was held tight in its sheath strapped farther down his hip.

But Marc Rakken's prized balisong, the Venturi, was right there, in a narrow pocket much higher on his hip.

Sorry, Marc.

In the span of two heartbeats Vatz had the Venturi in his hand, pinky-popping the bottom latch, bite handle dropping then swinging up to lock the blade in the open position.

The Russian was sliding the pistol out of his holster—

Vatz dove forward for the kill, thrusting his blade deep into the soldier's neck to sever his spinal cord.

Gunfire resounded over his shoulder, and Godfrey was there. He put a bullet in the guy's head as Vatz withdrew the balisong's Damascus blade.

"I put out the word to mask up," said Godfrey. "Now that they know we're here."

Vatz rose, covered in blood. He closed the balisong and returned it to his pocket, then slid off his light pack to fish out his mask.

They didn't have full nuclear, biological, or chemical protection, part of the micro-climate conditioning sub-systems of the full MOPP 4 helmets and suits, but the lightweight masks would help.

He froze as more footfalls sounded in the stairwell.

Silently, he motioned for Godfrey to halt, then reached into his tactical vest, tugged free a fragmenta-tion grenade, pulled the pin, and tossed it down the stairs.

Major Stephanie Halverson and the boy reached the barn and darted inside, then moved to the window to catch sight of the remaining troops.

She'd been right. Just three left now, and all charged forward, widening the distance between one another, rifles held menacingly.

With three of their brothers dead, they wanted much more than a downed pilot.

The boy's face was scrunched up in agony, tears fi-nally slipping from his eyes. "They killed my mom and dad."

"And they'll kill us."

"My parents are dead *because of you*!" He leveled the automatic rifle on her.

She slowly raised her hands, one still clutching her pistol. "Well, Joey, we got about ten seconds before they get here. They don't care. They'll shoot—both of us."

The barn door beside them burst open—

But no one charged in.

"Yankee pilot? Come out with hands up!"

Halverson bolted to the wall, then sprinted for the door on the opposite end of the barn. She already knew at least one more troop had to be waiting there.

Joey charged behind her, reached for the door handle.

"No!"

He looked at her.

"Wait," she said.

She reached out, opened the door, and rolled back inside the barn—

Gunfire ripped though the doorway. At the same time, a trooper appeared in the opposite doorway. Joey spotted him first.

Just hours ago the kid had been an innocent farm boy living in rural paradise. Now he jammed down the trigger of his rifle, wise enough to aim for the guy's legs because the Russian wore body armor.

Then Joey rushed across the room, since the soldier was still moving, getting ready to draw his pistol.

Halverson wanted to scream for him to come back, but it was too late. He rushed forward and shot the guy in the face, even as the other two soldiers burst into the barn, immediately cutting him down.

Halverson, who was near the door, came in behind the first Spetsnaz troop, shot him point-blank in the neck.

But the second guy whirled, aimed his rifle at Halverson.

I'm dead.

She flinched, but the troop suddenly staggered back, rounds punching into his chest and neck.

Halverson slammed onto her gut, dirt and hay wafting into her face.

She glanced over into the lifeless eyes of the Russian. Then she lifted her head.

Joey was on the ground, clutching his rifle with one hand, his chest with the other, blood pouring between his fingers.

"Joey?" She rose slowly, making sure all three troops were not moving, then she went to him, took his head in her lap.

"It's not fair," he said, coughing up blood.

Halverson's voice was gone.

No, it's not.

He grew very still, and then . . . he was gone.

She couldn't move. Couldn't breathe.

But she couldn't lose it. Not now. More troops would come. She had to get the weapons, a snowmobile. She had to get moving!

Gingerly, she slid out from beneath Joey, placed his head gently on the ground.

Then, frantically, she grabbed a couple of the rifles, another sidearm, two more clips, and rushed from the barn, her mind racing as quickly.

Get inside. Get her clothes, civilian clothes. Activate the beacon or they'll never find you.

She reached the house, stormed into the master bedroom, tore through the woman's closet, and found herself jeans, a sweatshirt, a heavy winter jacket, hat, scarf, gloves.

Back to the kitchen. She grimaced and stepped over the father's body to tear through the refrigerator, grabbing a couple bottles of water and some apples.

Then, still trembling, she went to the cupboard and seized an unopened package of cookies and some canned goods. She went to the drawers, throwing stuff everywhere, trying to find a can opener. Then she cursed, tossed the cans, and grabbed the rest.

She gathered more ammo from the soldiers, tucking it all into a pillowcase like some burglar, then found the keys to one of the snowmobiles in the pocket of a dead troop.

On the table in the entrance foyer sat a picture of the happy family. Halverson stared at it for a few seconds before charging outside.

After using bungee cords to fasten the gear inside the snowmobile's small rear basket, she donned the helmet, fired up the engine, and ordered herself not to look back.

She sped away, heading due south, leaving a rooster tail of snow in her wake. The cold wind on her face began drying her tears, and after another moment, she slid down the helmet's visor and leaned into the machine.

The fuel tank held about five liters, just over a gallon of gas, and the Russians had already used a liter to get to the barn. She wasn't sure how far she'd get, but she'd ride until the tank was empty.

A broad, flat plain of snow lay ahead, and more trees stood on the far horizon. She steered for them.

TWENTY-EIGHT

"You're wasting my time, Colonel." Major Alice Dennison sat at her station in the command post, arms folded over her chest, and sneered at the broken and defeated Russian on the screen.

"I did not talk under the influence of your drugs."

"Sorry, but you did."

"I did not!"

"You told us everything you know—which is, unfortunately, not enough."

Colonel Pavel Doletskaya's brows came together, and he began nervously pulling at the white whiskers on his chin. "You tell me what I said."

"All right. Operation 2659 is the invasion of Alberta."

"That's shocking," he said sarcastically. "I can't believe you beat that out of me."

"The twenty-six represents the duration of time you've given yourselves to gain full control of the province. But if, after twenty-six days, you've failed in that mission, the second part of your plan takes place, activation code five-nine."

Doletskaya's mouth began to open, as he realized that he had, in fact talked, but not willingly, as he pretended he wanted to do now.

She went on, "The snow maiden was, in fact, Colonel Viktoria Antsyforov, with whom you were having an affair until she went home one night and set fire to her apartment, killing herself and four of her neighbors."

"I didn't tell you that!"

"Yes, you did. Maybe you thought you were remembering it, but you were telling us. I'll ask you one last time, but I don't expect you know the answer: The activation code is for what? A second invasion? A tactical missile attack? What?"

He sighed loudly for effect. "I'm not aware of any activation code."

"Yes, you are. She told you about the code. But she never told you what it meant. And then she died. So we're finished talking, you and I."

"Wait a moment, Major. If I told you everything already, then why did you agree to meet with me?"

She shrugged. "Just for confirmation."

"No, I don't believe that. I think . . . I think you are attracted to me."

"You're a sick bastard."

"No, I think you are attracted to me because I have control over you. And you like that. You are always in control. And it's so hard, isn't it? Wouldn't it be better to let me take care of everything? Maybe we can work together. Maybe there's still hope for you and I."

She rolled her eyes and thumbed off the call.

But she was trembling, visibly trembling. He was under her skin again, coursing through her veins like a poison.

She wanted to kill him.

Because maybe . . . he was right.

"We'll split up and flank them," said Black Bear over the radio. He looked up at Sergeant Raymond McAllen. "I'll need you guys up top."

McAllen nodded, but he had other plans.

Sergeant Rule had gone to another back door and had spotted a chopper on the ground, just behind the fire crew's garage. The pilot and co-pilot were still inside, the rotors spinning. McAllen wasn't sure if they were having a technical problem or just waiting to pick up troops, but he didn't care. All he saw was an enemy bird worth capturing and taking back into enemy territory to pick up that fighter pilot.

Better to fly in with a big red star tattooed on their butts instead of a bull's-eye.

But he was still torn between helping out these SF guys and the mission.

Oh, damn, he had to go with the mission; it came down from The Man himself.

He had to do . . . what he had to do. The apologies would come later, if these guys made it out.

"Khaki, you think you can fly that thing?"

The pilot made a face. "Don't insult me. If it's got a rotor, I can fly it."

"All right," McAllen said, eyeing the entire group. "We make a run for the garage. I don't think they can see us from this angle. Then from the garage we move to the bird." McAllen looked once more at Khaki. "Will a couple of holes in the canopy be a big deal?"

"Don't chance that. Just show 'em a grenade and get 'em to open up."

"All right then. Palladino? Gutierrez? You set up outside to cover."

The sniper and medic nodded.

"Let's go!"

During the 1970s there was a secret military research facility near Leningrad, where according to some former Soviet chemical weapons scientists Kolokol-1 was developed. The drug took effect within a few seconds and left victims unconscious for two to six hours.

In 2002, Chechen terrorists took a large number of

hostages in an incident known as the Moscow theater siege. Kolokol-1 was used against them; however, large doses of the drug might have contributed to the deaths of more than one hundred of the eight hundred hostages.

Intelligence gathered from Russian Federation defectors between 2018 and 2020 indicated that the Russians had made further refinements to the incapacitating agent in order to make it "more safe," though they had thus far not used it against civilian populations.

Consequently, Vatz felt a deep sense of dread as he and Captain Godfrey stepped over the soldier they had killed with the grenade and headed down to the ground floor of the town hall, where they found the mayor and half a dozen other town leaders lying on the floor, a beer can–size canister still emitting gas beside them.

They checked for pulses. "Still alive over here," said Godfrey, voice muffled through his mask.

"Here, too."

"Looks like they're hitting them where they find them with small concentrations."

"Good. We may not need our masks outside."

They hustled out of the building, rushed around to the corner, both slamming themselves against the wall as two Spetsnaz troops wearing masks rounded the opposite corner themselves.

Vatz caught the first one with his rifle, rounds stitching up the soldier's armor and reaching his head.

But the second troop was already firing, his rounds drumming into Vatz's armored chassis and knocking him off his feet.

Captain Godfrey stormed forward, unleashing a vicious salvo, drawing within a couple meters of the guy until the Russian went down, blood spraying inside the mask.

With his chest sore from all the fire, the wind still knocked out of him, Vatz pushed himself up on his elbows, blinked hard.

Just as Captain Godfrey sank to his knees, then fell forward, his rifle clacking to the frozen pavement.

Wrenching off his mask, Vatz got shakily to his feet and staggered forward, reaching the captain. He rolled Godfrey onto his back, removed the mask.

"Captain . . . sir . . ."

Vatz undid the quick release straps of Godfrey's armor, tossed the vest aside, saw the two bullet holes in the captain's neck, another just under his earlobe.

He checked the captain for a carotid pulse, got one: weak and thready but there.

"Band-Aid, this is Bali, over?"

The team's senior medical sergeant, Jac Sasaki, answered, his voice tense, gunfire echoing behind him. "Bali, I can hardly hear you, over?"

"I need you here, south side town hall. Berserker Six is down, over."

"What? I can't hear you."

"Berserker Six is down!" Vatz repeated his location.

"Roger that! On my way!" cried the medic.

Vatz switched channels to call Warrant Officer Samson. "Black Bear, this is Bali, over."

"Bali, this is Black Bear, make it quick!"

"Berserker Six got hit. He's still alive. I say again, Berserker Six was hit. Got Band-Aid on the way."

"Roger that, Bali. I'll notify Zodiac Six and coordinate with him. Looks like they're spreading out now, some heading for the neighborhoods. We need to take out as many as we can, right here, right now, before they all turn into snipers, over."

"Roger that, and they're using gas. Looks nonlethal, over."

"Yeah, what they call nonlethal just kills you slower. Tell you what. You stay put. I'll send over a truck."

"Roger that, standing by. Bali, out."

Vatz checked Godfrey's neck again for a pulse, put his ear to the man's mouth, listening.

They wouldn't need Band-Aid now.

He swore, and dragged Godfrey's body to the side of the building.

The guy was a good captain, not the usual token officer sent to do his time with an ODA, then go on to lead brigades. He'd really wanted to learn. And hell, he wasn't even thirty years old yet.

Band-Aid called on the radio to say he was almost there. Vatz didn't stop him. They'd pair up, get down in the alley between the town hall and another office building, and remain there until Black Bear's truck arrived.

The sounds of whomping rotors kept Vatz tight to the wall. He looked up, saw one of the civilian birds banking overhead at just two hundred feet.

Just behind it came one of the Ka-29s, narrowing the gap, its four-barreled machine gun blazing until the civilian bird's tail rotor was chewed apart by 7.63 mm rounds, its engine beginning to smoke, fuel leaking from its tanks.

But then a glorious sight from the ground: a Javelin missile rose to cut across the blue midday sky, its exhaust plume trailing.

Before Vatz could fully turn his head, the Ka-29 burst apart, the fireball so close that Vatz knew he had to get out of there. He shoved arms beneath Godfrey's armpits and dragged the captain's body toward the back of the building to escape the secondary explosions.

Good thing he did. The debris was already crashing down along the wall, and just as the larger parts of the helo's fuselage hit with echoing concussions and multiple booms, Band-Aid hustled up and dropped down to the captain.

The medic was a Japanese-American with a sparse beard who never seemed relaxed, always "on." He dropped his medical bag, about to get to work. "How long has he been unconscious?"

"He's dead."

"Aw, hell. I liked him."

"Just move up front, look for Black Bear's truck. They're coming for us."

"You got it, Sergeant."

Vatz glanced once more at the fallen captain. And once again, it was always somebody else.

Cursed? Lucky? He didn't want to think about it anymore. He wanted to close his eyes and sleep.

And for just a second, he did just that.

There in the darkness of a dark, damp alley in Moscow lay his old friend Zack with a gaping bullet hole in his head.

Zack's eyes snapped open. "Vatz, man, it's not so bad here. If you want, we could hang out."

"What do you mean?"

"I mean you're just delaying the inevitable. Those boys from the Tenth probably won't get here in time. Maybe you'll weaken this recon force, but once their BMPs come rolling down, you guys are all dead. Unless, of course, you run for it."

"We won't leave these people."

"I know. So I guess I'll be seeing you soon."

"Sergeant!"

Vatz took a deep breath, heard the sound of an engine.

"Sergeant?" cried Band-Aid.

Vatz snapped awake with a chill. He immediately hoisted the captain in a fireman's carry, then rushed around the corner, toward the street, where a pickup truck was waiting.

TWENTY-NINE

Sergeant Raymond McAllen, Sergeant Scott Rule, and Khaki rushed up to the idling Ka-29. McAllen held up the grenade, as Khaki had suggested.

Meanwhile, Rule was on the other side of the helo, pointing his weapon at the co-pilot on the other side of the canopy.

Both pilots were in their late fifties and seemed more annoyed than scared. They raised their hands, and McAllen motioned for the pilot to go to the back, open the bay door.

"You smell that?" cried Khaki. "That's fuel."

The pilot reached for the side door and inched it open, just as McAllen seized it, glanced up, and aimed his SIG P220 pistol, screaming in Russian, "Don't move!"

With a gun to his head, the pilot was most accom-modating, and McAllen climbed up into the helo, took the pilot's sidearm from his holster, then motioned him back toward the cockpit.

"Something's wrong with this helo," hollered Khaki.

McAllen ignored him for now. "Rule, get everybody else in here," he ordered his assistant. "Khaki, come on up, get in the co-pilot's seat. But I don't think you're flying."

After ordering the co-pilot to turn over his sidearm, McAllen moved back, allowing Khaki into the cockpit. The co-pilot vacated his chair and slowly headed into the troop compartment, Khaki's pistol trained on him until Rule got back inside and took over.

McAllen and Khaki donned headsets, then Khaki spoke quickly to the pilot in Russian, his language skills even better than McAllen's. In fact, the two spoke so quickly that McAllen only picked up a word here and there.

"All right, he doesn't care, he'll fly us where we want to go so long as we don't shoot them, but it's no coin-cidence they were just sitting here."

"How bad?"

"He says they're having trouble with the gear. And there's an electrical problem along with a fuel leak somewhere. Remember, these Russians have some new gear, but the old stuff is *very* old."

"So we just got into a flying bomb."

"Pretty much."

McAllen lowered his voice, even though he didn't need to. "Don't tell the other guys."

Khaki winked and said, "We're screwed."

"Less screwed than before. At least we got a ride now. How's the fuel?"

"They filled it up before leaving Behchoko, but we'll find out just how bad this leak is."

McAllen spoke slowly to the pilot, asking him more about the fuel problem.

The pilot threw up his hands, shrugged.

Bastard wasn't telling.

"It's about a two-hour ride up to your pilot's last known coordinates," said Khaki. "We might make it there, but if we don't refuel, this won't be our ride home."

"Just get us there. My CO's working on the rest."

Friskis, Gutierrez, Palladino, and Szymanski piled into the bird, and Rule shut the door behind them.

Then the assistant team leader rushed up, slapped a hand on McAllen's shoulder, and shouted in his ear, "Do we have to take the co-pilot?"

"No, you're right. Good call. Ditch him." While Rule took care of that, McAllen ordered the pilot to take off.

The rotors began to kick up as Rule shoved the co-pilot outside, then slammed shut the door.

After jogging a few yards away, the co-pilot whirled around and raised his middle fingers.

"He's not happy!" Rule cried.

"He's lucky we didn't shoot him," added McAllen.

As the engine began to roar even louder, and the floor began to vibrate, McAllen grabbed onto the back of the pilot's seat as the gear left the ground.

"This helo is a piece of crap!" shouted Rule.

McAllen smiled darkly. "But it's all ours!"

While Khaki ordered the pilot to bank away and head north, McAllen wrestled with the idea that they could use the helo and its weaponry to assist the SF guys.

What a surprise that would be, seeing a Ka-29 swoop down to take out Spetsnaz infantrymen on the ground, not Canadians and Americans.

But they didn't have the fuel, might need the weapons later on, and there was always the chance that they could be accidentally taken out.

So there it was. Despite the pure, unadulterated frustration, they would stick to the plan.

Of course, those Special Forces boys weren't about to let him live down that decision. "Outlaw One, this is Black Bear, over!"

"Go ahead, Black Bear."

"Is that you in that Russian helo, over?"

"Roger that. Sorry we couldn't stick around for the cake, but I think your operators got it under control, over."

"If this channel wasn't being recorded, you know what I'd be telling you right now, don't you?"

McAllen knew. And he'd probably say the same thing. "Understood. Outlaw One, out."

"Don't let it bother you, Sergeant," said Khaki over the intercom. "Every player has his part."

"Yeah, but you know, you can't help but ask—what's more important? One pilot? Or helping secure an entire town?"

"That's not your question to answer."

"No, but it's still mine to ask."

The driver of the pickup truck had introduced himself as Barry. He was three hundred and fifty pounds of flannel-clad Canadian hunter/firefighter, and he barreled down the street at sixty-plus miles per hour, with Vatz buckled into the passenger's seat, Band-Aid jammed into the backseat.

Vatz had contacted the other four guys he had posted downtown, and they were already en route to the airport in another truck.

Meanwhile, some of Captain Rodriguez's men were reconnoitering the roadblocks, while others attempted to fall back into the neighborhoods to see just where those Spetsnaz troops had moved. Rodriguez had said he'd already lost four men, and that he still hadn't heard when the Tenth Mountain Division's first troops would arrive from Grand Prairie.

They drove in silence for a minute, then Barry suddenly blurted, "This is like something out of a movie. I mean, this stuff doesn't happen to folks like us."

"Well, it does now," said Vatz.

"I got a condo in Florida. What am I doing here?"

"Saving your town," said Band-Aid.

"Speaking of which, I heard we destroyed all of their helicopters."

"I didn't hear that," Vatz said.

"I also heard that a squad or two went off into the neighborhoods. They're using gas."

"What else did you hear?" asked Band-Aid.

"They shot down the two choppers we had up there."

Vatz rubbed his eyes, and the tension in his shoulders began to loosen. "I saw one of our birds go down. But we also took out the helo that was after it."

A crash and muffled *thud* made him snap up.

Suddenly, the truck was drifting to the left, cutting into the wrong lane and now racing toward a building.

Vatz glanced sidelong at Barry.

He'd been shot in the chest by a sniper, and blood had splattered all over the cab. A gaping hole had opened in the windshield.

Band-Aid was screaming that the round had missed him by a few inches. Most of the rear window was gone.

Before Vatz could grab the wheel, the truck plowed through the glass door and adjoining wall of the Canadian Imperial Bank of Commerce, cinder blocks and glass tumbling down onto the hood, crashing through the windshield and onto Vatz as he ducked, burying himself in the floorboard.

But the truck kept on moving, blasting through decks and counters until Vatz reached up through the debris on his lap and threw the gear into park, then switched off the engine.

"Jac, you all right?"

The medic came up from behind the seat. "I'm good. I'm good."

Vatz lifted pieces of cinder block from his lap, opened his door, and forced himself outside, coughing.

Dust-filled beams of light shone in from the shattered entrance. With his rifle at the ready, Vatz moved shakily forward, along with Band-Aid.

"He's out there, somewhere . . ."

"Only way to tell is to draw his fire," said Band-Aid. "I'll run across the street."

"Hold up." Vatz got on the radio to inform Black Bear what had happened.

"Too tied up now to send another truck, but I need you here! There's a squad out there in the trees. Our snipers got them pinned down, but for how long I don't know. We can't move till we take them out. I need you here, over."

"Roger that, on our way, out."

Band-Aid frowned. "On our way?"

"Get back in the truck."

"Damn, I like your style." The medic rushed to the rear cab door, tugged it open, hopped inside.

Vatz yanked the driver's door, reached in, and hauled Barry out of the seat. He dropped hard to the floor, and Vatz had to turn away. Sure, he'd seen his share of blood and gore, but all that blood and brain matter, coupled with the guy's weight, was just too much.

Repressing the urge to gag, he hauled himself into the driver's seat and fired up the engine. Damned radiator was cracked and hissing. Ignoring it, he threw the shifter in reverse, floored it.

Rubber burned as they shot back through the bank and exploded onto the street, trailing dust and tumbling pieces of concrete.

Not a second later, another round punched through the side window; Vatz ducked, threw it in drive, floored it again.

A third round struck as Vatz kept low and steered blindly.

After two more breaths, he popped up and cut the wheel hard left, turning down a side street. "We're out of his bead now, I think."

Band-Aid did not answer.

Vatz stole a look into the backseat, couldn't see the medic. "Band-Aid?"

Nothing.

Vatz's heart skipped a beat. My God. He was a magnet for death.

"Hey, Sergeant, yeah, I'm good." The medic popped his head up and leaned back in the seat, one eye shaded by his monocle.

Vatz sighed in heavy relief. "Damn it, bro, you gave me a heart attack!"

"Sorry, I was just checking the Cross Com. You know, if you and I can get in behind those squads near the terminal—"

"Yeah, I know. That's what Black Bear has in mind."

THIRTY

The snowmobile's engine began to falter, and Major Stephanie Halverson knew she'd be back on foot very soon.

"What do you think, Jake?" she asked aloud. "Still think I'll make it?"

She imagined Jake Boyd in his cockpit, flying just off her wing, flashing her a big thumbs-up.

"Well, I won't argue with that."

Halverson estimated she had covered between sixteen and eighteen miles, and she now rode through tall pines; beyond the woods she could see a frozen river whose opposite shoreline lay a half kilometer away.

With an unceremonious cough, the engine died. She tried to start the snowmobile again. The tank was bone-dry.

She hopped off, checked the forest behind her, then unloaded the gear, jamming what she could into the pillowcase she'd taken from the farmhouse.

That poor family. Halverson now wore the mother's clothes, which smelled like laundry detergent. She slung the survival kit over one shoulder, the pillowcase over the other, then started toward the river.

At this time of year the ice should be thick enough to support her, she thought. If she followed the river, her GPS said she'd reach another broad plain offering no cover, but more forest lay on the opposite shore. However, getting to that better cover meant crossing the river and placing herself in the wide open.

Her whole life had been a risk, and there were very few she hadn't taken, save for the one with Jake.

She paused at the very last tree before heading down onto the snowy bank. She took a long pull from her water bottle, stowed it, then thought, *I got this*.

For a few moments, it was eerily quiet. Just the sounds of her breathing and snow crunching faintly beneath her boots.

Then she heard it: a humming in the distance. Was that an engine?

"Outlaw One, this is Hammer of Tampa Five Bravo, over."

Sergeant Raymond McAllen, who was seated just behind the pilot's chair inside the Ka-29, had already been notified by radio operator Friskis that Major Alice Dennison was calling, so he put on a headset and adopted his all-business tone to answer, "Hammer, this is Outlaw One, go ahead, over."

"Outlaw One, I'm sending you updated GPS coordinates for your package. We picked up the survival beacon about ninety minutes ago, over."

"Outstanding. At least it's a rescue now and not a recovery, over."

"Roger that. However, be advised that mechanized infantry forces are homing in on that location. Intel from one of our drones indicates two BMP-3s, over."

"Roger that, Hammer. Coordinates just received. Stand by." McAllen got on the intercom. "Khaki, you looking at that GPS?"

"Yeah, I got it," he said, tapping a finger on his own unit's screen. "I think we're about thirty minutes away." He leaned forward and rapped a knuckle on a gauge. "But look at this fuel. She's leaked a lot, come down fast. We'll be riding on fumes."

"All right." McAllen switched to the radio. "Hammer, this is Outlaw One. Note we're approximately thirty minutes out from the package, but we're nearly out of fuel. I put in a request for an exfiltration helo over an hour ago, but haven't heard anything from our CO. Can you follow up, and we'll send an updated GPS of our location at that time, over?"

"Roger that, Outlaw One. Understood. I'll check on that pick up and get back to you. Hammer, out."

The lights inside the chopper flickered. They'd been doing that sporadically for the past fifteen minutes, leaving McAllen's men even more restless.

Since the noise was so loud in the troop compartment, McAllen got the team's attention by raising a fist, then he traced a big 3 0 on the back of the pilot's seat, mouthing the words: thirty minutes. He gestured going down to snatch up the pilot.

Each man flashed a thumbs-up, then each went back to checking his weapons and inspecting the rest of his gear.

"Hey, Sergeant," called Khaki. "These GPS coordinates . . . you know where she is right now?"

"Do I want to know?" he asked, his tone already darkening.

"She's crossing a frozen river."

"Why?"

"There's a huge wooded area on the other side. Only good cover around."

McAllen swore through a deep sigh. "Well, that gives us two problems: if she's still on that river when we get there, then *we'll* be out in the open."

"But we'll be quick."

"And if she's not," McAllen went on, "it'll be interesting trying to find her in the woods while you hang back with the chopper, which might run out of gas before we find her."

"These are the things we think about but do not say," said Khaki. "Got some good news, though: I think we can intercept her before she reaches the tree line."

Just then, several blinking lights shone on the cockpit panel and the chopper began to lose power.

"What is it?" McAllen asked.

"I'm not sure," said Khaki.

The pilot was speaking so fast that his words became a blur, like the ground racing by at just a thousand feet below, then nine hundred, eight hundred.

"He's talking about that electrical problem again," said Khaki. "But I'm not sure what he means. I don't know all the technical terms in translation."

With a jolt, the power returned, and the rotor spun back up hard, the fuselage shuddering a moment before they began to regain altitude.

Khaki glanced back at McAllen and beat a fist twice on his chest, as if to say, heart attack averted.

McAllen nodded, then told the pilot in Russian that he'd buy him a lifetime supply of vodka if he could keep them aloft until they reached their destination.

The pilot rolled his eyes and in broken English said,

"I will make deal. But you will take me with you. I want to see America . . . before my government takes over everything."

McAllen exchanged a look with Khaki, then said, "Well, my friend, you'll get your wish, but it'll be a cold day in hell before a Russian flag is flying over the White House."

"Or flying over the Canadian Parliament," added Khaki.

The pilot laughed under his breath. "Gentlemen, I think you should prepare for some cold days ahead."

Sergeant Nathan Vatz and Band-Aid took the truck along a dirt road running parallel to the wooded area opposite the airport terminal. While that section of forest was thick, it was only about a thousand yards wide, cut into a perfect rectangle when the airport had been constructed.

"All right, this is close enough," said Vatz, bringing the overheating truck to an abrupt stop.

They hustled out and skulked their way into the forest, threading between clusters of firs and pines, their limbs drooping with snow. Intermittent cracks of gunfire boomed ahead.

At the next tree, Vatz signaled for the medic to crouch down. "How many frags you got?"

"Three."

"I got two. Now listen very carefully."

Vatz unfolded his plan, then studied the medic's face. Was there any sign of fear? Would this guy lock up at the most dire moment? Damn, if only Vatz had spent more time training with these guys. Well, the medic had made it this far and had even taken all those extra qualifications courses. Sometimes you had to let go and place your trust in the machine that produced operators of the highest caliber.

"Sergeant, are you all right?"

Ironic. Maybe Vatz was the one who couldn't be trusted.

"Sergeant?"

"Yeah, sorry, just going over it again in my head." He called up Black Bear, let him know what was happening, and the assistant detachment commander said he and the men inside were ready.

Vatz proffered his hand to Band-Aid. "Let's go get 'em."

The medic shook vigorously. "Hooah." Then he trotted off, working to the north side of the woods to place himself in a flanking position of the enemy.

Meanwhile, Vatz kept low, shifting as gingerly and stealthily as he could straight toward the enemy position. He came within fifty yards of the Russians, his breath shallow as he settled down beside a tree.

His binoculars told the story. It was a full squad all right—at least ten troops visible. One Russian shouldered a rocket launcher, either an RPG-7 or a Bumblebee, but they were probably saving that as a last resort. They would've blown up the terminal already. They probably had some mortars as well, definitely two machine guns, plus the usual assortment of rifles, pistols, and undying love for the Motherland that had been brainwashed into them during training. They hadn't wasted any gas. They were masked up, as was everyone inside the terminal. So it was what it was: a standoff.

But not for long.

"Band-Aid, I'm in position, over."

"Roger that, me, too."

"All right. Wait for it."

Vatz called Black Bear. The boys inside were ready.

He switched his MR-C rifle to single-shot mode, raised it, then stared through the scope.

The squad leader would be the guy doing the most talking through his headset.

After panning down the line, Vatz found him. The Russian had his mask off and lay on his gut, balanced up on his elbows, reading images from a small tablet computer on the snow in front of him. He spoke quickly into his boom mike.

In truth, military snipers rarely engaged targets closer than three hundred yards, but Vatz's plan depended upon a perfect shot. So he'd come in much, much closer, and he would do everything possible to ensure that perfection. Yes, at this range he could probably just lift and fire, but he had a moment to be sure, so he took it.

Vatz couldn't use the laser target designator on his assault helmet because the Russian would detect it. So Vatz would need to compare the height of the target to its size using the mil dot reticle on his scope.

Time for math homework. The average human head was six inches wide. The average human shoulders were twenty inches apart, and the average distance from a trooper's crotch to the top of his head was one meter.

The height of the target (in yards) × 1000, divided by the height of the target (in mils), gave the range in yards. Bullet drop and gravity wouldn't be issues.

Consequently, the perfect shot was all about the simple range and dialing in the scope to set those crosshairs on target.

He made the calculations, the adjustment to the scope, and settled into his breathing pattern.

He considered himself a good shot, not a great one. He could fight an ODA team better than most of them, but again, he was no record holder on the firing range.

His finger got heavy on the trigger, and it appeared the squad leader was about to get up.

Vatz held his breath.

And fired.

The shot caught the Russian in the back of his neck, just below his helmet, blowing that helmet off and taking a large piece of skull with it.

As the dead man hit the snow, the two troopers nearby spun back in Vatz's direction, like good little soldiers, exactly as they should.

Vatz switched to full automatic, bolted to his feet, shifted out from behind the tree, and hosed them down with his first salvo, dropping one before he dodged to the next tree.

A pair of explosions resounded.

That was Band-Aid, initiating his part of the plan. While their attention was drawn to the rear by Vatz, Band-Aid was moving in from the left flank and lobbing his frags.

And then Black Bear and the men inside joined the fiesta.

It was up to Vatz now to make sure he got out of their line of fire. He sprinted off to the south, making a wide arc through the trees, gunfire tracking his steps, shaving off bark, whistling by.

Vatz ran on currents of electricity, viewed the world through high contrast, smelled every particle of gunpowder. He suddenly turned, weaving through more trees, heading directly toward their right flank.

He spotted two troops, both trading fire with the guys in the terminal, who'd all in unison opened up with a barrage of rifle fire.

Vatz put the MR-C's grenade launcher to work, thumping one off to fall at the trooper's knees—

Boom! The explosion tore them up, and they rag-dolled it to the snow.

The remaining Spetsnaz seemed unorganized now, with at least three more turning tail and running straight toward Band-Aid. Vatz hit the ground, called up the medic.

Two seconds later, Band-Aid's rifle echoed.

"Black Bear, this is Bali, over."

"Go ahead, Bali."

"Hold fire. Move in. We got 'em on the run!"

Black Bear keyed his mike, and Vatz heard the hoots and hollering of the others. "Roger that, Bali. Great job!"

Vatz took a deep breath and smiled inwardly. It was about time something went right.

But the victory celebration lasted only a few seconds before Band-Aid's tense voice came over the radio:

"I'm hit! I'm hit!"

THIRTY-ONE

Major Stephanie Halverson's eyes had grown so heavy, her muscles so sore, that she staggered to a halt in the middle of the frozen river, leaned forward, and tanked down air.

Ten seconds, she told herself. *Just ten seconds*.

The wind had picked up and had been blasting snow in her face. Her cheeks and nose were going numb. She shivered and pulled up the scarf, turned back, squinted at the shoreline she'd left behind.

Through veils of snow she made out two Russian BMP-3s rumbling on their tank-like tracks down toward the riverbank.

Her little trek on the snowmobile had helped buy her time, but once she'd switched on the beacon, the Russians had also picked it up. Those infantry squads had probably been tasked with both finding her and performing a reconnaissance mission in this area, killing two birds with one stone, unfortunately.

Reflexes took over. She turned, broke into a run. The opposite shoreline seemed impossibly far away. Her legs were back to burning as she imagined a sniper somewhere behind her casually lining up to take his shot.

At least the end would be quick.

What was she thinking? She wouldn't give up. Not yet. Not after coming this far. Not after three innocent people had already died!

Screw the pillowcase, the supplies. They dropped into her wake.

She would reach the forest by sheer force of will. They couldn't stop her.

Anticipating a gunshot, she veered right, then left, still jogging, her boots nearly slipping on the ice beneath the powdery snow.

She glanced back. The Russians were still coming, frozen river notwithstanding. The BMP drivers were testing the ice, while dismounted troops started toward her.

As the snow rose to her shins, her pace slowed, but she swore and kept weaving erratically, kicking forward now. Then, suddenly, a crack made her flinch and gasp.

The gunshot echoed off.

She didn't feel anything. Maybe he'd missed. Or maybe it'd take a second for the pain to come.

Automatic weapons fire resounded—

But it was joined by the strangely irregular thumping of rotors.

The afternoon sun blinded her for a moment, but out of the glare came a helo swooping toward her.

For a split second her spirits lifted. They'd sent someone. She'd make it.

Then the chopper banked slightly, and she got a better look at the fuselage, the red star, the terrible and familiar outline of a Ka-29. Now those rotors seemed to pound on her head, made her want to scream.

"Oh, yeah?" she cried aloud. "I don't think so." She kept on running as the chopper came around once more, descending from behind.

As its shadow passed directly overhead, she extended her arm and fired, the round ricocheting off its hull.

They would land in front of her, cut her off from the forest.

She fired again, smelled fuel, and thought maybe she'd scored a hit.

The helo slowed to a hover, began to pivot, and Halverson wasn't sure what to do now. Break left? Right?

"She's firing at us," hollered Sergeant Scott Rule.

Sergeant Raymond McAllen didn't need the young superstar to tell him that. But damn, McAllen hadn't anticipated this part, where the pilot assumed they were

Russians about to capture her and decided to shoot at their already malfunctioning helicopter.

They were still hovering, and McAllen ordered the pilot to land, but the Russian shook his head, second chin wagging. "How thick is the ice?"

"It's thick. Land!"

"I don't like this ice."

"Khaki, can you land this thing?"

"Okay, I put down," said the pilot with disgust. "But if ice breaks, your fault!" He leaned forward and spoke rapidly into his microphone.

"Damn it!" Khaki jolted forward and switched off the unit.

McAllen shoved his pistol into the back of the pilot's head. "Put this bird down!"

Then he called out to Rule, telling him to open the bay door and throw down one of his Velcro patches, the American flag.

All their uniform patches and other black insignia could be removed via the Velcro, depending upon the mission and what the lawyers had to say about operations in a particular nation. Sometimes you had to show the patches, sometimes not.

Rule slid open the door, and as they got even lower he tossed down the patch, then started closing the door, just as she fired again, the round pinging off the jam.

Rule cursed and fell back onto the floor.

"Is he hit?" asked McAllen.

"I don't think so," shouted Gutierrez.

"Look, she's got it," said Khaki. "She sees us! She knows. Here she comes."

Halverson thought she was dreaming as she ran toward the helicopter, its gear just setting down on the ice. She clutched the patch in her hand and broke into a full-on sprint.

For a moment she had doubted the patch, thought maybe the enemy was luring her into the helo, but that was thinking too hard. If there were Russians on board, they would rather take her by force, not cunning. It would be a matter of ego. This was her rescue.

The gunfire behind her had ceased. Those fools thought their comrades in the helo had captured the "Yankee pilot." They had no idea that somehow, some way, Americans had taken control of an enemy helicopter. She had almost waved after picking up the patch but thought better of it. The troops behind would find that highly suspect.

With the rotors now blowing waves of snow into her eyes and clearing a circle around the helo, Halverson leaned over, ditched the survival kit, and made her last run for it, coming onto the rotor-swept ice.

Just twenty yards now, and her gait grew shaky as her boots found little traction. It was all she could do to remain upright.

Boom, down she went. Took a hard fall. Right on her butt. The impact sent tremors of pain through her back.

Get up!

The helo's side door slid open, and a helmeted soldier was waving her on.

She rose. Gunfire began pinging off the chopper. Damn it. The Russians had figured it out.

Okay, back on her feet now. A few rounds sparking here and there.

Ten yards. Five. That soldier was right there, his face obscured by a visor.

Abruptly, the helo tipped slightly away from her, rotors lifting back—

Then she saw what was happening. The ice below had cracked, and the helo's gear was sinking into the water, chunks of ice already bobbing around it.

But the cracks were on the back side of the helicopter, so Halverson kept on running. Just fifteen feet now. Ten. Five.

The soldier's mouth was working: *come on!*

Halverson increased her stride.

The soldier leaned out as far as he could, extending his gloved hand.

What was that sound? *Oh, no* . . . The ice began splintering at her feet.

She took three more steps, heard a chorus of cracking sounds, then she began to slip and tried shifting to the right—

Only to find herself atop a small raft of ice that floated freely, her weight driving one side down.

Instinctively, she reached out. Nothing to grab on to, no one to help. She began to fall.

Oh, God, no . . .

The water rushed up her legs, over her chest, and broke over her face, the sensation like a billion fingernails of ice poking every part of her body.

Completely underwater now, the shock having robbed her entirely of breath, she panicked and kicked frantically for the surface.

Only then did the extreme cold hit her.

In truth the water was probably not colder than what she'd experienced during water immersion tests during her training, but combined with the stress of the moment, the stress of the past night, it was liquid death.

Her head hit something hard. More ice. She pushed up, tried to find an opening.

Where was the surface?

She made a fist, punched the ice, looked around, punched again.

Rule had already yanked the quick straps on his boots, toed them off, and had zipped off his combat suit, leaving him in his black LWCWUS (lightweight cold weather undergarment set) and socks.

No way would they let that pilot drown.

Rule would die first.

Friskis had already found a nylon rescue rope, and Rule made a loop in it as the chopper began to rise from the river.

With the looped rope in one hand, he jumped out, dropping six feet toward the broken ice. Before he even felt the water, he screamed at it like an animal raging against nature.

Just as he broke through, about to be swallowed, the rattling of the helo's machine gun sounded against the rotors.

That's right, boys, let 'em have it!

Rule sank deep, popped up, and cried out again as the chill seized him in its grasp. He told himself, *not so cold, not so cold*, as he swam forward, didn't see her, dove under, widened his eyes—

And there she was, just off to his left, a few feet back and struggling to push through the ice, unable to see the opening nearby.

He paddled to her, grabbed her wrist, and pulled her back with him, kicking as hard as he could.

They burst up, both tanking down air, gasping, the rotor wash whipping over them. "Grab on to my back!"

She wrapped one arm over his right shoulder, tucked the other arm beneath his left, and locked her hands. Smart girl. "I'm ready," she said through her intense shivering.

There wasn't time to ascend the rope and climb back into the helo—not with that incoming fire.

So Rule flashed a thumbs-up, seized the loop with both hands, and braced himself.

From the open door, McAllen gave the Russian pilot the go-ahead, and the rope snapped taut. Rule and the woman were wrenched from the water and swung hard under the chopper.

"Go, go, go," McAllen cried over the intercom.

The helo's nose pitched down, and they veered off, still drawing fire from the infantrymen behind them.

One of the BMP-3s even fired a round from its big gun but missed by a wide margin. The Russians were at once desperate, embarrassed, and mighty pissed off.

"This is it," said Khaki. "We're on fumes now."

"Just get us to the other side of this forest and put us down there. We have to get them inside."

McAllen wished they could turn back for just a moment and launch rockets, but not with Rule and the pilot dangling below.

"Hang on, buddy, just hang on!" shouted Palladino, even though the sergeant below couldn't hear him.

They all began shouting, and maybe it made them feel better, McAllen wasn't sure, but he joined in and remembered the conversation he'd had with his young assistant:

"Just want you to know that I'm giving you a hundred and ten percent. Always," Rule had said.

"We'll see how long it takes for you to create your own shadow. And I hope it's a pretty long one."

Yes, indeed, Sergeant Scott Rule had just cast a very long shadow. And McAllen would make sure to commend him for that.

Rule's arms were frozen, his hands locked onto the rope. The pilot was tugging hard on his shoulders, and tears were beginning to form in his eyes from all the exertion.

"Don't . . . let go . . ." she said in his ear.

She was half dead, but even then she sounded kind of sexy. Leave it to him to be thinking of sex at a time like this . . .

He closed his eyes.

I am a Marine. This is my job. I will not fail.

But the feeling had escaped from his arms, and the rope began sliding through his fingers.

"He's losing it!" shouted McAllen. "Khaki, how much longer?"

"We're almost there!"

McAllen began stripping out of his combat suit so he could give it to the pilot, once they had her inside. The suit's life critical layer had a narrow network of tubing that would provide one hundred watts of heating A-SAP. Rule's suit waited for him.

Talk about being hung out to dry. McAllen couldn't imagine how cold those two must be.

The helo broke past another long stretch of trees, then the engine stuttered like a misfiring lawnmower.

"No choice now," said Khaki.

"Try to put them down easy," McAllen said.

"Easy is not possible," grunted the pilot. "Maybe you pray now. Because we go down hard!"

He wasn't kidding. The chopper began dropping like a rock as she lost power.

McAllen clung to the back of the pilot's seat, watched as Rule, who was one-handing the rope now, slammed into a snow bank.

"They're down!" he shouted. "But he's still holding the rope. He's not letting go! Cut it! Cut it!"

Gutierrez immediately unsheathed his Blackhawk Tatang, a thirteen-inch-long serrated blade that he lifted high in the air, then—

Thump! He cut nylon like butter, leaving a deep scar on the helo's deck.

"They're clear!" cried McAllen.

"Everybody, brace for impact!" warned Khaki. "Three, two, one!"

THIRTY-TWO

"He's been shot in the leg. Caught him just above the armor. Looks like it missed the artery, though. Get Beethoven over here A-SAP," Vatz told Black Bear.

The warrant office acknowledged, then Vatz finished cutting open the medic's pant leg with the Mark I the medic had given him. The Masters of Defense knife had a secondary blade at the butt that was specifically designed for cutting cord or clothes off an injured combatant.

As Vatz worked, his attention was divided between treating the medic and checking the perimeter for remaining troops.

A couple of gunshots sounded from somewhere south.

"That's our guys," said Band-Aid.

"You have a good ear."

The medic nodded, then flinched in pain.

Vatz had the morphine injection ready. "Okay."

Band-Aid tensed, took the shot, then relaxed a little and said, "Thanks, Sergeant."

"Don't thank me yet, Jac. I'm no medic. I could still kill you."

"Please don't. I'll tell you what, though—you're some damned operator."

"Nope. Just doing my job like everyone else."

"Your plan worked."

"Sometimes you get lucky."

"Like me." The knot of agony that had gripped the medic's face began to loosen. "Could be worse, right?"

"Right. Morphine kicking in?"

"Yeah. Feels good. Next time make it a double."

Vatz cracked a slight grin.

"Bali, this is Beethoven, over?" called the team's assistant medic, Staff Sergeant Paul Dresden. "Coming right up on you, over."

"Come on, out."

The assistant medic arrived. He had a scruffy blond beard and wore an expression of deep concern. He'd been given the call sign Beethoven by the captain since he was, in fact, an accomplished pianist.

Vatz gave Beethoven an update of what he'd done so far.

Band-Aid thrust out his hand. "Thanks, Nathan."

"Any time, brother." He turned to Beethoven. "I'll

get the portable litter ready. We'll get him back to the terminal."

A voice sounded in Vatz's earpiece. "Bali, this is Black Bear. Just got a report from Zodiac Six. We have at least a battalion-size force coming down from Behchoko. ETA on their first elements is four hours, six for the rest of the battalion. We need to get back to the roadblock, see how much damage has been done. Zodiac wants to take a few men into the neighborhoods to recon their sniper positions. I want you to lead the roadblock team, over."

"Roger that. Any word yet from the Tenth?"

"They have sorties in the air, some already on the ground. Air support is en route, too, but no one's committing to an exact ETA yet. I've pressed them hard. I'm sure that battalion coming down has stepped up their plans."

"Roger that. We're bringing up Band-Aid to the terminal, then I'll organize the team. Send down some guys to get Captain Godfrey's body out of my truck. See you in a few, out."

"Hey, Sergeant, you know they're all talking about you," said Beethoven as he helped Vatz get Band-Aid onto the litter they had just unrolled.

"Who's talking?"

"The rest of the team, that's who."

Vatz's tone turned defensive. "They all talking smack about the new team sergeant, eh? Heard about what happened to me in Moscow?"

"They're saying you might be the best operator they've ever seen."

"Excuse me?"

"I'm not kidding."

Vatz gave a little snort. "You guys haven't been around much."

"All I know is, I'm sticking close because you don't die. Put me on your roadblock team."

"My luck will run out. Either way, I always draw a lot of fire."

Beethoven grinned. "Sign me up."

"We'll see."

The Ka-29 slammed into the ground so hard that the booms supporting the landing gear snapped off.

The chopper slid forward, then came to a sudden halt, driving Sergeant Raymond McAllen hard against his seat's straps as a wave of snow crashed down over the canopy.

"Palladino? Gutierrez? Go get them!" ordered McAllen, bolting from his seat and opening the door. "Friskis? Szymanski? Security outside!" McAllen crossed toward the cockpit. "Khaki, how we doing?"

"I think we survived," mused the pilot, studying the gauges. "Still got some battery power. Good news: the fuel leak has been fixed."

"Yeah, since the tank is dry. You're a comedian."

McAllen turned and slammed a palm on the Russian pilot's shoulder. "Well, Boris, you might get to see America after all."

"My name is Captain Pravota. Address me as such."

"All right, Captain, you can get up now, get to the back, and we'll fit you with a nice little pair of zipper cuffs."

"No need. I won't resist. Have I?"

"Just follow orders. You can take orders from a lowly sergeant like me, can't you?"

The old pilot frowned. "Just leave me here."

"Nah. You're coming. Everybody loves a defector."

"As one soldier to another, do me honor and shoot me."

"Aw, Captain, don't be so dramatic. The conditions in our prisons are way better than your barracks. You're going on vacation. Did you bring your bathing suit?"

It didn't matter that the helicopter had practically crashlanded and that Major Stephanie Halverson felt certain that it wouldn't be taking off anytime soon. It was all about getting out of the wind, getting out of the wet clothes, and getting warm.

The big Marine with the olive skin, who had introduced himself as Sergeant Gutierrez, carried her on his back into the helo. The other guy named Palladino carried the Marine who had rescued her. His name, she had learned, was Sergeant Rule, and his face was blue. If that was any indication of what she herself looked like, maybe frostbite had already set in.

They frantically pulled off her clothes, and for once she could care less about being naked. But they were gentlemen about it, ignoring her body and just helping her get into the long johns and then into the combat suit.

Oh, God, the heating system was unbelievable. She sat there on a rear seat, legs pulled into her chest, riding wave after wave of heat.

"I'm hoping you're Major Stephanie Halverson," said a steely eyed man with a touch of gray at his sideburns.

"Good guess."

"I'm Staff Sergeant Raymond McAllen, United States Marine Corps." He offered his hand.

She took it. "Thanks for . . ." She broke off.

"Well, yeah, I know, it's not much of a rescue. And we'll need to get moving pretty soon. I know you've been out there a while. We can set up a litter, turn it into a little sled, and drag you if we need to."

"I'll be all right. Moving is good. Thanks for the combat suit. But what're you going to do once we're out there? Sun's up, but it's damned cold with that wind."

"Guess I'll have to cuddle with the Russian."

"Don't make me smile. It hurts."

"Sorry, Major. Can I ask you something personal?"

"Uh, okay?"

"Are you a relative or friends with Becerra?"

She drew her head back in surprise. "I've never met him."

"Funny, because this TRAP mission came down from him. The President of the United States ordered my team to rescue you. Any idea why?"

She frowned. "You think I'm carrying secret intel that could end the war tomorrow?"

"Who knows?"

"Sergeant, I'm just a pilot who was training at the wrong time, in the wrong place. The president contacted me directly while I was up there. He wanted a SITREP. I don't know. Maybe he thought I was worth saving."

"Damn . . ."

"What, not a good enough reason?"

The sergeant shrugged. "I was just hoping for something . . . I don't know."

"Something more important than my life?"

"I didn't say that."

"It's okay, Sergeant. I am just a pilot."

"You must be one hell of a pilot."

Her brows lifted. "That I am."

He nodded then regarded his men. "All right, people. We'll assume those mechanized troops are still coming for us, on foot or otherwise. Let's get ready to move!"

"Sergeant?" called Halverson. He glanced back to her. "Thank you."

"You're very welcome. And if you need anything—"

"Just get me home."

He winked. "Count on it."

It was midnight when General Sergei Izotov was wrenched from sleep by a video call from President Vsevolod Vsevolodovich Kapalkin.

The president appeared disheveled and incensed. He rubbed sleep grit from his eyes and said, "General, I have Snegurochka on the line."

"Does she know what time it is here?"

"Obviously, she does."

"What does she want?"

"She wouldn't say. She wanted to speak to both of us together. I hope, for your sake, General, that everything is going as planned."

"I'm sure it is."

"All right, I'm putting her through."

The screen divided into two images: Kapalkin on the left and Colonel Viktoria Antsyforov, that dark-haired beauty, on the right.

Antsyforov was wearing an expensive fur coat and hat, and stood near a tree in a wooded area draped in snow. Her breath steamed in the cold air. "Hello, gentlemen."

"Hello, Snegurochka," said Izotov. "I hope you've called with good news."

"Yes. There is no way we will lose this war."

"Very well, then. Stand by, and we will contact you with the confirmation code—"

"Uh, no, General. When I said *we*, I wasn't talking about you." She shifted, to the left, allowing a man dressed in a green cowl to appear: Green Vox. "I was talking about the Green Brigade Transnational."

"Hello, purveyors of death," said Green Vox.

Izotov threw up his hands. "Colonel, what now?"

"There is a suitcase in Edmonton, another one in Calgary. Ten kilotons in each. As planned. But now we control both of them. And again, when I say *we*, I mean us—not you."

Izotov spoke through gritted teeth. "Colonel, this terrorist scum is merely a subcontractor, nothing more. I'm unsure what you're trying to say."

"I'm saying, dear General, dear President, that our plan has changed."

Izotov leaned farther forward on his bed and widened his eyes on her.

Colonel Viktoria Antsyforov was, in his opinion, one of the most brilliant and trusted GRU officers in the history of the organization. When the security leak involving Doletskaya had been exposed and the Euros had alerted the Americans, it'd been she who had gone underground by staging her own death with their help.

She had erased herself from the organization—all in the name of restoring the Motherland to greatness.

And now she was saying it was all a lie?

She had even given her body to Izotov, pleasured him in ways that no woman ever had.

Now even that meant nothing to her?

They were going to use the threat of tactical nuclear weapons to bluff the Americans and Euros into giving them Alberta, should the conventional ground war fail.

"What are you talking about, Colonel?" asked Kapalkin.

"I'm saying that this oil has become the root of all evil. I'm saying that Mother Gaia can no longer survive if this struggle continues. I'm saying we are going to detonate both of the nuclear devices. And there's nothing you can do to stop us."

Izotov noticed how Green Vox reached over and clutched Antsyforov's hand.

The president sighed deeply. "All right, Colonel. You've sacrificed a lot. You want money. I understand. Let us go back to sleep, and we'll begin negotiations tomorrow."

"There will be no negotiations."

"Excuse me?" asked Izotov.

"Within forty-eight hours, the reserves in Alberta will be contaminated, the cities of Edmonton and Calgary uninhabitable. We will ensure that the Russian Federation is held responsible for this by fully revealing your plan. And forget using this call as evidence. I've taken care of that as well as the deactivation of my chip. You can't kill me."

"Colonel, have you gone insane?" asked Izotov.

"No, General. I have never seen things more clearly."

"Enough games," said Kapalkin. "We will call you in the morning, and you will name your price."

"No price. Only a clock for you to watch . . . and time for you to think about what you are doing to our world."

Izotov dug fingernails into his palms. "What are you waiting for then?" He threw up his hands. "Detonate the nukes!"

She took a deep breath and sighed. "We will wait until as many civilians as possible can escape. Then, with all of those military units in the area, we will achieve maximum effect against the Federation."

"Name your price!" cried Kapalkin.

She took a step toward the camera, opened her slightly chapped lips. She suddenly grinned, glanced away, then looked up. She said very slowly, "No . . . price . . ."

"So you're going to do it," said Izotov. "You're terrorist scum now."

"No. You have no idea who I am, and why I do what I do. No idea. Good-bye."

Izotov sat there a moment, stunned. Kapalkin was equally speechless. "I could not have anticipated this," Izotov finally said.

"Nor I. But what do we do now? We can't let her destroy those reserves."

"No, we can't."

"We'll send in two teams to find the weapons, pull out all of our forces."

Izotov shook his head. "If we pull out, and the weapons are detonated, there will be no denying we are responsible." Izotov thought a moment. "We could lie and say we were tipped off, but that would still mean we are in bed with the enemy. Also, our nuclear search teams would never make it in time—especially if they have to penetrate American defenses. I'm at a loss. There is no one in the GRU I trusted more than her. No one. This is . . . unbelievable."

Kapalkin bolted up, walked away from the camera, then cursed and said, "Do you know what I'm going to do now, General? I'm going to do something that will shock you."

"At this moment that will be difficult."

"Oh, *this* will bring you to your feet."

THIRTY-THREE

The Russians had cleared a path through the roadblock of demolition derby cars that Vatz and the local boys had constructed across Highway 35. Enemy rockets had reduced more than half of the vehicles to heaps of blackened and burning wreckage, though the hulks themselves could still be pushed back into place. It would take at least an hour or two for Vatz's team to repair and reinforce the obstacle. Thankfully, the team's little surprise for the Spetsnaz mechanized infantry had remained intact. Sadly, the eight Mounties who had been defending the area had been killed; Vatz put two of his men in charge of picking up the bodies, which would be taken back to the airport. The atmosphere was at once tense and grim.

Band-Aid had been stabilized and moved into the

terminal, where one of the medics from Zodiac team had established a makeshift infirmary. Consequently, assistant medic Beethoven was cut loose and able to come along with Vatz.

He and the medic drove a civilian car nearly three kilometers north along the highway. They pulled over into a ditch and hopped out to survey the plains in the distance. Twice Vatz had tried to use the Cross Comm to pull up imagery from drones flying over the area, but the Russians were back to jamming their frequencies.

They both lay in the embankment with binoculars pressed to their eyes. Vatz asked, "Got anything?"

"Thought I saw a reflection. Gone now."

"You all right?"

"Sergeant, I can barely keep my eyes open."

"Me, too."

"Can I ask you something? What if the Tenth doesn't show up? What if they get new orders?"

"New orders? I don't think so. They'll be here."

"And if they don't come, the Russians will roll in and pounce on us."

"I like your positive attitude."

"I'm a realist. There's no way we can hold this town. No way."

Vatz closed his eyes a moment. The guy was right. They could delay the battalion, but hold them off entirely?

"Hey, Sergeant?" called Beethoven. "Wait a minute. Think I got something."

Vatz snapped open his eyes, squinted through his binoculars.

President David Becerra wasn't sure how to feel about the request for a conference call with President Vsevolod Vsevolodovich Kapalkin and General Sergei Izotov.

The Russians had thus far been ignoring all such requests from the JSF and Euros, and now *they* wanted to talk? Would it be a final threat? Would they demand surrender and want to talk terms? Would they suggest something even more ridiculous?

Becerra's impulse had been to ignore them. Let them stew a while. But within an hour after the Russians' request, he had asked Mark Hellenberg to get General Kennedy on the line and contact Moscow.

Three windows opened on Becerra's screen. Kapalkin wore an odd expression. Izotov appeared so disgusted that he could barely look up. General Kennedy was, of course, her impeccably groomed self and the consummate professional, ready for battle.

"Mr. President, General," Becerra began, acknowledging each man with a curt nod. "I'll first say that I'm shocked by your request to talk."

"We are shocked, too," said Izotov. It was obvious he'd been forced into the call.

"Mr. President, we have a matter to discuss that is of grave importance," said Kapalkin.

"Yes, we do. Get your forces out of Canada. Otherwise, I promise, you won't recover from this one. Not this one."

Izotov began to smile.

"You find this amusing, General?" Becerra widened his eyes, about to raise his voice.

"Mr. President, we will do as you ask," said Kapalkin.

"Excuse me?" Becerra nearly fell out of his chair. He glanced across the cabin at Chief of Staff Hellenberg, who shrugged in confusion.

Kapalkin went on: "I said, we will comply. However, we must first work together to address another problem."

"Work together?" Now it was Becerra's turn to smile. "If you'd like to do that, then first you'll cease all military operations around the globe. Your desire to expand the Russian Federation ends today."

"Shut up, Becerra!" cried Izotov. "You have no idea what is at stake here!"

Kapalkin fired off a sharp retort in Russian, silencing Izotov. He took a moment to catch his breath, to compose himself. Then he said, "Mr. President, we've learned that the Green Brigade Transnational has planted two nuclear weapons in Canada, one in Edmonton, the other in Calgary. The exact locations are unknown. These are suitcase bombs, ten kiloton. We are certain they are there. The terrorists are trying to blackmail the Russian Federation and, of course, destroy the reserves."

Becerra folded his arms over his chest. "Prove it."

Kapalkin raised an index finger like a weapon. "You can do one of two things. You can doubt us, ignore us, and in less than two days you will have your proof because the Brigades will detonate the weapons. Or you can trust me and send in two of your NEST teams, one to each city, to find and deactivate the bombs. Your teams can get there before ours can."

The Nuclear Emergency Support Teams that Kapalkin had mentioned were nuclear physicists and scientists working in the nation's weapons labs. They were heavily equipped and highly trained at sniffing out bombs.

"Why hasn't the Brigade contacted us directly?" asked Becerra.

"As I said, they're trying to blackmail the Russian Federation and blame us for the destruction. They believe we are the instigators of this war. They will detonate the nukes in less than two days. They're waiting for more civilians to be evacuated and more military forces to move into the cities. If we attempt to pull out our forces, we assume they will detonate the nukes. Mr. President, the loss of those reserves would be catastrophic to your economy *and* to the world's. So this time, we must work together to stop them."

Becerra's thoughts were flooded with what-ifs. "Mr. President, if you don't mind, I'd like to have a word in private with General Kennedy."

"By all means."

Becerra switched to a private channel. "General, I'm at a loss here. Are they playing us?"

The general's gaze went distant. "Hard to say. Our NEST teams could verify the presence of nukes, that's for sure. We can't trust the Russians, but it wouldn't hurt to send in those teams."

"If they're lying to us, then what would they gain by all this? Do they need our teams for some other purpose?"

"I don't know. But if they're being honest, and the nukes go off —"

"That's what bothers me," Becerra interrupted. "The nukes go off and the reserves are lost. What happens? The price of Russian oil and gas skyrockets."

"Exactly. So it's odd they come to us with this story. You'd think they'd let the reserves be destroyed."

"But that's short-term. Long-term, they'd have much more to gain if they controlled them."

"Definitely."

Becerra thought a moment. "I'm just shooting from the hip here, but here's what I think. The Russians are still in bed with the Brigade. They used them to plant the nukes and intended to bluff us. They figure if their ground war fails, they can threaten nuclear destruction."

"But their deal with the terrorists went south."

"And that's the real shock to them. They must have had some people on the inside working with the Brigade, GRU officers they fully trusted, maybe this agent with the codename 'Snow Maiden.'"

"Now they need us to bail them out," Kennedy concluded. "And if the nukes *were* to go off, then you're right, the price of Russian oil and gas would skyrocket—but the Russians are also trying to court the North Koreans and the Japanese, who've been buying more and more oil from the Canadians."

"So in the long term, if the nukes go off and the world believes the Russian Federation is at fault, then this becomes a major economic blow to their government."

"Exactly. Alienating future allies and taking the blame for nuclear destruction could finish them. We could turn those neutral nations, and they know that—which is why they've come to us."

"My God, General, I hope we're right." Becerra switched back to conference channel. "Gentlemen, it seems you have everything to lose, and we risk only a couple of search teams. Those teams will be marked with locator beacons, and you'll need to communicate with your forces so that our teams are not engaged."

"We will do that," said Kapalkin.

"But it will be difficult," added Izotov. "Both of our forces are using electronic countermeasures and jamming. We will try, but we can make no promises."

"Well, General, I hope for your sake your people don't kill them. Now, it's my understanding that we'll need to continue ground operations so the terrorists don't prematurely detonate the nukes. But you will *not* send in any more forces. The planes you have in the air? Turn them around. Do I make myself clear?"

"We will agree to that," said Kapalkin.

"Finally, if by some small miracle we're able to pull this off, I would expect that you would withdraw all troops from Canada. Completely. And then, once the Canadians have assessed their damages, we will discuss reparations."

"Becerra, let's not get ahead of ourselves," said Kapalkin.

"Oh, we won't. We'll also discuss reparations for every nation involved in the construction and operation of the International Space Station."

"Perhaps we should have kept to ourselves," said Izotov. "You Americans are all the same—always with your hand out. The world does not owe you anything."

"In this particular case, General, you owe us something: the truth. And if you're lying now, then the hand coming at you will not be empty—if you understand my meaning."

Izotov snickered. "I understand."

"President Becerra, protecting those Canadian reserves is in the best interests of both of our governments," said Kapalkin. "Let us focus on that and not use this situation as a bargaining tool to address other conflicts or desires."

"We're going to put everything on the table here. But you're right. We can't do anything until we're sure those nukes have been deactivated. General Kennedy? I'd like you to coordinate with General Izotov."

Kennedy nodded, though the awkwardness in her expression was clear.

"Gentlemen, we will be in touch with further details." Becerra broke the link with them and returned to the private channel with General Kennedy. "Let's get those NEST teams called up and in the air."

"Yes, sir. But, sir, have we just climbed into bed with the Russians?"

"They say to keep your enemies close. Can't say I like sleeping with them, though. Let's get to work."

THIRTY-FOUR

Sergeant Raymond McAllen and his Marines, along with Khaki, the Russian helicopter pilot Pravota, and their rescued pilot Major Stephanie Halverson, had been hiking away from the chopper for about four hours, following the woods south, taking short breaks roughly every forty-five minutes.

The snow was knee-deep in a few spots, and it was slow going to be sure. Halverson had warmed up and refused to be pulled in the litter, though McAllen could tell she wouldn't last much longer. The Russian wasn't faring much better.

McAllen called the next halt, and they gathered below a stand of white spruce, hidden by the dense evergreen branches, while Gutierrez and Palladino took off ahead to reconnoiter the path and report back. Szymanski was keeping an eye to the rear, which thus far had been clear of pursuing ground forces.

Halverson's survival kit had been left behind, but the Russians began dogging them from the air, with the occasional Ka-29 passing over the forest, driving all of them into the snow for cover. McAllen had been forced to break radio silence to get an update on their pickup, and they learned they had at least two more hours to wait until their bird arrived. They could shave off some of that time by continuing to head south.

McAllen was qualified to guide in the chopper, but so was Khaki, so when their taxi arrived, the Canadian had volunteered for those honors.

As they sat there, huffing beneath the trees, McAllen offered up the last few pieces of his chocolate-coated energy bar to anyone willing.

Halverson took a piece and said, "You look like you're freezing. You want the suit?"

He shook his head. "I've been accused of being cold-blooded, so it all works out."

"I will take your suit," said Pravota, wincing over his zipper cuffs.

"She's not offering," snapped McAllen.

"That's right," Halverson growled.

McAllen turned back to her. "So, is this rescue everything you dreamed it would be?"

She glanced away. "They killed everyone at my base. Killed my wingman. Killed this poor family who was trying to help me. Damn, Sergeant. If you didn't pick me up, I would be dead by now. Don't sell yourself too short."

"Thanks. I just, uh, I'm not thrilled by the prospect of two more hours of hiking."

"Me neither. And can I ask? Why are we dragging along this guy?" She flicked a dark glance in Pravota's direction. "Why didn't we leave him back at the chopper? Or just shoot him and be done with it."

"A POW's a bonus in my book. And he's an officer. Not sure my boys will ever get a crack at capturing an officer again."

She grinned crookedly. "I'm sorry I interfered in your little professional development project."

Her sarcasm stung. "Hey, relax. We'll get you out of here." McAllen leaned forward to brush snow from his boot.

A shot rang out, punched into the tree trunk at his shoulder.

He threw himself forward and cried, "Get down!"

They were finally rolling into downtown Calgary, Ninth Avenue Southwest, and Staff Sergeant Marc Rakken signaled his rifle squad seated inside the Stryker to make their final gear checks.

Navy SEALs already in the city had asked that at least one Stryker platoon enter Calgary Tower, a tall column of concrete supporting a huge, conical-shaped observation deck. The tower was the city's most identifiable landmark, and it had been seized by several squads of Spetsnaz troops who were using it as an observation post.

After all, the tower was famous for offering the best views of Calgary, and those Russians knew it'd only be a matter of time before someone entered to flush them out.

And with no way to escape, they also knew they would be fighting to the death.

As Rakken sat there, waiting for the platoon to pull up outside the tower, he nervously flexed his gloved fingers. It had been an exhaustingly long ride. With some shuffling after the bombs had gone off during their trip up 95, his platoon was now spread among three Strykers, down a squad, and certainly a little demoralized.

Still, no more bombs had gone off after the initial ones, and their road march had proceeded without incident. Thorough searches of every vehicle had turned up nothing. Most of the officers were convinced that the bombs in question had been cleverly disguised as Stryker parts.

Hassa and Appleman were on the intercom, discussing two civilian choppers that for some reason had been allowed to circle overhead, when Appleman suddenly broke off and said, "All right, Sergeant. We're here. Get ready!"

The Stryker rumbled to a halt, the ramp lowered, and Rakken and his men charged outside, onto the street, then up and onto the sidewalk—

Where they were suddenly accosted by their company commander, Captain Chuck Welch, who was joined by a group of five civilians, two women, three men, all middle-aged and being fitted into body armor by two vehicle gunners from the master sergeant's platoon. They each carried a heavy backpack.

"Sergeant Rakken, these folks have just put down and it's your job to get them up and into that tower."

"Yes, sir." Rakken's confused expression was hard to conceal. "But sir, they know we're coming. Power's been cut. No elevators. Got like eight hundred stairs to climb. They'll probably gas us, drop grenades, and—"

"You need to get them up top. Period. Do you read me, Sergeant?"

"Yes, sir."

"We're putting snipers in the building next door, see if we can take some of them out from there, lob some flash bangs and gas inside the deck. We're going for a surgical removal here with minimal damage to the tower itself. Let me repeat: minimal damage. They've made that clear."

Rakken pursed his lips, gestured the captain away from the civilians. "Sir, what's going on?"

The captain sighed. "I got orders to get these folks

up top and not destroy this beautiful landmark. I don't know any more than you right now. Off the record? Take a look at these people. Geeks with backpacks, heading up into a tower heavily defended by Russians. Think they might be looking for something?"

Rakken was no rocket scientist, but it didn't take him more than a few seconds to blurt out the word: "Nukes?"

Captain Welch gave him an ominous look. "They were circling overhead for thirty minutes before they put down. And they got carte blanche wherever they go. I asked for ID. They said they don't have to show us anything. There was a JSF XO here to vouch for them."

"Damn."

"Good news is I'm issuing all of you MOPP 4 suits and Cross Coms, with access to a pair of small recon drones we'll fly up each stairwell. They'll walk point as you go up."

"Nice."

"Get your men over there, get on those masks and protective suits, and finish gearing up."

"Yes, sir."

Captain Welch thrust out his hand. "Good luck, Sergeant."

Rakken shook hands, then his gaze swept up the tower, toward the top, reaching the impossibly high observation deck. He stood there a few seconds more, forgetting to breathe.

Everything about this said: get those people up there, but you are expendable.

Rakken had never felt more uncertain about an operation. But he couldn't show that. "All right, Spartan team! Here's what's happening . . ."

"Stay behind me!" shouted McAllen.

"No, I see one right there," cried Halverson. She knew that the next time that Spetsnaz troop behind the tree rolled out, she'd have him.

And she wasn't going to let Mr. Macho Marine rob her of a little payback.

"Major, get your butt back here! We didn't come this far to lose you now!"

The Russian appeared, raised his rifle, and Halverson, who was armed with McAllen's pistol, fired two shots, striking the Russian in the left cheek. He slumped. She ran—

Right back behind McAllen's position.

"Jesus, lady!" he cried.

"I ain't no lady," she shouted back. "Not today!" She dropped down at his side and said, "Two squads. I saw a few of them shifting to our flank."

"I know," the sergeant said. Next to McAllen sat Pravota, who'd been gagged since he'd been screaming to the Russians after they'd fired their first shot.

The rest of the Marines were out there, somewhere behind them, engaging more of the Russians. They must have been spotted by one of the chopper crews, who'd set down and dropped off their troopers.

"Any chance of our ride coming a little early?" she asked him.

"Yeah, right. Hold on." He got on his radio, began talking to the others. Outlaw this guy, outlaw that guy. All Halverson wanted was to bail. Now. She'd drawn her blood, was ready to go home now.

If it wasn't too late.

When he finished on the radio, he glanced sidelong at her and said, "We need to make a break for it. Ready?"

She nodded.

"Let's go!"

Major Alexei Noskov stood in the hatch of the BMP-3K Rys, the reconnaissance version of the infantry vehicle equipped with a 30 mm gun and radar. His was the lead BMP of the entire battalion. And much to the chagrin of all the other officers, he'd insisted on riding at the tip of the spear.

The other officers were afraid of him, aware of his contacts in Moscow, aware of his temper.

Of his rumored insanity.

He chuckled aloud as he glanced right toward the

sun lowering on the horizon. He took in some meager warmth, then lifted his binoculars once again.

The town of High Level stood just a kilometer away, with a pathetic roadblock strewn across the highway.

Ignoring the order for communications silence he had just given, he got back on the radio and cried, "Great soldiers of the Motherland, this is Werewolf. Tonight we expand our empire! Tonight we make Canada bow to Mother Russia!"

He thrust his fist in the air, glanced back at the vehicle commander in the BMP behind him, who returned the fist.

Good man. If he hadn't, Noskov might've shot him.

His smile grew even broader.

Someone would write a history book about this battle. And Noskov would lean over that man's shoulder, making sure N O S K O V was spelled correctly.

"All right," he said into the vehicle intercom. "When we draw close to the obstacle, we will shift to the embankment and let the engineers begin breaching operations."

"But, sir?" said the driver. "I thought you wanted us to blast on through. I thought you wanted the glory."

"Yes, but as I look at that obstacle now, I see a trap, not glory. The engineers will go in first."

"Yes, sir."

"Do you think me a coward?"

"No, sir. And my girlfriend back home in St. Petersburg thanks you for this."

"I'm sure she does. Now pull over."

Noskov waved on the BMPs carrying the engineers, those great heroes and saints who would roll out a carpet stained with blood.

THIRTY-FIVE

Sergeant Nathan Vatz had left six of the Canadian hunters in charge of the roadblock team, and they had done a remarkably fine job organizing and positioning the men.

Once the Russian engineers pulled up in front of the obstacle and got out to inspect the area, they received some immediate Canadian hospitality.

From the piles of snow lining the embankment there suddenly emerged more than two hundred local boys, armed with shotguns, .22s, and grenades given to them by Vatz's team. These rural boys had about as much heart and attitude as any men on earth.

This was their land. Their country.

The grandfathers of these invading Russians had fought in Afghanistan in the 1980s, and now their descendants would be taught the same lesson—that sheer numbers and technological superiority will still not triumph over a foe trying to protect his home. Never underestimate sheer force of will and the heart and courage to win.

Vatz stared through his binoculars from his position about a half kilometer west atop the roof of a small gas station, watching as the Canadians brought down about fifty Russians, killing many of them at point-blank range. It was like medieval carnage out there.

Grenades dropped into open hatches.

Buckshot blasted into red-nosed faces.

And Vatz could almost hear "O Canada," the national anthem, playing in his ears as several BMPs lit up, smoke and flames pouring from their hatches.

But then some of the other Spetsnaz vehicles behind the engineering team made their move. The drivers floored it, rolling hard and fast to plow through the long piles of cars.

As they approached, their gun tubes flashed and boomed, sending 100 mm HE-FRAG (high explosive fragmentation) rounds at the roadblock. Pieces of flaming derby car debris sailed into the sky, taking flight like NASCAR racers forced into the wall and tumbling wildly.

The BMP gunners opened up with their machine guns, chewing into those patriotic and ferocious hunters, the drivers continuing on at top speed—doing exactly what Vatz expected they would when faced with the ambush.

And they were in for an even bigger surprise.

"You seeing this?" Beethoven asked him. "I think they got six, maybe seven BMPs! Those boys are hardcore!"

"They're doing one hell of a job, but it's a one-way trip. They knew it. You could see it in their eyes when we left. But that's what they wanted." Vatz got on the radio, told his pair of snipers posted on the rooftops nearby to lend a hand.

The cracks of thunder commenced. And for some of the Russians, God was a bullet.

Hallelujah.

Vatz checked in with Black Bear, who had taken the other half of Berserker team to the neighborhoods to join Zodiac team in flushing out the remaining snipers—no small task—and they most certainly needed more time, which was being bought by Vatz and his group of hell raisers.

The majority of the local force had been given to Vatz to delay the oncoming battalion, though a handful of residents were scattered throughout the town and remained within their homes, all at the ready.

It was, of course, imperative that Vatz's team remain alive so they could be the eyes and ears of the 10th Mountain Division as their first elements arrived. Soon. He hoped.

"All right, here we go," said Vatz, resuming his surveillance. "Suicide run."

The first few BMPs had blown a pretty deep hole in the obstacle, with only about ten cars left in their way. Two drove up side-by-side and began ramming the pile.

Impatience was a beautiful thing, and the Russians behind exhibited that perfectly. They made the obvious choice of taking the paths of least resistance on either side of the road, unwilling to wait for the first two vehicles to open the lane. Those frustrated drivers assumed that the snow couldn't be very deep, that their vehicles would make it across that terrain and they could return to the road behind the stretch of cars. Why blow through all those vehicles when you could go around them?

If the Russian engineers had survived, they would have cautioned those drivers not to veer around any enemy obstacle.

But the engineers were dead. And the recon troops inside those lead BMPs would join them for shots of vodka in the afterlife.

Two BMPs had broken off from the convoy, one heading left around the pile of cars, one heading right.

"Just like you said, Vatz," muttered Beethoven. "Just like you said."

Vatz tensed.

And almost in unison explosions lifted beneath both vehicles, destroying the forward wheels and tracks and stopping them as the clouds of fire obscured the area.

All right, the secret was out: both sides of the obstacle were mined. But this was no ordinary minefield.

The next two BMPs trundled up, started to swing wider around their burning counterparts, wider and wider, believing they could arc so far around that they would avoid the field.

Those Russian drivers didn't realize that the mines were communicating with each other and literally hopping into alternate positions to repair the first two breaches and keep the enemy within the kill zone, no matter how far they drifted off. Each mine was capable of two-sided mobility and able to maneuver up to ten meters with each hop. They were all being carefully monitored by one of the weapons sergeants on Vatz's team, who sat in the back of a pickup truck parked below, reading data on the computer.

If the enemy managed to jam the signals between each mine, the system would enter autonomous response mode and maintain minefield integrity for several more hours.

Either way, the Russians had stumbled upon a convoy's worst nightmare: a self-healing minefield that could only be breached by a continuous number of suicide runs and the unloading of a significant cache of ordnance.

ODA 888 and their crew of Canadians could never wipe out an entire Spetsnaz battalion. Not this gentle few. But they sure as hell would delay them.

"Now we've really stirred up the hornet's nest," said Beethoven.

"Yeah, that's the scary part." Vatz keyed his mike. "This is Bali, everybody get ready to move."

A series of explosions rose on both sides of the obstacle, as all of the BMPs that had moved in began rolling backward, away from the fields to fire their main guns into the ground.

Showers of rock, snow, and dirt whipped into clouds that began to blanket the entire area, the rounds themselves bursting into brilliant fireballs that flashed like heat lightning within the clouds.

Vatz sniffed and crinkled his nose over all that ordnance going off, a smell that reminded him of Moscow.

There were fifty mines on either side of the cars, and it would take those Russians a while to detonate them all, so long as the mines kept shifting to repair breaches.

Meanwhile, the entire battalion would come to a halt. While they were most likely prepared to engage in conventional minefield breaching operations by using mine plows and MICLICs (mine clearing line charges) attached to long ropes and fired over the minefield to create a breaching lane, these measures were ineffective against the team's high-tech surprise.

The Spetsnaz officers riding out there had to be mighty upset. Vatz smiled as he imagined them growing flush and cursing at their subordinates.

"All right, this is it. Time to fall back to our secondary position," he told his men. "Move out!"

"Your NEST team in Edmonton has narrowed their search to the legislature building," said General Amadou de Bankolé. "But my Enforcers Corps commanders tell me that another Spetsnaz battalion is heading up from Red Deer—and they will roll directly into the downtown area."

"I understand, General," said Becerra. "And let me emphasize that we truly appreciate all of the assistance the European Federation has provided to us in Edmonton."

"You can thank us, Mr. President. But it's not enough. My troops dropped in light. They've engaged the Spetsnaz in the city, but at least a company-size force remains in and around that legislature building. My troops are facing heavy sniper fire. Our first attempt to secure the building has already failed. Furthermore, if that battalion from Red Deer reaches the downtown area, my troops on the ground—and your NEST team—won't have a chance. They need more time, and I don't have enough assets in place."

"General, you may not like me, but I've admired you. I read one of your articles on Hannibal Barca, and I'm well aware of your reputation as a strategist. You're not telling me you can't do it, are you?"

He snorted. "Of course not."

"Then what is it you have in mind?"

Sergeant Raymond McAllen was muttering a string of epithets as he and Major Stephanie Halverson charged through the forest, working directly between Rule and Gutierrez, who were laying down fire to cover them.

He wasn't swearing over the fact that the Russians had landed and had ambushed them. He just couldn't believe that he'd forgotten about Pravota. Now they'd lost their prized POW, who was probably running off to rejoin his comrades.

They hit the snow and dropped down behind Rule and Gutierrez, and then—to McAllen's utter astonishment—the Russian pilot came shambling toward them, still gagged and cuffed.

"Captain? What the hell?" cried McAllen over all the gunfire.

"He wants to come," said Halverson.

McAllen untied the Russian's gag. Pravota coughed then asked, "Why are you sitting. We must escape."

"Are you kidding me?" asked Halverson.

Pravota shook his head. "I changed my mind." He faced McAllen. "I want vacation, like you said."

McAllen smiled. "Me, too."

Friskis came running up behind them, hit the snow.

"Contact from the helo. They're only five minutes out now. I can already hear them."

"All right, get back there. You guys cover Khaki while he guides in our bird. We'll hold them here. Pravota? You go with him."

"Yes, Sergeant," said the Russian.

As they ran off, Halverson turned to McAllen. "You got a new friend."

"And it's not you," he snapped. "Next time, you listen to me. If you die, you'll really piss me off."

"So this is all about you."

"Look, don't give me that. Just stay close. We're going to fall back another fifty yards. Ready?"

She nodded.

"Break!"

Major Alice Dennison was studying the maps of Calgary as she listened to the Special Forces company commander on the ground just north of the city issue his update.

The Stryker Brigade Team from Fort Lewis was in the city, and evacuation operations were well under way, along with the systematic targeting of at least ten Spetsnaz strongholds. Power had already been restored in several areas except downtown.

That was the good news.

The Russians had kept their word and aborted all

sorties currently under way into Canada, while their ground forces continued operations to put on a show for the Green Brigades.

Dennison was now faced with a serious request from the commander: a call for a kinetic strike on the Russian mechanized force heading south down Highway 2 from Red Deer.

Within thirty minutes that force would reach the Country Hills Boulevard overpass, then roll right toward the downtown area. The SEALs and Special Forces already had their hands full, as did the Stryker Brigade.

She told him to stand by and took the request up to General Kennedy, who in turn wanted to discuss the matter with the president.

Within a minute, Dennison once more found herself speaking directly with Becerra.

"Hello again, Major. The general has briefed me, and I have to say I've already turned down a similar request from General Bankolé. The collateral damage is just too severe."

"I know, sir, but our people on the ground tell me they can't stop the Russians. Engineers could bring down the overpass and block the road to buy some time, but the Russians will breach fairly quickly. Our air assets won't reach the battalion in time. The Russians will already be rolling into Calgary, and if you're worried about collateral damage, well . . ."

"Where are those Russian forces now?"

Dennison went over to the touch-screen map table, tapped the appropriate commands, then sent the map's images to the president as she brought up real-time streaming video from one of their drones.

The long column of vehicles lumbered steadily south, gun tubes held high like chins in defiance. In a window next to the video, the computer created a sophisticated graphic showing the convoy's estimated path and probable attack plan, dotted lines flashing red.

"As you can see, sir, they're rolling down Highway 2 right now, but the surrounding terrain is mostly slight hills and extremely rural along this eighty-seven-mile stretch. Now is the time to strike, when collateral damage will be at a minimum."

"General Kennedy?" called Becerra.

Dennison shifted back to her station, where the screen had split between the general and the president. "Sir, I concur with the major," said Kennedy. "We should take out those ground elements before they near the overpass."

"Very well. General, tell those platform commanders to stand by for my order to launch."

"Yes, sir."

The president regarded Dennison with a polite nod. "Excellent work, Major."

"Thank you, sir."

"And Major, I'd like to speak to you after the strike.

I have new information that I'd like you to share with Colonel Doletskaya."

"You do?"

"Yes, and I'm curious to see his reaction."

"All right, then."

He nodded, and the screen abruptly switched to the call log report.

Dennison leaned back in her chair, wondering what the new information was. Deep down it excited her, and she hated herself for that.

Because the excitement wasn't professional.

She would get a chance to see him again.

THIRTY-SIX

After sinking the Russian task force, Captain Jonathan Andreas had taken the *Florida* to the Dolphin and Union Strait, where he and his crew had continued to patrol silently and swiftly, listening with all their electronic ears for ships coming through the choke point.

They had poked their nose up every two hours to receive text messages from COMPACFLT—

And their most recent one sent Andreas's pulse bounding. He had even taken the risk to call back Admiral Stanton. That conversation had been interesting—to say the least.

They now had orders to return to Coronation Gulf.

"Are you going to tell me, sir, or keep me in suspense?" asked the XO as he stood in Andreas's quarters.

"Have a look." Andreas was seated at his desk, where on his computer he had pulled up some photos and schematics of High Level Bridge in Edmonton—not to be confused with the small town of High Level much farther north of that city.

The bridge spanned the North Saskatchewan River and was located next to the Legislative Assembly of Alberta. In the summer months, a waterfall created by artist Peter Lewis dropped one hundred and fifty feet off the side of the bridge, casting mist and rainbows across the waves. It was a beautiful piece of architecture and a significant landmark in Edmonton.

"High Level Bridge," said the XO with recognition. "I've actually driven over that."

"Yes, and it seems a large Russian ground force is looking for the same experience."

"Oh no."

"Oh yes. And you know what they want us to do."

"They can't be serious. What about collateral damage, aren't they worried about—"

"The Euros asked for a kinetic strike."

"That would take out the surrounding buildings—including the legislature. Couldn't engineers rig the bridge?"

"I'm told that was the first plan, but they realized they can't get it done in time."

"I see."

"So we're going to deny the enemy that avenue of approach, but we'll need to do it like surgeons. If we're successful, Enforcers Corps troops on the ground will continue the delaying operation. I get the impression from the admiral that something even bigger is going on down there and that it's imperative we do our part."

"Well, he can count on us, sir."

"My words exactly. So we're under way for the Gulf. And XO, the second we're in our firing position, I aim to let our Tomahawks fly and destroy that target."

The XO nodded. "The crew will happily oblige, sir."

In 1703, Peter the Great laid the cornerstone of the fortress he named St. Petersburg, in honor of the guardian of the gate of heaven. He later built a shipyard across the Neva River from the fortress.

In 2015, *Pyotr Alexeyevich Romanov,* a Project 955 Borei-class submarine was launched to honor the great tsar.

Five years later, Captain Second Rank Mikhail A. Kolosov was given command of that sub. Kolosov was thirty-nine, never married, and known by his colleagues as a pensive loner. He was a graduate of the Tikhookeansky Naval Acadamy and the Paldiski nuclear submarine training center.

His first assignment was as communications officer

on a diesel-electric Foxtrot class. Next he was an engineering officer aboard the last remaining Alpha nuclear attack sub. He later served four years as XO onboard a Typhoon-class SSBN until it was sold to the Chinese.

Despite eighteen years in submarines, Kolosov was still the youngest officer to be given command of the *Romanov*, and he was now on the mission of a lifetime.

Just two days previously, the *Romanov* had slipped her moorings at Severodvinsk's Sevmash shipyard, transited the Neva River, and disappeared under the polar ice. Kolosov knew that JSF spy satellites had photographed *Romanov*'s empty berth and that her movement had triggered a worldwide alert.

Now they were about to pass through the Dolphin and Union Strait, bound for the Coronation Gulf, utilizing their shaftless propulsors called RDT—rim-driven thrusters. The super quiet, all-electric *Romanov* did not require noisy main reduction gears to convert high-speed main turbine rotation into low-speed propeller shaft rotation, and Kolosov was certain that he and his crew of 110 would pass unnoticed into the Gulf, carrying their full complement of twelve R-30 Bulava (SS-NX-30) ballistic missiles.

Kolosov reached into his breast pocket and removed the picture of Dimitri. He stared at it a moment, then rubbed the back for good luck, a ritual he had performed countless times. His older brother, twelve years his senior, had died back in the mid-nineties.

Dimitri had been working on the clean-up of the 70 MWe and 90 MWe pressurized-water training reactors in Paldiski, Estonia, and had suffered radiation poisoning while constructing the two-story concrete sarcophagus that now encased the two reactors. Officials and administrators had been grossly negligent, and Kolosov had lost his brother because of them. Dimitri's death was a devastating blow to the family, one from which his parents had never recovered. They had gone to their own graves grieving his loss.

Kolosov returned the photo to his pocket and regarded his executive officer.

"It won't be long now, sir," said the younger man. "Today will be a great day for the Motherland."

Kolosov averted his gaze. "Yes, comrade."

Sergeant Marc Rakken and his team moved up the Calgary Tower stairwell, climbing farther into the uncertain darkness. The Spetsnaz troops had gassed the entire stairwell but to no avail. Rakken and his squad were masked up and determined. Another squad was coming up behind his, with two more in the other stairwell.

The staircase seemed to go on forever, the teams' lights shining up until they seemed to run out, beams clogged with the still-lingering gas.

Every man on Rakken's squad was now equipped with a concave-shaped Ferrofluid shield behind which they could duck in the event of a grenade being tossed into the stairwell. The shields also protected them from incoming rifle and rocket fire, though a significant explosion's concussion would send them tumbling back down the stairs. If the blast didn't kill them, the fall might.

Real-time video from the drone showed two heavily armed Spetsnaz troops posted on the landing outside the main door to the observation deck. Both were staring down into the stairwell with digital binoculars pressed to their masks. They resembled darkly clad aliens, armored and deadly. A third troop appeared and reached into a satchel.

"Grenade!" one of Rakken's men cried over the radio.

Rakken already had an image from his point man's helmet camera. The grenade had been dropped at an angle intended for their landing, but it flew wide, and plummeted toward the very bottom—

Two seconds later it exploded, the staircase and railings reverberating.

"Sparta Team, they still can't get a decent angle on us. Let's pick up the pace!" Rakken cried.

However, every man on his rifle squad was already breathless, including himself.

And they were only halfway up the tower.

"Incoming, shields up!" yelled Rakken's point man.

Dozens of rounds began pinging and ricocheting down at them, and Rakken crouched down behind his shield, feeling the vibration of several impacts as the shield's liquid outer layer grew hard, absorbed the blow, then returned to its fluid state. The Russians were simply delaying them now, and Rakken wouldn't stand for that.

"Sparta Team, I don't care about that fire! Move out!"

Not two heartbeats after Rakken gave the order, the entire tower began to shake, as though from some massive earthquake.

"Sergeant!" cried one of Rakken's team leaders. "What the hell is that?"

Major Alice Dennison was riveted to her monitors. She had just watched the Rods from God platform commanders line up for their shot. Then the rocket-and-fin-equipped tungsten rod had streaked away from the cylindrical platform, its engine glowing as it reached a speed of nearly 36,000 feet per second—about as fast as a meteor until retro rockets kicked in to prevent it from burning up. The rod was nearly twenty feet long, one foot in diameter, and its heat-shielded nose cone had grown cherry red as it had vanished into the atmosphere.

The rod had all the destructive effects of an earth-penetrating nuclear weapon without all of the radioactive fallout. It relied upon kinetic energy to destroy everything in its path.

Dennison had views from several cameras on the ground when the rod slammed into Highway 2, directly in the middle of that long convoy of Russian vehicles.

And now a swelling sphere of destruction spread from the impact site, the ground heaving up in great torrents, as though a billion subterranean explosions were going off in succession, chutes of fire and smoke lifting hundreds of feet into the air. The kill zone continued to spread, vehicles instantly pulverized by the unstoppable force.

She could only imagine what it must feel like on the ground, commanders popping out of their hatches, only to look up as the sky turned black. A breath later, they were incinerated or torn apart or buried under tons of dirt.

Dennison wasn't sure what the quake would measure on the Richter scale, but the entire province would feel some kind of effect.

It was hypnotizing to watch, even though she'd seen kinetic strikes before. Every one was a little different, all awe-inspiring and even a little sad. No one on the ground had even a remote chance of survival.

Their ride home was nothing fancy: just a good old HH-60G Pave Hawk, which in truth was a highly modified Black Hawk whose primary mission was to conduct combat search-and-rescue operations into hostile environments.

Well, Sergeant Raymond McAllen mused, his current situation fit quite nicely into the air crew's mission parameters.

Khaki had assisted the two pilots, one flight engineer, and one gunner into putting down in a clearing about five hundred yards south of their position; at the moment, McAllen, Halverson, and Pravota were charging toward the waiting bird, now less than a hundred yards away.

Rule and Gutierrez ran past them to provide a final few salvos of covering fire, and McAllen forced Halverson and Pravota to run ahead of him, placing himself between them and the incoming fire.

He'd read it a hundred times in the biographies of other Marines, had experienced it himself, and now, at this very moment, he knew it would hit him.

When you were just seconds away from safety, those last few seconds were the hardest.

You saw yourself getting shot at the last moment.

Saw yourself dying just as you were about to be saved.

Many combatants said they were never more scared than in the moment they were about to be picked up.

McAllen's group cleared the forest, and Halverson and Pravota made a last mad dash for the waiting chopper, rotor whomping, engine thrumming, snow blowing hard. The gunner was at the ready near the open bay door, pivoting his .50 caliber, hungry for kills.

Halverson pulled ahead of Pravota, then she suddenly slipped and hit the ground. The Russian stopped and, though still handcuffed, tried to offer help. But Halverson got back up on her own and together they made the final twenty-yard leg and were helped inside by the flight engineer.

"Outlaw Team, this is Outlaw One. Everybody fall back to the pickup site. Package is loaded. Say again, fall back now." McAllen turned and dropped onto his gut. Between him and the chopper's gunner, they had good coverage of the tree line.

Palladino and Szymanski came bursting from the forest first, then came Friskis and Gutierrez. Khaki was already onboard the chopper.

"Outlaw Two, this is Outlaw One," McAllen called. "Everybody's loaded up. Come on, buddy, let's go."

But there was no answer from Sergeant Rule.

McAllen tried again. Then he cursed, rose, and charged back toward the tree line.

THIRTY-SEVEN

Sergeant Raymond McAllen spotted his assistant team leader lying prone beside a tree, his head low.

He wasn't moving.

But suddenly McAllen's attention was torn away to the trees, where several troops were darting from trunk to trunk—moving in. Gunfire immediately sounded, and McAllen crouched and charged for Rule's position.

He took a flying leap and crashed into the snow just as Rule's rifle boomed.

"Sergeant?"

Rule regarded him. "They're moving up!"

"I ordered everyone to fall back."

"I didn't hear that." The Sergeant banged on the headset fitted below his helmet.

"Let's go!"

Rule fished out a grenade, pulled the pin, hurled it at the oncoming troops, then burst to his feet.

He and McAllen charged back through the forest, leaving behind an onslaught of fresh fire from the Russians.

The grenade exploded with a satisfying boom, just as the two rounded a pair of trees and spotted the chopper ahead, eclipsed by the last few pines.

Something pinged off McAllen's helmet, then a few more pings struck his back. Aw, hell, he was taking fire.

Then a pair of sharp stings woke in his legs. He took three more steps, the pain growing unbearable.

He collapsed to his belly as Rule kept on running.

What they thought had been an earthquake turned out to be a successful kinetic strike on the Russians coming down from Red Deer, and Rakken used that good news to boost the morale of his men in the stairwell. And God knew they needed a boost.

They had about two hundred more steps to climb, and if Sergeant Marc Rakken's legs were any indication of how the others felt, then they all could hardly stand.

But they forged on, with the Russians up top sending down bursts of fire and the occasional grenade. They also continued lobbing smoke to obscure the entire stairwell. If they had any rockets, they were waiting until Rakken's men got closer to use them.

So up they went, stair after stair, in the smoke-filled darkness, only the sounds of the radio and their own breathing now filling their ears.

The company commander informed them that snipers in the building across the street were attempting to pick off any troops they spotted on the observation deck, but thus far those Russians had kept out of sight.

And twice Rakken had attempted to gain information from one of the five civilians ascending just behind them, a bearded, middle-aged man with the call sign "Nimrod One."

"You just get us in there, Sergeant, and we'll do the rest," the man had said.

"I can help you more if I know what your job is."

"I think you'll figure it out pretty quickly once we're up top."

"Well, I have my ideas."

"I'm sure they're not too far off base. Now, if you don't mind?"

Rakken almost wished this were the simple destruction of a Spetsnaz observation post. Then again, what kind of bragging rights would that earn him?

"Grenades!" shouted his point man. "Two more! Three!"

They all dropped down behind their shields as the explosions resounded—

And then, as the smoke cleared, Rakken's men reported that a four-meter section of the staircase had been destroyed and that they would need the ropes to ascend to the next landing.

Delays, delays, more delays. That's what the Russians wanted. The teams in the other stairwell weren't faring much better, according to reports.

"All right, people, let's rig this up and get climbing!"

As Rule ran toward the Pave Hawk, he couldn't understand why Gutierrez and Szymanski were waving their hands and pointing. He tried his radio, but it was dead: either the battery was gone or he'd damaged it out there.

But it only took another pair of seconds for him to realize that they were indicating to the trees behind him. He stole a look back and saw McAllen lying in the snow.

He turned around, raced toward the sergeant, even as the chopper's door gunner opened up on the trees to give him some covering fire.

McAllen pushed up to his hands and knees, trying to stand, as Rule opened up with his own rifle, hosing down a pair of troops who burst from behind a trunk to confront him.

But two rounds struck Rule's armored chest, knocking him backward. He lost his footing, fell on his rump. He got up, started once more toward the sergeant, the .50 caliber still churning behind him, ripping up bark and limbs ahead.

It dawned on Rule that the sergeant wouldn't be lying there, shot up, if it weren't for him and his damned busted radio.

So he poured every ounce of energy he had left into his legs. He reached the sergeant, dropped, returned more fire as rounds stitched lines in the snow just a meter parallel to them.

"Rule, you idiot," gasped McAllen.

"I know," he said. "Ready?" He rolled the sergeant over and hoisted him up over his back, legs buckling under the man's considerable weight.

He walked three steps and collapsed.

Meanwhile, Szymanski, Palladino, and Gutierrez had hopped back out of the chopper, dropped, and were providing more covering fire.

"You're going to kill me if they don't," said McAllen. "Drag me!"

"Thought a carry would be faster." Rule stood, came behind McAllen, grabbed his pack's straps and began sliding him over the snow.

A sudden *thud* on his chest sent Rule back to the snow, his hands snapping off the pack. He groaned in pain.

"Rule?"

"Yeah." He gasped. "Got my armor. Damn I'm going to be sore tomorrow."

He returned to dragging the sergeant, whose legs were leaving a blood trail in the snow.

"Hey, Rule, I didn't tell you this before, but you cast a *big* shadow, Marine. A *big* shadow."

"You're just saying that so I drag your shot-up butt out of here."

"That, too."

Even as Rule continued hauling the sergeant forward, McAllen lifted his rifle and fired several bursts.

After a few more tugs, Rule suddenly felt the sergeant grow lighter as Gutierrez joined him. Within a handful of seconds they had McAllen into the bay, where Gutierrez immediately cut off the sergeant's pants legs and got to work.

Rule shoved himself into the back of the Pave Hawk as the chopper roared up and away, leaving the Russians on the ground firing wildly at them as they cleared the trees, their muzzles now winking in the half-light of dusk.

"How is he?" he shouted to Gutierrez.

The medic gave him a look: *Not now. I'm busy.*

McAllen gestured for Rule to come close so he could shout in his ear. "You did good. I give you a B plus."

Rule rolled his eyes. "Thanks!"

"Make your depth one-five-zero feet," ordered Commander Jonathan Andreas.

"Make my depth one-five-zero feet, aye," repeated the officer of the deck.

It was all business in the *Florida*'s control room, though Andreas noted a hint of excitement in the OOD's tone. They were in launch position in the Coronation Gulf and about to punch their Tomahawk land attack missiles out of their vertical launch system tubes.

Despite the outbreak of war, Andreas assumed that most members of his crew had never live-fired those missiles; they had only practiced simulations. Andreas recalled when he could only launch while at periscope depth, but design improvements now made it possible to fire from the safety of 150 feet.

He reviewed the sequence in his head: The tube door would open, the gas generator would fire up to boil the water pocket inside. The water would flash to steam, forcing a pressure pulse to the bottom of the tube. The pressure pulse would then push the missile up through its protective membrane enveloped in a steam bubble, and eject the bird completely clear of the surface.

Then, as the Tomahawk cleared the surface, the first stage would ignite, lifting the bird to three thousand feet.

At its apex, the first-stage would jettison and the missile would plummet into free fall, spinning the missile's jet engine on the way down. The increasing flight speed would turn the compressor and build up pressure and heat in the combustion chamber. Fuel would be injected, and the missile's engine would then be up and running.

Andreas could see it all in his head.

Now it was time to make it happen. He gave the firing order, and the entire submarine rumbled.

Once the first missile left the sub, Andreas lifted his voice and said, "Watch your trim, Officer of the Deck. Keep your eye on the bubble."

The *Florida* had to adjust her buoyancy and trim to compensate for the sudden loss of weight after each missile left the sub.

The remaining five Tomahawks, spaced three minutes apart, would follow the first down a bearing of one-seven-eight degrees while cruising at subsonic speed roughly fifty feet above the surface.

The one-hour, forty-nine-minute, thousand-mile flight included a pre-programmed midpoint correction as each Tomahawk passed over Wild Buffalo National Park.

Packed into each missile's computer memory were final destination landmarks: pictures of the Alberta Legislative Assembly building, the exact interchange point where 97th Avenue NW, 109th Street NW, and 110th Street NW converged and provided sole access to High Level Bridge.

Onboard TV cameras would accurately identify the final orienting landmarks as each missile plummeted toward the Saskatchewan River and the High Level Bridge below.

After the last missile blasted away, Andreas congratulated the crew, then he gave the order to head back to the Dolphin and Union Strait to continue their patrol, even as they monitored the missiles' progress.

Just one hour into that journey, the sternplanesman cried, "Jam dive, sternplanes!"

The sternplanes were horizontal rudders, or diving planes, extending from each side of the submarine near the stern. They had lost hydraulic pressure and had slammed into the dive position, where they would remain locked until hydraulic pressure could be restored and control reasserted.

With miles and miles of steam, electrical, and hydraulic lines running up, down, and through bulkheads, it was just a question of time before something broke, got damaged, wore out, or operator error occurred.

Now the *Florida* was headed straight toward crush depth.

"All back full!" yelled the OOD and Andreas in unison.

The bow planesman jerked his joystick to full rise, trying to counteract the effects of the sternplanes.

"Passing one thousand feet, thirty-one degrees down bubble," reported the chief of the watch, his hands hovering over the controls to blow the forward main ballast tanks.

The sternplanesman immediately switched to auxiliary hydraulics and pulled back on the sternplanes. Nothing.

"Passing twelve hundred feet, forty degrees down bubble, sir," cried the chief of the watch.

The sternplanesman switched to emergency hydraulics, pulled up, when suddenly the sonar operator lifted his voice:

"Torpedo in the water, incoming torpedo bearing three-two-zero! WLY-1 classification—a Shkval—range thirty thousand yards, speed two hundred knots!"

Sergeant Nathan Vatz and his men had shifted farther back into the town to their secondary positions along the rooftops of some local businesses on 97th Street, parallel to the highway.

For the past hour the Russians had been pounding the hell out of the obstacle, and Vatz figured they'd destroy the remaining mines within thirty minutes, maybe less.

Once that happened, Berserker and Zodiac teams could make a last stand or withdraw and live to fight another day.

Because if they didn't withdraw, they would eventually exhaust all ammo and be overrun. Vatz felt sure those Spetsnaz forces would not take them prisoner.

In fact, Russian political officers might order the public execution of the captured ODA teams to keep High Level's civilian survivors fully intimidated and in line.

Moreover, if watching a group of military men forced to their knees and shot in the head wasn't enough, they'd shoot a few civilians, as well as threaten the use of biological and chemical weapons.

"Black Bear, this is Bali, over."

"Go ahead, Bali."

He gave the assistant detachment commander a SITREP regarding the obstacle, then added, "What's the status of the Tenth, over?"

But before Vatz could get a reply, the channel went dead. Damn it. The Russians were jamming again.

"Hey, look!" cried Beethoven, pointing up at the northern sky. A dozen or more Ka-29s were inbound, flying in an arrowhead formation.

The lead chopper, along with one other, pulled ahead, swooped down, and began unloading rockets on the remaining cars in the obstacle, blasting a clear lane through the burning wall.

Even as the choppers peeled off, one on either side, the first few BMPs broke through.

The weapons sergeant on Vatz's team, who was now posted atop a machine shop two buildings down, cut loose with the team's last Javelin.

With a powerful *whoosh*, the missile streaked skyward, came down, homing in on the lead BMP, then struck it perfectly, blasting apart the vehicle and sending pieces slamming into the BMP behind it, killing the vehicle commander who'd been standing in his hatch.

Vatz rose, jogged to the edge of the roof, and gave the signal to fall back. The signal was passed on to the other four men as Vatz and Beethoven got moving.

Once on the ground, they piled into their pickup truck, with Vatz at the wheel, Beethoven riding shotgun.

"Are we headed to a third fallback position?" asked the medic.

"I'm not sure yet."

"We're low on ammo. We can't stay."

"Black Bear figured the Tenth would be here by now. We'll have to wait right here till those choppers fly by, then I'll get us to the south side of town, find some cover there. And after that, well—"

"This is it. We won't make it out of here. Not with them dropping troops on the ground now."

Vatz didn't respond.

Part of him was getting awfully depressed, whispering like the Reaper in his ear, *It's about time you died. You're long overdue.*

He shoved his head out the open window, lifted his binoculars, and watched the helos streak overhead, descending hard and fast.

Before darkness fully settled, High Level would belong to the Russians.

THIRTY-EIGHT

Back inside Calgary Tower, Sergeant Marc Rakken sent two of his men forward, told them to use their rifles' attached grenade launchers.

He'd been ordered to cause minimal damage to the tower. Well, tell that to the troops up there, four on the top landing now, dishing out a steady stream of rifle fire punctuated with the occasional smoke and fragmentation grenade. The Russians had already destroyed several landings that the team had strung ropes across.

Another explosion rocked the stairwell, and suddenly three of Rakken's men tumbled by, having been blown off the stairs. Two had probably been killed by the explosion, but a third had keyed his mike as he fell, screaming at the top of his lungs as he plummeted to his death.

"Sergeant, we can't go on," cried one of his grenadiers.

Rakken, his face covered in sweat now, the MOPP gear practically suffocating him even as it protected him, could stand no more. "Sparta Team!" he barked loudly. "Follow me. We're going in!"

With the civilian geeks huddling behind their shields to the rear, Rakken pushed past the others and pounded up the stairs, firing steadily until he neared the final landing.

All four Spetsnaz troops were positioned there; reacting instinctively, Rakken pumped off a grenade from his rifle's launcher.

Three, two . . .

He hit the deck as the burst rumbled hard through the concrete and steel above.

Before the smoke cleared, he was back to his feet, thundering up to find two of the troops blown apart, a third missing his legs, the fourth lying on his back, half his torso gone. He groaned and reached out to Rakken for help.

Rakken answered his request with a bullet.

"Sparta Team, clear up here, come on up." He checked the door leading into the observation deck and souvenir shop: locked, of course.

He called up his engineer to blow the door. As the charges were being set, he returned to the civilians, told the guy known as Nimrod One that they would need to clear the observation deck first before he could allow them to enter. The guy understood but urged Rakken to hurry.

After issuing another SITREP to Captain Welch, Rakken checked in with the engineer: good to go.

"Fire in the hole," warned Rakken.

With an appreciable bang, the C-4 blew the door from its hinges, and as the gray smoke rose, Rakken and his men charged onto the deck, a huge, circular-shaped room with panoramic windows offering a wide view of the city lights. The souvenir shop was in the middle, obscuring some view.

Two Spetsnaz troops burst from the shop, firing at Rakken and his men as they fanned out.

Rakken returned fire as he dropped to his gut and propped himself up on his elbows.

One of his men shrieked in agony. Then another. Yet there were no sounds of gunfire.

Rakken reached down to the belt at his waist, withdrew his Blackhawk Gladius, activated the thumb switch. The brilliant light pushed back into the shadows to find an unmasked Spetsnaz troop brandishing a large combat knife.

He was slipping up behind one of Rakken's men.

Rakken screamed out—

But the knife came down into the back of the man's neck. His man shrieked and fell, either dead or incapacitated.

Rakken bolted to his feet, one hand detaching his

own mask as he charged along the windows, firing and dropping the guy. Then he whirled at the sound of more gunfire on the other side of the deck.

He made a mad dash along the windows, spotted three more Russians firing ahead at his men.

Dropping once more onto his belly, he used the laser designator in his helmet to target the exposed necks of each man and delivered one, two, three shots.

Blood and brain matter flew, and two men collapsed, but he'd missed the third. That troop turned back.

Just as Rakken was about to fire again, a metallic clang caught his ears.

He glanced to his right.

A grenade hit the floor and rolled toward him.

Just beyond it, the second team was moving in, along with the civilians, who were running toward him.

"Get back!"

He threw himself on the grenade.

Just as it went off.

Sergeant Nathan Vatz and his men raced in the truck down 97th Street, unaware that one of the Ka-29s had wheeled around until a pair of rockets tore into the asphalt behind them and exploded.

The two operators seated back there leapt over the side, just as a wall of flames filled the pickup truck's rear window.

Then, as the truck reached the next corner, Vatz hung a sharp left turn—

Just as another rocket hit, blasting them up onto two wheels.

Beethoven shouted something but Vatz's ears were still ringing from the explosion.

They hung there for a million-year second until the truck slammed hard onto the passenger's side, safety glass shattering. They slid up onto the sidewalk, caromed off a building, then sideswiped a light pole before coming to a screeching halt, engine still running, glass still tumbling, flames crackling from somewhere outside.

As smoke began to fill the cabin, Vatz coughed and unbuckled. He called out to Beethoven, whose head was bleeding but who was conscious.

The two operators in the back of the crew cabin were already hauling themselves outside, where they took near-instant machine gun fire from the helo as it swooped down again.

Vatz figured that on the next pass the pilot would launch rockets again. He and Beethoven had only seconds to get out of there.

Holding his breath, he forced open the door and climbed out onto the crew cabin door. He gave Beethoven a hand, hoisting the medic up and out. They jumped down to the sidewalk—

Just as the chopper finished its turn and began to descend directly toward them.

Vatz glanced over at Beethoven.

They both knew there was no time to run. The helo would launch rockets, and their lives would be over in a heartbeat.

Yet in that second, in that shared look, they knew what they had to do. If they were going to die, it wouldn't be running; it would be defying the enemy until the end.

So, without a word, they crouched down and began firing at the chopper, as did the rest of his team—if only to rage against the enemy.

And as his clip was about to empty, Vatz closed his eyes, thought of Zack back in that alley. *Get ready to buy me a beer, my friend. I'm coming home.*

Commander Jonathan Andreas drew in a long breath as tension mounted in the *Florida*'s control room.

The VA-111 Shkval racing toward them was a solid rocket torpedo that generated a gas cavity, which gave it great speed but precluded a guidance system. Its eight-mile short range classified it as a last-ditch weapon and earned it the title of revenge weapon. The torpedo was most often fired as a "snap shot" back down the bearing of an incoming enemy's torpedo.

At the moment, Andreas assumed that the commander who had ordered its launch was as surprised to discover him as he was to discover the Shkval.

"Sonar, go active, single ping on bearing three-two-zero!" he ordered.

"Torpedo has rapid right-bearing drift, headed across our bow," reported the sonar operator.

"Passing fifteen hundred feet, Captain," said the chief of the watch, making direct eye contact with Andreas.

The sonar operator chimed in again. "Sonar contact, bearing three-two-four, range thirty-five thousand yards, designate contact Sierra One, sir."

"Emergency blow main ballast—" cried the officer of the deck.

"Belay that!" barked Andreas. "Check the bubble. The bow's coming up. The planesman has control. Ahead two thirds. Keep water moving across the control surfaces, make your depth eighteen hundred feet."

"All ahead two thirds, make my depth eighteen hundred feet, aye, sir," repeated the OOD. "What about that torpedo, sir?"

"He launched an out-of-range snap shot when he heard our emergency backdown. We were sinking like a rock with virtually no forward motion. A two-hundred-knot Shkval can't be guided. If he cranked in any lead angle, he aimed where we aren't."

"Let's hope his aim continues to be that poor, sir."

"I think it will." Andreas regarded the sonar operator. "Talk to me. Anything from Sierra One?"

"Nothing on broadband or narrowband, sir," replied the operator.

"Engineering, get somebody on that hydraulic glitch. I want a healthy sub when we attack this guy." Andreas silently scanned the control room, gauging the tension level once more as the hull groaned under the pressure. "All right, consider this a moment to regroup—and remember, if God didn't want us down here at eighteen hundred feet *she* wouldn't have given us HY-100 steel."

He got one or two chuckles and observed some easing of posture among the men manning the various stations.

After a few more breaths, he added, "Now gentlemen, we might've found that missing Borei, the *Romanov*, and I have every intention of taking her out." Andreas checked his display. "Flood tubes one and four, equalize the pressure, power up both units, and open muzzle doors."

The *Florida* could still operate at virtually any depth with two Mark 48 ADCAP torpedoes powered up and two muzzle doors open.

"Come left to three-two-zero," he ordered. "We'll close on datum and see what sonar can sniff out."

He had ordered them to the target's last known location. Now *they* were on the hunt.

Vatz snapped open his eyes at the sound of a terrific boom, followed by a dozen other pops and cracks and groaning sounds, all rising above a tremendous rush of air that knocked him flat onto his back.

As the sky panned overhead and a wave of dizziness crashed over him like a twelve-foot breaker, he rolled onto his side, blinked hard, and looked up again.

The Ka-29 had burst apart and crashed into the street, long draperies of fire and smoke rising high.

Beyond it, engines booming, soared an A-10 Thunderbolt II, better known as a Warthog or just Hog, a twin-engine jet designed to provide close air support for ground troops.

A second A-10 followed closely on the first one's wing, and then, off to Vatz's left, he spotted a half dozen Apache attack helicopters, along with several Chinooks, V-22 Ospreys, and the redesigned RAH-66 Comanche recon/attack helicopters.

Beethoven started hollering and cursing, unable to contain his emotions. "Ladies and gentlemen! The Tenth Mountain Division has arrived!"

A flicker of movement from the buildings on his left caught Vatz's eye. Down at the next intersection, a squad of Spetsnaz troops had just rounded the corner and crouched to fire.

"Troops right there!" cried Vatz.

Shots rang out; blood sprayed over the pavement as Beethoven fell, multiple wounds in his face and neck. He died quickly.

Vatz returned fire, darting behind the burning pickup truck; the rounds tracked him, thumping hard into rubber and steel. "Black Bear, this is Bali, over!"

He swore. Comm was still jammed. He slipped around the back of the truck, where he spotted three of his men holed up in another doorway. He waved them on, and they charged down the street away from the fiery wreck, the Russians moving up behind them.

Rakken flickered open his eyes. They were talking about him. He recognized the voices: medics from his platoon. He was lying on his back, staring up at the observation deck's ceiling. Flashlights panned everywhere. There was no more gunfire, only the sounds of his men.

"He won't make it, will he," said a bearded, unhelmeted civilian, leaning over Rakken.

"Shhh," ordered one of the medics. "He can still hear you. And there's always a chance. But he's not in pain. We took care of that."

Rakken's gaze came in and out of focus.

"Sergeant, if you can hear me, squeeze my hand."

The guy took Rakken's hand, and he squeezed.

"Listen to me. We wouldn't have made it in here if it weren't for you. Right now my people are trying to disarm a ten-kiloton suitcase nuke. If they fail, we're all going to die anyway. But I wanted you to know that what you did . . ." His voice cracked. "I just wanted you to know. Thank you."

Rakken managed to nod ever so slightly. He squeezed the man's hand again, just as Captain Welch knelt down beside him. "Sergeant, the chaplain's on his way. Hang in there for me. You got no permission to die."

Rakken wasn't one to disobey an order, but the intense cold creeping into his chest would not cease. He closed his eyes. The mission had been accomplished. His work here was finished.

Suddenly, all the lights snapped on in the room, causing him to open his eyes.

Was he leaving his body now? Or was he beginning to hallucinate?

"They've restored power to the cell network as well," someone shouted. "They might be trying to trigger the device that way now!"

"Get someone to shut that power down. And move it!"

Rakken wanted to sit up, see what was going on. He turned his head slightly, where the civilians were gathered around something on the floor, the nuke maybe, all working under intense, battery-operated lights.

And then, quite suddenly, the world grew dark around the edges, and he closed his eyes.

THIRTY-NINE

Viktoria Antsyforov and Green Vox were in the tiny town of Banff, just off the Trans-Canada Highway as it traversed the Banff National Park, seventy-eight miles west of Calgary. They had chosen the location to be upwind from nuclear fallout once the detonations were made.

They had checked in to The Fairmont Banff Springs, a lavish getaway nestled in the Canadian Rockies. The Fairmont was styled after a Scottish baronial castle, with ornate spires and castle-like walls. Antsyforov's time there had made her feel very much like royalty. But that time had come to an end.

Green Vox—who went by so many aliases that even Antsyforov didn't know his real name—was downstairs, checking on their ride out to the heliport.

Their sources in Edmonton and Calgary had said that the JSF and Euros had located both bombs and were attempting to dismantle them. And while she had wanted to wait the full forty-eight hours to ensure as many military casualties as possible, the JSF and Euros had moved more swiftly than she'd anticipated—meaning that Kapalkin must have tipped his hand to the Americans.

Antsyforov had already tried triggering the nukes via her Iridium satellite phone, but she couldn't believe it: the entire network was down. Impossible!

She had told her sources to pass on word to get the conventional cell phone network up and running.

Vox returned to the room. "They're waiting for us. Is it done?"

"The entire Iridium network is down. I have to try my cell."

"No power."

"They're taking care of that."

"And if they don't?"

"They already have," she said, studying her cell phone. "My call to Calgary is going through right now." Once she heard the familiar hum, she need only dial two numbers: 5 9.

Confirmation that the weapon was armed to detonate in twenty seconds would come as three beeps.

But the humming continued.

She hit the numbers again. And again.

She cursed.

"I told you this would happen," Vox cried.

"No!"

"Yes! They've already dismantled the nuke because you let your ego get in the way. You didn't need to contact Kapalkin and Izotov."

"After all those years, I deserved that much," she said through her teeth.

"Well, now what? Do you really believe your brother can come through for us?"

"He will."

"Are you ever going to tell me who he is? What the plan is now? We're in this together."

She cocked a well-tweezed brow. "We all have secrets."

Vox grabbed her by the throat, shoved her up against the wall. "You stupid . . ."

He didn't finish. Instead, he came in for a violent kiss, and she offered no resistance.

When he finally pulled back, his voice lowered to warning depths. "Tell me what's happening."

"If you only knew . . ."

"Tell me, otherwise—"

"What?" She glared at him. "We just made love. Now you're threatening me?"

"You have no idea how much money is at stake."

She snorted. "Oh, yes I do. This will happen—one way or the other."

"We're not leaving until you talk."

"All right. You want to know it all, huh? It doesn't

matter anymore. Listen closely. My brother is commander of the *Romanov*. He *will* launch a salvo of Bulava missiles. They'll fly low, and the JSF's missile shield can't stop them. It'll destroy a series of decoys while the live missiles reach their targets in Alberta."

"This has never been tried before."

"Until now."

"How did you manage this?"

"Very carefully."

"And you're so very sure."

"I am."

"And you don't care about how many innocent lives will be lost if you're right."

She smiled darkly. "I am Snegurochka. What did you expect?" She shoved him away, drew the silenced pistol tucked into her pants.

"Viktoria, what are you doing?"

"Did you *really* think I was working with you?"

His mouth fell open. "You can't be serious."

She grinned and extended her arm.

Vox's face filled with hatred. "Go ahead, kill me. Green Vox will return. He always does."

She shot him between the eyes. He dropped hard to the floor.

"Yes," she said, staring down at his body. "You always come back—and always as a man. What a pity."

* * *

After ducking down the next side street, Sergeant Nathan Vatz sent two of his operators across the street, where they kept low in a doorway, while the team's senior communications sergeant paired up with him.

They set up behind two parked cars, both so beat up that it was clear why their owners had abandoned them, and waited for the pursuing Spetsnaz troops to round the corner.

Five seconds. Ten. Twenty. They didn't come.

Vatz immediately assumed they had doubled back in an attempt to catch them from behind. Now he had two choices, neither good: he could avoid the ambush and head back to the truck—but the air support no doubt had moved on. Or they could rush ahead, try to catch the enemy by surprise, ambush the ambushers.

The decision was obvious.

He ordered the group to move out, to keep moving forward. They kept tight to the walls, were twenty yards from the corner when the Russians burst into view, just as he'd expected. All six of them.

Vatz jammed down his trigger, spraying the soldiers, as did his men.

The Russians fell back around the corner, but one spun and cut loose a last burst.

Vatz was about to order his men to drive on, but a second group of troops, four in all, appeared behind them and opened up, driving Vatz and his partner into the next doorway.

Across the street, one of Vatz's operators had taken a round in his thigh. He lay there clutching the wound, a dark stain growing on the sidewalk.

They were now cut off, with the Spetsnaz troops at both ends of the street.

Vatz had been taught that it was moments like this that separated the good team sergeants from the great ones. Despite all the stress and heightened senses, you needed to clear your head, analyze the situation, and use cunning, speed, and maneuverability to your advantage.

Calling for help was a good idea, too.

He switched to the team's channel. Maybe Murphy would allow him to get through. "Black Bear, this is Bali, over."

"Go ahead, Bali."

He sighed over the small miracle. "Check the Blue Force Tracker. I'm pinned down here with one wounded, over."

"Roger that. Cross Com's back up now. Tenth's got people on the ground. I'll send a squad or two your way, over."

"That would be nice," Vatz answered matter-of-factly. "Misery loves company. Bali, out." He turned to his commo guy. "We can't stay here."

"But they have us cut off."

"Which is why we can't stay here." He pointed over at his two men across the street. "Cover them. I saw a staircase on one building. I'm going to check it out."

"You're going alone?"

Vatz bit back a curse. "Cover them. Do it."

As Vatz jogged up the street, he realized his team-mate wasn't questioning orders but genuinely concerned about his safety.

Well, Vatz was also genuinely concerned about his safety, and it puzzled him why he wasn't drawing any fire.

Racing to the end of the building, which appeared to be some kind of factory or warehouse, he turned left, found the metal staircase leading up to some heavy machinery on the roof.

He slipped onto the stairs, controlled his breathing, and took it one step at a time.

At the top, he spotted the four Russian soldiers that had been behind them, skulking along the edge, preparing to move along the rooftop to ambush his men below.

One poorly placed step would give him away. He eased off the stairs and onto the ice-covered roof, his boots barely finding traction. He shifted over to a tall aluminum venting system, crouched down, and raised his rifle, just as footfalls rumbled on the staircase and the sounds of the battle grew louder.

"Captain, I'm picking up flow noise from Sierra One on narrowband, bearing three-three-nine," said the *Florida*'s sonar operator.

Andreas's breath grew shallow with excitement. "Where's the thermal layer?"

"Two hundred feet, sir."

"We couldn't pick up his flow noises if he wasn't below the layer with us."

"Concur, Captain."

Andreas called out to the officer of the deck. "Come right to three-three-nine, slow to one third, make your depth sixteen hundred feet."

He waited until the OOD repeated and executed his order, then switched his attention back to sonar. "What's your best guess on that flow noise source?"

"I think it's flow-induced resonance, Captain. That snap shot might've unlatched a stowage bin outside on his hull. It sounds like blowing into an empty Coke bottle. He has to hear it himself. I'm surprised he hasn't slowed down to make it go away."

Andreas squinted and thought aloud: "He knows we're still alive, but he's not sure of our status or where we are, so he's risking some noise to put distance between himself and our contact point. Then he'll slow to a crawl and acoustically vanish."

"I agree, Captain."

"Stay on him, Sonar. That's two mistakes he's made."

"Two, sir?"

"Yeah, taking a cheap panic shot at us during our emergency was his first. On the other hand, we'd most likely have missed each other if we hadn't had that jam."

Andreas had to assume that the *Romanov* would behave like the SSBN it was and try to skulk away and hide—

Because a Joint Strike Force nuclear attack sub was a Russian SSBN crew's worst nightmare.

Major Alice Dennison's monitor showed streaming video from the High Level Bridge in Edmonton, just as Spetsnaz mechanized forces were making their way over it—

And just as the Tomahawks launched from the *Florida* made impact.

As explosions flashed in a string of lights festooning the bridge's lines, Dennison nodded. A perfect strike.

Sure, the nuke there had already been deactivated, but the Euros had reported that the Russian ground force moving in was much larger than initial intel had indicated, and cutting off their main avenue of approach would now allow the Euros to better engage and delay them, until more follow-on forces arrived, or until the Russians decided to pull out.

The bridge broke apart in three distinct pieces and dropped to the river, creating tremendous waves and sending fountains high into the night sky.

And along with the bridge came the Russian vehicles, tumbling end over end, crashing into the pieces of bridge before they sank or simply splashing hard into the water.

At least a dozen more vehicles had been moving so swiftly that they couldn't stop, and like elephants herded to a cliff, they plunged over the side.

She took a long pull on her coffee cup, leaned back in her chair, and continued to watch as, in another set of windows, images came in from Calgary Tower, where wounded or killed infantrymen were being evaced away.

She'd spoken to one of the company commanders there, a man named Welch, who'd said one of his rifle squad leaders had saved the entire NEST team by throwing himself on a fragmentation grenade. Stories of men doing this in order to save their brothers in arms were common during times of war.

But that kind of bravery was not.

That solder's name was Sergeant Marc Rakken, and Dennison would make sure that he received the full recognition he deserved.

A call flashed on her screen. "Yes, General Kennedy. What can I do for you?"

FORTY

"Captain, we've got a passive range solution of twenty-six thousand yards and a computed course and speed of three-two-zero, fifteen knots, for the target," reported the *Florida*'s attack coordinator.

"Sonar's lost contact with Sierra One, Captain," said the operator. "He's definitely slowed down."

Commander Jonathan Andreas nodded. "Weps, set the unit in tube one on low speed, passive search, transit depth fifteen hundred feet. Set the unit in tube four on low speed, passive search, transit depth one thousand feet."

While the Navy called them units, Andreas still thought of the Mark 48s as torpedoes and would refer to them as such when in the company of nonmilitary friends and family.

However, it hardly mattered what they were called when one was bearing down on you.

The Russians would soon testify to that.

Andreas continued: "Gentlemen, I want to sit back here in his baffles and straddle him with our 48s. Let both units achieve ordered depth during their run-to-enable. With units one and four walking point, we'll follow behind, right down to fourteen thousand yards if he doesn't hear us. Now here's the plan . . ." Andreas paused, solidifying the tactical picture in his mind before voicing it. "I'm going to send unit four out onto his port quarter, maybe just abaft his beam, turn it toward him, then switch it to high speed, active mode. If he thinks he's under attack from the west, he'll turn east to evade and concentrate his snap shots and countermeasures toward the west—not at us. Meanwhile, unit one will be out on his starboard side, waiting. He'll never know what hit him."

The weapons officer flashed a knowing grin. "Reminds me of growing up on the sheep ranch. We had two smart border collies. One would outflank the flock, bark, and charge, then turn the flock back toward his buddy."

"Exactly," said Andreas. "Now you've got the bubble, Weps. We American cowboys and sheepherders will show these Russians how it's done."

"Yes, sir!"

* * *

Sergeant Nathan Vatz wasn't sure who was coming up the stairs behind him, but he needed to make his move. He charged across the roof, coming up to the rearmost Spetsnaz troop making his way along the edge.

Vatz covered the troop's mouth with one hand while the Caracara knife in his other hand tore through the Russian's neck and into his spinal cord. This soldier died as quickly as that one had back in Moscow. As he went down, Vatz folded up his knife, slung around his rifle, and jogged off.

The other three still hadn't noticed him. It was pitch-black up there on the roof, no power in the entire town now, and the temperature was dropping rapidly. His nose was runny and frozen, his lips growing more chapped.

He rushed up to the next guy, the drumming of helicopter rotors all over the sky now, along with the whooshing of jet engines, sporadic gunfire, and near-and-far explosions. The din fully concealed his thumping boots.

Vatz was about to dispatch the next guy with his blade when the trooper turned around, and gaped at Vatz. All Vatz could do was throw himself forward, knocking the Russian to the rooftop.

They slid across the ice, rolled, still clutching each other, then Vatz forced the man back while driving his knife into the trooper's neck.

The guy let out a scream.

The last two Russians came charging back, rifles coming to bear.

Maybe thirty feet away, they grew more distinct, two unmasked men in their late thirties or early forties loaded down with gear but shifting as agilely as bare-chested jungle fighters. These two were seasoned Spetsnaz troops.

Vatz grabbed the bleeding Russian beneath him and rolled to his left, using the troop as a shield—

As the others opened fire, riddling their squad mate with rounds, some thudding off his helmet and armor, others burrowing into his legs and neck. Vatz flinched hard, knowing it would take only one lucky round to finish him. He lay there a moment, unmoving, playing dead, as they ceased fire and came closer.

While Vatz couldn't see them, he reached out with every other sense, and just as those boots sounded close enough, he threw off the body and came up with his rifle.

They were ten feet away, firing as he did, the rounds striking his chest hard, the armor protecting him, the impacts breath-robbing.

Both Russians dropped to the roof, clutching their wounds and firing one-handed into the air.

Unsure if he'd been hit in the arms or legs, Vatz pushed himself up, checked himself, then turned toward the other side of the roof, where a half dozen silhouettes appeared:

More troops. Running toward him—

While a chopper swooped in behind them, its powerful searchlight bathing the Russians in its harsh glow.

Vatz squinted while beginning to move back. Was that an enemy helo or not?

He got a better look and shouted, "Yeah!"

Trailing the troops was, in fact, a JSF Black Hawk helicopter, its door gunners delivering the .50 caliber early bird special to the Russians below.

Two troops were cut down hard and fast.

A third threw himself behind a rectangular-shaped duct but was torn to ribbons.

Vatz broke to the left, out of those gunners' line of fire, reaching the other side of the roof, when he was nearly knocked off his feet by a Russian troop coming around another aluminum vent.

He shoved the guy back in order to bring his rifle to bear, but the wide-eyed troop reacted as quickly— grabbing him by the collar and swinging him around.

Vatz tried to wrench off the troop's hands, but the kid had a death grip, which was fitting, since their forward momentum carried them both off the roof—

And into the air.

"Captain, Sonar. Regained contact on Sierra One, bearing three-four-one, narrowband tonals, twin ship turbine generators. WLY-1 matches to a Borei class. You were right, sir. It is without a doubt the *Romanov*.

Range, twenty-five thousand yards, computed from prior *Romanov* SSTG detection tables."

"Excellent. We're sure who he is, and now we got him," cried Andreas, slamming a fist into his palm. "Officer of the Deck, come right to three-four-one, make your depth eighteen hundred feet, speed four knots. Make tubes one and four ready in all respects. And when ready, match generated bearings and fire!"

"Unit in tube one fired electrically. Unit in tube four fired electrically," reported the weapons officer.

For the next two minutes there was utter silence in the control room, then the attack coordinator abruptly jarred Andreas from his introspection: "Units one and four enabled and conducting spiral searches."

"Turn unit four twenty degrees left. Then, once clear of the baffles, turn it right—directly at the target—changing speed to high and switching to active search mode," ordered Andreas.

"Aye-aye, sir!" cried the weapons officer.

Vatz and the Russian plunged twenty feet to the ice-covered pavement below.

During the fall, Vatz had been able to roll the Russian slightly, so that he was on the bottom.

It was interesting how Vatz's mind emptied in the two seconds it took to drop. He was at complete peace, because the part of him that wanted to die would soon be satisfied. The guilt of living would be gone. But in the last quarter of a second, as the ground came up hard and fast, the other part took over, the Special Forces soldier trained to live at all costs, and a four-letter word blasted from his lips.

He gasped as they made impact, which was far less severe with one hundred and eighty pounds of Russian cushion beneath him.

The guy's head snapped back, his neck probably broken.

That wasn't so bad. I'm alive.

But then Vatz felt a tremendous pain rushing up his legs, and now he couldn't move them. He'd probably fractured both.

He rolled over, groaned, looked up as someone approached, shone a light in his eyes.

The light shifted to expose a Spetsnaz troop with a pistol in his hand. "Good-bye, Yankee."

The *Romanov*'s reaction was immediate and textbook. The sub turned right, went to flank speed, and launched countermeasures.

"Second detect on unit one," called out the weapons officer. "Unit one is homing!"

Andreas inhaled deeply. There'd be no more signals from unit one's wire.

At "homing," the Mark 48 increased speed to sixty knots, armed itself, and activated its proximity detector. The torpedo's high-explosive warhead would detonate once it sensed the high concentration of the earth's magnetic field caused by the close proximity of the steel mass of the *Romanov*'s hull.

Andreas literally held his breath.

Captain Second Rank Mikhail A. Kolosov closed his eyes and tensed every muscle in his body. He and Viktoria were going to exact their revenge on the Russian government for Dimitri's death. It was going to be simple. Magnificent. Memorable.

And there were several other governments who'd paid dearly to help them along in their quest—because many others stood to benefit from their plan. But he had failed them. Failed his siblings.

Dimitri was the brother with a heart of gold who'd sacrificed his life to do a good job for his employer.

Viktoria was the sister with a brilliant mind.

But what was he now, except a failure?

His boat was in a dive, descending through twelve hundred feet, trying futilely to escape. His men were overwhelmed by what their instruments told them.

"The torpedo is locked on!" cried the executive officer.

Kolosov opened his eyes. "I know."

"Then we die with honor for the Motherland!" the XO shouted.

Kolosov shook his head, removed the picture of his brother from his pocket, and whispered, "I'm sorry."

"Detonation, detonation!" shouted the sonar operator.

Their torpedo had been rising up from thirteen hundred feet, and Andreas imagined it striking the *Romanov's* keel with a massive explosion, the submarine breaking apart, sections tumbling away into the cold darkness.

Andreas sighed, took in a long breath.

"I've got popping noises and secondary detonations from Sierra One, sir," reported the sonar operator.

Whatever was left of the *Romanov* had reached crush depth.

"It's a kill, Captain. We got a kill," announced the sonar operator, switching from headset to speaker for all to hear.

"Please, shoot me," Vatz told the Spetsnaz troop in Russian.

That Vatz spoke the bearded man's language surprised him. He drew back his head, but then grinned. "I will help you die, Yankee soldier."

"Thank you. You see, I'm tired of killing you guys. You are the worst soldiers I have ever seen." Vatz frowned deeply. "You are Special Forces? I don't think so. You fight like little girls."

"Sergeant!" hollered one of the Spetsnaz troops.

The Black Hawk had banked hard and was descending for another pass.

But the troop was pointing at the two rifle squads from the Tenth Mountain fanning out across the street and already engaging the half dozen men standing above Vatz.

And it was in that second of distraction that Vatz drew the LC pistol from his hip, and just as the soldier turned back to finish him, Vatz lifted his arm and fired a 4.6 mm projectile into the Russian's face.

As the troop tumbled back, a glorious cacophony of gunfire filled the street, the Russians scattering like roaches.

After a minute of withering fire, Vatz forced his head up at the approach of someone.

"Hey, man, nice shot," said one of the riflemen, a corporal, now at Vatz's side. "What's your name?"

"I'm Sergeant Nathan Vatz, Special Forces." He tried to move; the pain was excruciating, bringing tears to his eyes.

"Easy, Sergeant. We'll get you out of here."

"I know you will."

As the corporal radioed back for help, Vatz tried to take his mind off the pain. He leaned back, rested his head on the pavement, and gasped.

He'd never known there were so many stars. It was, indeed, a heavenly view, and it reminded him of that terrible night before the rains had set in.

"Are you worth it?"

Those words had never stopped echoing in his mind, and now, as he considered them once more, he wondered if it wasn't about placing value on the Russians or the terrorists.

Maybe it was about valuing the mission.

Is what we do worth it? Worth our lives?

His hands tightened into fists.

Of course it was worth it—worth every drop of blood, sweat, and tears. They had been soldiers to the marrow and had died being true to who they were.

It *was* worth it.

FORTY-ONE

Commander Jonathan Andreas brought his boat to the surface. They were calling in their After Action Report to COMPACFLT. He stood outside on the deck with the XO, the weapons officer, and the communications officer. It was a star-filled night, brutally cold, but Andreas was certain his men had never felt warmer.

After sharing the good news with Admiral Stanton, Andreas lifted his voice. "Gentlemen, let's get below and break out the medicinal brandy. As morale officer, I'm concerned about the crew's well-being in these arctic climes. But before that, I want you take in a deep breath and remember this day. I'm unsure if there ever was or ever will be a boat as busy as we've been in the past twenty-four hours or so. If we carried it, we launched it.

If it came near us, we killed it. I'm proud of each and every one of you."

The men shouted their agreement, then Andreas noticed that both photonic masts were up and the BRA-34 antenna was extended.

Worse—the running lights were on. His grin faded.

Someone would catch holy hell for that.

"XO, we have a problem!"

The Pave Hawk had transported Sergeant Raymond McAllen, his Marines, Pravota, and Major Stephanie Halverson back to Fort McMurray, where McAllen received treatment for his wounds at a field hospital. He sat up in bed, warmed by the portable heater and sipping on a cup of strong coffee inside the rickety tent.

His wounds were minor, one in each leg, and the rounds had been removed. In a few weeks—and with a little physical therapy—he'd be back on his feet. Palladino, Szymanski, Friskis, and Gutierrez had come by to see him, but strangely, Sergeant Rule had not, and the others had not seen him in the past hour. But then, finally, the sergeant came loping down the long aisle of beds, holding a small plastic bag.

"Here," he said with a smile. "Souvenirs. The slugs that were in your legs. Took me a while, but I got them for you."

"Uh, thanks. Maybe I'll make a necklace."

"Really?" Rule grimaced.

"No, you idiot."

Rule thought a moment, then finally chuckled. "Sergeant, I just wanted to thank you for the opportunity to prove myself."

"You're thanking me for getting shot?"

Rule shrugged. "I guess so."

McAllen widened his eyes in mock seriousness. "Well, I hope I can return the favor."

"That's okay."

Just then Halverson, who'd changed into a spare Marine Corps uniform with heavy jacket, approached the bed. "How're you doing?"

McAllen smiled. "Better, thanks."

"How are *you* doing?" asked Rule.

She shivered. "Finally thawed out."

McAllen gave Rule a look: *Go!*

But the guy didn't get it.

"Did you see the Russian when we left him?" Rule asked her. "That guy cracked me up. He was all smiles. Never seen a POW so happy."

McAllen raised his voice. "Sergeant, you mind if I talk with the major?"

"Oh, yeah, oh, okay. Be good, man. See you later." Off he went, with a little hip-hop rhythm to his gait.

"He's a character," said Halverson.

"He's like a new pair of dress shoes. Stiff and squeaky. But he's doing better than I thought."

"I just came to tell you that you should expect a phone call. And this is one you don't want to miss."

"Oh, yeah?"

"American Eagle wants to thank you."

"No kidding?"

"Yep. I have no idea why he's made such a big deal of this, but when it comes to politicians, you never know what they're thinking." Her tone grew cynical. "Maybe we're symbols of the American spirit."

"Don't sell us too short. Maybe we are."

"That works well for your ego, huh?"

"And yours, too."

She proffered her hand. "Well, thank you. I mean it. I hope we can stay in touch."

He took her hand, shook firmly. "I hope so, too. Do fighter pilots ever date Marines?"

She grinned, turned away, then glanced back over her shoulder and said, "Only the cute ones."

Sergeant Nathan Vatz had been evaced back to Grand Prairie, and the nurses were applying the cast to his left leg when he got the call from Sergeant Marc Rakken's vehicle commander, Sergeant Timothy Appleman.

Twenty minutes earlier Vatz had tried to call Rakken, who wasn't answering his cell. Then Vatz had put a call in to Appleman, whose number he also kept in case of emergencies.

In a somber tone, the sergeant described how Rakken had saved the entire NEST team through his selfless act of courage.

And Vatz just lay there, listening to the sergeant call his name over and over—because he just couldn't respond to the news for a few seconds. "Yeah, I'm here. Thanks, Tim. I'll call you tomorrow."

"Nate, I'm giving this to you for two reasons: first, if one of us is going to make it, it's going to be you."

Vatz reached into his pocket and withdrew Marc's balisong. He clutched the knife in his fist and closed his eyes.

You knew it all along, didn't you, Marc. And you knew it was worth it. You didn't have any doubts. Not a one.

"We've still heard nothing from Moscow," said General Laura Kennedy.

President Becerra leaned back in his chair aboard Air Force One and nodded. "I didn't think we would."

"They are, however, beginning to withdraw their forces from Alberta."

"Good."

"Yes, sir, but it'll still take months to flush out all the special forces. And who knows how many spies could have infiltrated the area."

"Understood. We'll work with Emerson to address that issue and the reconstruction issues. I suspect he'll be quite upset over the highway and the bridge."

She winced. "Oh, yes, sir. I'll update you again in one hour."

"Thank you, General. Now I need to call a very skilled Marine Corps sergeant who got our pilot out."

"He'll appreciate that, sir."

General Sergei Izotov massaged his bloodshot eyes as he sat in President Vsevolod Vsevolodovich Kapalkin's office.

"It's confirmed," said the president, his cheeks growing fiery red as he turned away from his computer screen. "The *Romanov* has been destroyed."

Izotov shook his head. "She had a deal with her brother, and that fool got himself killed."

"She needs to join him in hell. I don't care how many agents you employ. I want her found. And if they can't capture her, they should kill her. Do you understand, General?"

"Completely. They'll return the body to me. I want to look into her dead eyes and be sure."

Kapalkin glanced back to his screen, began tapping away on his keyboard. "Now, there are other ways to gain control of those reserves. Has Vasiliev called you back?"

"Just two hours ago."

Alexi Vasiliev, aka William Bullard, was a Russian mole and member of the Canadian Parliament.

"How much money and time will it take?"

"He's not sure yet, but Prime Minister Emerson's handling of our invasion has been very unpopular. I'm confident that Mr. Bullard will one day become the next prime minister of Canada. But as we discussed, this is the much slower, perhaps even more expensive route."

Kapalkin nodded slowly. "Well, General, I'll leave you to your interrogations."

Izotov nodded and dragged himself from the chair. The conversation could have been handled via video phone, but Kapalkin wanted to punish Izotov for the Alberta debacle and force him down to the office.

Moreover, Kapalkin had ordered that every employee of the GRU be tested once more for loyalty—including Izotov himself. It was an act of sheer paranoia and an insult, but Izotov had his orders—and he had the Snow Maiden to thank for everything. His fingers itched to get around her throat.

At sixty-one, there weren't many things left in this world that truly moved General Sergei Izotov.

War was one of them.

And revenge was another.

The early morning flight to Cuba was thankfully brief— because during the entire time Major Alice Dennison wrung her hands and couldn't stop trembling.

Her pulse raced as she was escorted through security,

and by the time she reached the interrogation room, she was sweating profusely and had to excuse herself to the bathroom.

She splashed cold water over her face, glanced up in the mirror. "Be strong."

A minute later, she was escorted inside the interrogation room, where Colonel Pavel Doletskaya was waiting for her, his hands and legs shackled, head lowered.

She took a seat across from him, plopped the file she'd been carrying on the table.

His nose crinkled. "You smell very nice, Major."

"Look at me."

He raised his head, eyes weary, face still unshaven. "Have you been crying?"

"No."

"Your makeup—"

"Forget my makeup. I'm going to get you out of here."

He hoisted his brows, the color returning to his cheeks. "Where are we going?"

"Away from here."

"I kind of like it."

"Especially the food, right?"

He grinned and glanced away. "So you've reconsidered my offer?"

"Shut up, Colonel. Look at this."

She shoved the file toward him. He glanced down at it. "Interesting. A pity I can't open it."

She'd forgotten he'd been handcuffed and rose, opened the file, then placed the photograph on the table.

"This image comes from surveillance footage taken two days ago in Banff. That's in Alberta, Canada."

"My God . . ."

"Yes, she cut her hair, but she's still alive, isn't she?"

The colonel was beginning to hyperventilate.

"Calm down. I'm getting you out of here so you can help us find her—before your friends at the GRU do. She double-crossed them and the Green Brigade. She could be working for another organization more powerful than any we've encountered. Colonel, are you listening?"

He stared long and hard at the photograph, reaching out to it with his eyes. Eventually he looked up at her, those eyes now brimming with tears. "Yes, I will help you."

Dennison called for the guards to open the door.

Outside, she dialed a number on her satellite phone. "Hello, Mr. President. He's in. And no, I didn't tell him everything. We'll take it one step at a time."